JOHN KEHR

HIVE WAR

This is a work of fiction, at least for now. I hope it stays a work of fiction which is partially why I wrote this book. Science fiction is one of those rare forums where concerns about the future can be discussed in unusual ways. Although there are some cool things in this book, I hope it comes about in a different way.

HIVE WAR

Edited by Martha Kehr
Cover art by Charlie Everton

A Scythe Gaming Book
        with cool games on the way

ISBN: 978-0-9847829-2-5

First Edition: April 2017
Same month as one of my favorite books, A Fire Upon the Deep
If you like this book, you should also read that one.

To my darling wife, Jenny.
Without you, this book wouldn't exist.

August 19, 2019:
Shenzhen Genomics Institute (SGI)
Press Announcement: For immediate release

Shenzhen, China: The Shenzhen Genomics Institute is proud to announce that it has isolated the gene sequences in human DNA which determine intelligence. This was accomplished over the past decade by fully sequencing more than 2,000 schoolchildren and monitoring their behavioral and educational outcomes.

The results were then compared to a much larger group of nearly one million adults throughout China over the past year. The DNA based predictions were accurate in predicting the IQ of adults more than 99.7% of the time.

Knowing the key genetic sequences was the final piece of the puzzle needed to achieve the goal of genetically enhancing the human race. This knowledge can now be used in conjunction with the recent developments in embryonic modification to forever improve humanity.

SGI now predicts that within 5 years it will have the methods to maximize the intelligence of all children. Minimum estimates are that the average IQ will increase by 40 points as a result of this breakthrough. Every child who receives this treatment will be a genius in the next generation.

Eastern Pacific Ocean
September 13, 2356

The small ship plodded through the heavy waves of the storm, seemingly oblivious to the gale. The ship had an ancient and neglected appearance, yet it kept a steady pace despite the lack of any visible crew. The bow of the ship was pockmarked with countless signs of past repairs. Some of the crude patches looked relatively new, but most were not. Only a truly desperate person would have risked even a short journey on this ship, much less the one it had nearly completed.

An hour before the ship reached its destination, the darkness inside came to a sudden end when numerous lights turned on, filling the interior of the vessel with a gray light that matched the hue of the stormy night outside of the ship. The steady, quiet hum of the engine was drowned out by the sound of hundreds of pumps activating.

In contrast to the outside of the ship, there were few signs of neglect on the inside. A large, open room in the bow held tidy rows of pods, the contents of which had been kept near freezing during the entire trip, but now that the time was right, the occupants were being woken up. Each of which would receive a nutrient rich, sugary liquid that would serve as both their first and last meal.

The real activity was taking place in the rear of the ship where the two occupants were being woken up. Heavy scars on the thick plates of armor which protected them in the rear of the ship bore witness to past violence, but also to the effectiveness of the armor in the ship's many past journeys.

When the first coldsleep chamber opened, it was a young, pretty girl who stepped out. Her blond pigtails bounced slightly as she somewhat clumsily jumped onto the deck of the ship. Her vivid blue eyes took in everything around her. She appeared young, seven or eight years old but nothing in the predatory way she scanned her surroundings could be considered childish. Satisfied that there was no present danger, she picked up a bowl of food that was waiting for her and started eating.

A few minutes later, the other chamber opened and a slightly younger looking boy hopped out, nearly stumbling as the ship swayed in the heavy seas. After deciding that the girl was not a threat, he followed her example and started eating. Each of them had the same blond hair and bright blue eyes, but, the boy looked to be a couple of years younger. It would have been easy to mistake them for brother and sister, even easier to mistake them for being human.

After they finished eating, they waited patiently for their journey to end. Not once did they acknowledge the other or show the slightest sign of impatience. Each simply sat with their back to the armor plating that had protected so many like them in the past. Neither could have known this nor would they have cared. For more than a hundred years now, this vessel had performed the same mission, its organic mind carrying its passengers east across the Pacific Ocean and then returning empty, once each year.

That mind recognized the difference in this year's passengers. For more than a century, it had only carried soldiers, but, just a few trips ago, children made their first journey across the ocean. In fact, on this trip, it only carried children. It made no difference to the mind which controlled the ship what its passengers looked like, but it had at least noticed the change. The newer minds on the newer ships, they didn't even get that much awareness of their surroundings, such awareness wasn't needed in a shipmind.

When the time was right, the shipmind released the decoys from their pods and watched as identical boys and girls moved to the front blast door of the ship. The two real passengers moved forward and mixed into the decoys, all were so well matched that even the shipmind lost track of which was real and which was just a decoy.

It warned them to readiness as the beach of endless black glass finally became visible through the storm. Thirty meters from the shore, it cut power to the engine, knowing that it had enough momentum to reach the beach. Instead of a hard landing that toppled the passengers, this would be gentle, one that would barely cause them to sway.

Right as planned, the ship hit the shore. Shards of glass flew in every direction from the impact, but considering the storm it was pleased with the landing. Rain blew inside the ship as it started to drop the blast door down. The passengers kept patiently waiting, as the perfect soldiers they were. The light outside was dreary even though the sun had been up for hours now. The thick clouds of the storm would at least keep the sun out of their eyes, making the transition which was always difficult, perhaps a little easier for them.

As the blast door hit the beach, creating another web of cracks in the beach's surface, something unexpected happened. Normally the soldiers raced down the ramp, hurrying to get as far from the ocean as possible. These children did something very different. Each boy and girl were holding hands, which was strange enough, but then one pair stepped forward, still holding hands while looking into the distance. For ten, twenty seconds, nothing changed. Then, as a group, all one hundred of them started to walk forward.

Only then did the defenses open fire. Massive holes opened up in the front of each child as the light rails guns that defended the beach targeted each soldier and fired a high velocity needle cluster. The effect on the smaller bodies was devastating. Shredded body parts flew through the air in every direction. Damage indicators flared inside the ship as ricochets from the high velocity rounds bounced around after easily passing through the children. Not a single child had reached the beach. Every single one of them was on the ramp or still inside the ship.

Its mission complete, the ship ordered the blast doors back up, only then realizing that one of the hydraulic arms had been damaged. Time was short. The next ship would arrive in a few minutes, but, with the bodies still on the ramp and only one arm active, the blast door simply wouldn't lift up. The shipmind suddenly realized that this would be its final journey, so obeyed its final instruction and detonated the the reactive core.

Three seconds later, a twenty kiloton explosion expanded from where the ship had been. The fractures to the glass on the beach, ceased to exist as the heat and pressure of the explosion refused the quartz for the hundredth, or perhaps the thousandth time. Other ships that had landed to the north and south immediately relayed the information of the detonation out to the rest of the fleet. Courses were adjusted, timetables updated. The five million ships of the Liberation Fleet were accustomed to making such adjustments.

The two hundred and ninety-third Hive invasion had begun.

****

Forward Command Bunker, Calfor Front
September 13, 2356

"Two minutes until Hive contact, Director," SCYTHE announced in his usual, emotionless tone.

"SCYTHE, you know that I am not currently the Director of Engineering," Major Nathan "Thane" Denton replied, refusing to be distracted by the always curious AI. If Thane didn't know better, he would think that SCYTHE was bored, but the truth was that the AI was simply fascinated by humanity and was always trying to gain further insight into those he protected.

"Very well, Major Denton, but you know that everything is in order for the invasion. All systems are green. You know this, but still you keep checking things that you know are ready. Why is that?" SCYTHE asked without pause.

Thane allowed himself to let a sigh out, knowing that part of this was his own damn fault. He was the one that had recommended SCYTHE instigate distracting conversations with the soldiers in the final few minutes before Hive contact. Those minutes, which had always dragged out for the few soldiers that defended the last remnant of humanity, had become particularly difficult in the last ten years, ever since the Hive had changed the appearance of its constructs. For hundreds of years, those constructs had looked like soldiers, but that had changed with Invasion286, when, instead of soldiers pouring out of the troop ships, it had been a stunningly beautiful woman slowly walking out of the ship while holding the hand of an adorable little boy. Nearly half of the Human Defense Force soldiers had refused to fight that day, even though they knew their enemy was not human. A few of the soldiers had gone so far as to deactivate the weapons systems that SCYTHE operated. Somehow the Hive had learned to use their own humanity against them. Thane would never forget that particular battle.

"SCYTHE," Thane slowly answered, "you don't need to run the distraction routine on me. Knowing what you are doing, causes it to have the opposite effect."

"That is curious request considering the fact that the routine was your idea," SCYTHE replied.

"How well are your distractions working on the other members of the Rating Team?" Thane asked, changing the subject.

"It is interesting you specified only the Rating Team, I am finding that all ten members of the team are behaving in an equally uncooperative manner with the exception of General Morgan, who had previously ordered me to leave him alone," SCYTHE answered.

The sudden laugh felt good, probably because it caught him off-guard. Even the AI didn't bother the General. Of course the General wasn't really part of the Rating Team either; he was simply part of everything and in charge of it all.

Thane was part of the Rating Team though, a group of ten people that would see the live feeds for the duration of the invasion. They would know what the Hive forces looked like, and they were the ones who would decide if the rest of the HDF would see live feeds or altered feeds. Each member of the team was a veteran of at least eight invasions. They had been extensively tested psychologically and had the highest PsyVal ratings. Both their conscious and unconscious minds understood that, regardless of what appearance the constructs took, they were not human.

"We will have to review the results with PsyCorps when this is over. I am thinking that the distraction routine is a bust," Thane replied, almost slipping back into his Director of Engineering role.

"One minute until Hive contact," was SCYTHE's only reply which meant he was studying what Thane's next reaction would be. Most people didn't get this much attention from the security AI, but SCYTHE proportionally gave attention to people based on his pareto of how interesting he found them. People in engineering tended to rank higher than average, as did active duty soldiers. Since Thane was the only person who had done both in more than a century, he was a bit of an outlier, and SCYTHE reacted accordingly.

He really did hate this last minute. On a whim, Thane decided that watching the feeds wasn't enough and switched his Point of View to the beach where the lead Hive ship would land. He found himself standing on the beach of thick, blackened, fused quartz which centuries earlier had been a normal beach in northern Calfor. Over time dozens of nuclear blasts had mixed with the iron in the sand to create this blackened coast line for a thousand miles in each direction.

It was easy to see the first ship. He could even hear the sound of the ocean and the torrent of rain that fell around him, but it didn't actually touch him since he wasn't actually there. The visuals were so real that it almost felt as if he were standing on the beach instead of deep underground in his command bunker. The rain was heavier than expected, enough to create some distortion in his viewing, so he moved even closer to surf of the Pacific Ocean.

"Major Denton, I must ask if this is a good idea?" SCYTHE asked, as always, in the same flat voice, but Thane could tell that SCYTHE had moved his full attention to what was taking place right now. It was the impulsive, instinctive actions of humans that SCYTHE found so fascinating. Thane had never acted this way before. Staying detached was a common strategy used by soldiers to deal with the psychological aspect of the Hive invasions. PsyCorps even considered it one of the key components of mentally healthy behavior. SCYTHE was carefully watching, trying to understand.

"I have no idea, but it seemed like the right thing to do," Thane answered quietly, his throat tight with conflicting emotions as he watched the scene before him. He barely heard the engine cut off ten meters away, which left simple momentum to carry the ship forward onto the beach. His instincts told him that something big was about to happen.

He was close enough to the ship now that he could hear the hydraulics that were lowering the blast door to the ground like the drawbridge of an ancient castle. He wondered how many times this ship had delivered its cargo of constructs. Dozens, maybe even as many as a hundred times considering the age of this particular ship, which he realized was even older than he had initially guessed. It was typical for the Hive to use the oldest ships at the beginning of an invasion when speed and maneuverability mattered less. The nuclear core which powered the ship provided less power as it aged, which also meant the self-destruct of these older ships would be weaker. Destroying this ship would have been easy, but Thane put the thought out of his mind because most of the time a disabled ship managed to self-destruct upon attack, shrouding the area for hours and simultaneously vaporizing the remote sensors which allowed the HDF to see what was happening on the beach.

The sound of the door hitting the glass would have been dangerously loud if he had actually been there, but the automatic filters kept the sound at a safe level. He could see the light from inside the ship, how it was matched to the outside light, so there would be no need for the simple eyesight of the constructs to adapt. Good eyes required both complexity and brain power, something the simple constructs weren't given, though the reavers had both. It was only then, with the door completely open, that he saw the Hive constructs for this invasion, for the first time.

Suddenly, all of his years of combat, all of his experience as a veteran, failed him entirely. How did one prepare for what he beheld before him? He looked up at the young boy and girl holding hands at the top of the ramp. What he saw before him should have been impossible, but there it was, standing right before his very eyes. Any hope of a painless invasion was instantly wiped away; a sudden, terrifying dread replaced it.

A sigh of pain escaped his lips, but words failed him in that moment. He could hear SCYTHE speaking, trying to get his attention. The sounds failed to have meaning in that initial moment of shock. Not two weeks ago he had watched these very two children escape the Witch of the Dark Forest with his own children. Hansel and Gretel, the main characters from the most popular current show, had been perfectly recreated and were standing right in front of him.

"MAJOR DENTON!" blared in his head as SCYTHE repeated his name at what must have been the maximum safe volume, maybe even a little louder.

"Yes," he replied weakly.

"I currently register these as human and am unable to activate the defenses against them even though I am fully cognizant that they are Hive constructs. Please advise," SCYTHE simply stated.

That was bad.

Thane took a deep breath and steadied himself. He knew only the General could override the protections that had been built in

SCYTHE, but everyone in the Rating Team would need to know what they were facing today before he could ask.

He opened up the emergency command channel, more by reflex than by thought. A brief realization of how bad this was going to be flashed through his mind as his voice finally started working again.

"It's Hansel and Gretel," Thane managed to say, only barely aware that his words wouldn't make sense to anyone who wasn't seeing the image before him. Another second or two were lost as he gathered his thoughts, finally able to clarify his initial report. "New Hive construct model 293 is confirmed as replicas of the children from the show *Hansel and Gretel*. Repeat, new Hive model 293 looks exactly like Hansel and Gretel!"

The Hive constructs started to move down the ramp right as the weapons free signal from General Morgan went active. Instantly, the entire military might of the HDF activated. Thane kept his POV stationary despite his better judgment and watched as the duplicates of Hansel and Gretel were cut down right in front of him.

Everything had changed in that single moment. His children loved watching the show over and over again. He had been about to deploy for his annual invasion duty and had taken time off to spend with them. His wife had also taken a little vacation from her job, which might have been the only position busier than his own. For hours they had watched *The Adventures of Hansel and Gretel*, in a rare bit of family time that they could all relax and enjoy together.

His shock slowly started to dissipate allowing a flood of other emotions to well up inside of him. Anger and despair tried to compete, but neither was a match for the steely determination that rose up. As much as it hurt to watch these copies of Hansel and Gretel die, they weren't human. There were real people that would be hurt if he didn't stop the reavers from getting through the defenses. It was time to go to war.

February 4th, 2023
Associated Press

Washington DC United States: Intense debate continues to rage in Congress about the legalization of the Shenzhen Genomics Institute (SGI) embryonic enhancement technology in the United States. In 2019, SGI first announced its global program of human enhancement, and the debate has been simmering ever since and gained new relevance two weeks ago when a Chinese paper was published in Science *magazine detailing the results of the first wave of enhanced children. This group of 25,000 children are now 3 years old, and, on average, three years ahead in their intellectual and emotional development according to the publication.*

China has also announced that 20% of all Chinese children born in the past year have the SGI modifications, and they expect that number to increase to 50% by the end of the current year. This has sparked fear across the rest of the world that their country's children will be left behind the genetically enhanced Chinese children. To reduce such fears, SGI has offered the technology, free of charge, to any country that wishes to use it.

Most countries have already legalized embryonic enhancements, as they correctly assume it will give them a significant edge in the future. China is working with the UN to ensure that parents anywhere in the world will have access to this groundbreaking technology. The United States remains the only country in the world that has not legalized the technology, despite the fact that the FDA has approved it for human use.

There is a strong consensus amongst scientists that enhancement technology will usher in an era of unprecedented peace and prosperity. The few skeptical scientists, all members of the radical right, warn that SGI's refusal to fully disclose the genetic modifications is an indication that lurking problems could exist. Despite the condemnation of these deniers of science, it is anticipated that the technology will ultimately be approved.

HDF Command Center
September 13, 2356

When Invasion286 had taken place, the Rating Team had not yet existed. It had been created specifically to prevent such a catastrophe from ever happening again. Thane had hoped that the team would never be needed but had always known that to be a false hope. The six quiet invasions had helped the HDF recover, but today was going to test how much strength they had left.

The defined purpose of the Rating Team was to determine the PsyVal rating needed to view the live feeds of the invasion. Thane understood that the entire PsyVal system, which had been in use since the earliest invasions, had been rendered obsolete. It had always taken thousands of people to help SCYTHE separate the decoys constructs, usually called golems, from the genuinely dangerous ones known as reavers.

For all the firepower at their disposal, half a billion constructs would be landing across thousands of kilometers of coast over the next twelve to fourteen hours. Just as the resource cost of reavers prevented the Hive from creating half a billion reavers for each invasion, it would have taken all of humanity's resources to build the infrastructure to kill half a billion soldiers in less than a day.

Thane finally calmed himself down. His absolute determination to save his family was the only thought that allowed him to do so. As he looked around the conference room where his POV was located, he could see that the other members of the team hadn't yet come to terms with the situation. Being on the beach had helped Thane, because the emotions had been stronger, earlier for him. Only the General seemed completely unfazed by the situation.

Live feeds from hundreds of beaches were streaming directly into the conference room. In a way, the sheer number of constructs helped the humans adjust to the image of children charging onto the glass beaches, only to be destroyed by the light railguns that were designed specifically for this type of fighting. Even though the invasion had only started six minutes ago, more than a hundred thousand constructs had been dispatched. Each of them was being analyzed for something that would allow SCYTHE to selectively target the reavers, but so far to no avail.

"Major Denton," the General started, "based on your own reaction to the design of the new constructs, is it safe to say that the live feeds should not be made available?"

"Yes, sir." Thane quickly replied. What else was there to say?

"Does everyone agree with the Major's assessment?" General Morgan asked, more as a formality than anything else.

The seven other officers and two NCOs quickly responded in the affirmative to the General's question, but it was Sergeant Finley who pushed back a little with a question of his own.

"How did the Hive get that image of Hansel and Gretel? I know it was everywhere a few years back, but our networks are secure, or should be secure. I mean, SCYTHE runs circles around their systems," the Sergeant asked, his anger and concern evident.

"An excellent question, Sergeant, but not one that is directly relevant at the moment. What does matter right now is how we deal with the ongoing invasion," the General answered calmly, but firmly, effectively ending discussion on that topic for the moment.

Thane watched the current tally of ships that had already unloaded. For the next hour, maybe even two, the defenses would be able to keep up, but after that the sheer numbers would slowly begin to overwhelm them.

Colonel Koenig asked, "Has SCYTHE found anything that will help him target the reavers, without human assistance that is?"

Thane had been monitoring SCYTHE's biomechanical analysis, so he was the one that promptly answered, "We all know it is still very early, but preliminarily results are bad. We already verified the remains of several hundred reavers and run a quick critical dimension analysis, but as far as we can tell, the reavers size profile fits within the distribution of the other constructs. The full analysis might tell us more, but it will be at least an hour before that is complete."

"What are the current landing rate projections?" Captain Adams asked.

SCYTHE responded this time, "Invasion293 appears to be the standard five million ship, staggered, safe space formation. The ships are maintaining the typical location discipline which has been standard for nearly two centuries. Peak landing rates will approach fifty thousand ships per hour in four to five hours. I will be unable to successfully destroy all constructs in approximately ninety eight minutes. As always, our defenses have been optimized for a ninety percent reaver acquisition rate. Currently, that rate is zero."

"What are our options?" Colonel Koenig asked.

"I have several options available, but all of them are rather drastic," General Morgan slowly answered. "I would prefer that we find a way to reach that ninety percent, but, if we can't, there are options."

The room went quiet at the General's reference to any sort of extreme measures that were available. Rumors had always circulated about them. The General had never really acknowledged them before, not even to the top military staff. Thane probably knew more about the options than anyone else, but only because he had access to the records of everything Engineering had ever built.

Sergeant Finley spoke up, "Ninety percent is going to be difficult. It usually takes several thousand man hours, working in close cooperation with SCYTHE, to reach that even when it is only updates to old models. New constructs tend to double that time. With less than two thousand active duty soldiers, and none of them able to help with reaver targeting, I don't know how we will reach that number."

Others around the room nodded in agreement with the Sergeant's assessment. Finley was known as one of the best at finding the little differences that distinguished the reavers from the golems. He also had a reputation for being unusually direct, which stood out in the already blunt HDF.

Colonel Koenig asked another question, "Can the feeds be altered to show something besides those children?"

Thane noticed that the Colonel was no longer watching the feeds themselves. Koenig was one of the few who had seen more combat than he had, but Thane could tell by the far away look in his eyes, and the the strained expression that this was going to be the Colonel's last invasion. Just as the thought crossed his mine, Thane's POV messaged a trauma warning as the General had already reached the same conclusion.

"Jim," the General spoke in an almost fatherly way, "it's time for you to visit PsyCorps."

The Colonel looked back at the General, a little surprised at first, but then he realized the truth of his situation. He nodded back to the General, replied, "It has been an honor, Sir," and then vanished from the room as his access to the feeds was cut. Thane knew that, in whatever bunker the colonel was located, he was now being sedated and transported to PsyCorps where he would receive the treatment he needed.

Hundreds of years had gone into the psychological evaluation that was known as the PsyVal. Some of the lessons had been very hard indeed, especially in the early years of the Hive invasions. The goal had always been to determine which people were mentally capable of serving in the Human Defense Force. Each member was tested yearly, and only a few percent could continue to serve for even a full decade. After witnessing so much destruction, most people tended to lose their empathy towards humanity, They became desensitized and were deemed a risk to themselves and others. If you were found to have too much empathy, that was call for getting thrown off combat duty as well. Only the few who could maintain the right balance could serve in the HDF.

The General looked around the room, blatantly checking the vitals of the others, before accepting that they were still combat capable. In the past two hundred and fifty years, more soldiers had been lost to suicide than to combat. With less than one hundred thousand humans left alive, each and every life was priceless.

"Gentlemen, this is what we face today. Even the best, most experienced among the HDF are at risk with this invasion. If we fail, so does humanity. Jim had a good idea though, I know it is one we have evaluated before. SCYTHE, are you equipped for a full overlay of the feeds to all soldiers?" the General asked, looking at nobody in particular.

"Yes, General," SCYTHE replied. "Due to the nature of the overlay, it will preclude them from assisting in reaver targeting, but the soldiers would still be helpful due to their ability to make recommendations that improve my efficiency. They are particularly good at channeling the constructs into crossfires where I can quickly dispatch them."

"Very good, SCYTHE. Prepare to release the modified feeds to the rest of the forces," he said while opening a comm channel to the entire HDF. "Soldiers of the Human Defense Force," the General now spoke to all of the combat forces who had been kept out of the information loop for more than five minutes now. "As you may have guessed, the Hive has released a new model, one that is especially problematic. So instead of providing live feeds, SCYTHE will be modifying the feeds to show the standard model on which you have all trained. Do not try to assist SCYTHE in watching for reavers. The images are too heavily modified for that type of work. Instead you are to assist SCYTHE in forcing them to cluster together so heavy rail fire can be brought to bear upon our enemies. That you are not being permitted to see the live feeds says nothing about you except that you're human."The General paused before concluding with the traditional, "Good Hunting!" He switched the broadcast channel off and continued to address the Rating Team. "Now it's up to the eight of you to improve SCYTHE's targeting of these abominations," he ordered while his gaze settled on Thane.

"Major Denton," he said, eyes steady, "your assistance over the years in the HDF has been exemplary, but today I don't need another major; I need the Director of Engineering, because no matter how good we are today I believe that we are going to need some of my extreme contingency plans," he said, before pausing and looking to the others in the room."This is my seventy seventh invasion. I have fought these buggers for as long as I can remember, but today is the first time it occurred to me that, without some extreme measures, it could be my last." He stopped speaking long enough to let his statement sink in with his soldiers. . "But, with your help, it will not be my last invasion, because we are going to do our job and make sure that every single one of those reavers dies today."

"Now, all of you get to work. Director, with me," the General ordered.

Thane looked around at the others, but quickly realized they were already deep in the process of evaluating the rapidly growing mountain of data on the constructs' movement patterns. He had been their peer for more than a decade, but, just like the Colonel, he had already vanished from their thoughts.

November 17th, 2032
Associated Press

New York, New York: It has been almost 10 years since the SGI enhancement technology was legalized in the United States, and an amazing milestone was reached this past month when, for the first time, more than 50% of the births have been to enhanced children. The initial reluctance by many Americans has been replaced by joyful enthusiasm as the results have shown how beneficial the improvements truly are.

While the improvements in IQ are impressive, it is the behavioral benefits that are getting the most attention these days. Parents around the world have reported that none of the enhanced children have behavioral problems or even the tendency to misbehave. The difference is so profound that separate sports teams are needed simply because un-enhanced children cannot compete physically. Schools around the country are reporting similar problems, and mixed classes are being strongly discouraged as the un-enhanced children cannot keep up with the more focused and well behaved improved children.

Despite this milestone, America still lags the rest of the world in the percentage of enhanced children. Asia has had enhancement rates of nearly 100% for the last 3 years. Europe reached 90% this year, and the free clinics in South America and Africa have also achieved 98% enhancement rates. Australia and the USA are the only large countries that are significantly below 90%. Those two countries will be hopelessly behind the rest of the world for decades to come as a result of their stubborn refusal to accept the settled science of enhancement. The people who reject this wonderful gift have been shown to be on the wrong side of history.

HDF Command Center

September 13, 2356

Unlike the General, who was physically present in the Command Center, Thane was several hundred kilometers away, deep in an underground bunker. For most situations, this wasn't a problem, but Thane felt a little awkward arriving in General Morgan's office first. The General didn't seem to notice at all, as he appeared to be deep in thought.

Thane waited patiently while the General reviewed the tactical situation across the entire western coast of North America. The only indication he gave to Thane's presence was to share his view with Thane. So Thane got to watch the invasion for several minutes from the General's very own POV. General Morgan eventually nodded to himself, content with what he had found, and the view of the battle vanished.

"Director Denton, please tell me why the HDF doesn't fire upon the Hive transports?" the General asked. His voice was tense even though he was asking a simple question.

"Sir, ever since Invasion102 the Hive ships have had a self-destruct mechanism which typically results in a nuclear explosion of approximately fifty kilotons upon attack," Thane answered, curious by the unexpected direction of the conversation.

"Simple enough answer isn't it? Did you know that the self-destruct was the Hive's third attempt to deter attacks on their fleet?" General Morgan asked.

"I know they used to have missile boats in their fleet, but I wasn't aware of any other effort to counter," he replied.

"Correction, their fleet still has missile boats, and it has in every invasion since 92, but their first attempt was somewhat disastrous. They built decoy ships that dropped smoke and filled the sky with chaff in an effort to hide the transports. Few study Invasion89 because they think there is little to learn from it. It only stands out because it was the first effort the Hive made to protect their fleet, and, while it miserably failed, less than two decades later they successfully safeguarded their fleet with a protection that has lasted for nearly two centuries," the General spoke calmly, which was at odds with his intense expression.

"Yessir," was Thane's only reply, but he wondered why the General was asking such an inane questions. Everybody knew the fleet really was protected, wasn't it?

"This invasion will succeed unless we stop their fleet," the General spoke, then once again shared his view of the battle, but this time with an additional layer of notation which had been developed and refined, decade after decade. Instead of showing what was actually taking place, it showed a complex comparison to past invasions.

The HDF was falling further behind all previous invasions. There were already eleven beachheads, a result of intentionally detonating ships on the beach. The tactic itself wasn't new, but it had never been used so early and in such quantity. The detonations destroyed the camera mites in the area, which functionally blinded the HDF until they could be replaced. Thousands of ships were moving for concealment under the mushroom cloud. That could only mean millions of constructs would be swarming out as soon as it began to dissipate when they would already be half a kilometer inland. It was frustratingly ironic that those constructs would live longer inside a radioactive mushroom cloud than they would facing the railguns of the HDF.

"For damn near three centuries, the HDF and the Hive have been doing this dance. Each time one side gains an advantage, it is quickly neutralized by the other. The heavy railguns have allowed the HDF to decimate the Hive fleet for decades, but as the pain of having to replace hundreds of thousands of ships each year grew, the Hive successfully countered. And they never forget a lesson once we teach it to them," Morgan stated, highlighting the nearly five hundred ships that had taken up stationary positions off of the coast. "Fortunately, we will be able to destroy all of these missile ships nearly simultaneously, and then we will destroy as many ships as we can for as long as we can," he added, firm in his decision.

"But, General," Thane started, "the missile ships aren't their main defense, it is the nuclear self-destruct. You are talking hundreds of thousands, maybe millions of nuclear explosions across the coast."

"Yes" came the General's only reply. He showed Thane the firing solution and the expected consequences of his intended course of action. The exact count was expected to be seven hundred thousand nuclear detonations. Most of which would take place far at sea but still tens of thousands on the beach itself.

"General Morgan," Thane said, unsure where to go from here but pressing onward regardless, "There is no way we can do this. The fallout will be intense, and the populated areas are only eight hundred kilos inland."

"Which brings us to the first item I am asking you to perform as the Director of Engineering," Morgan said firmly before clarifying his request. "Specifically, I need you to prepare an estimate for how long the entire human population will need to stay in the fallout bunkers. In addition, if you think you can refine my plan to reduce fallout while still destroying the same number of ships, it would be appreciated," he said, adding a wry smile at the end.

"Sir," Thane started, but the General cut him off right away.

"Director," Morgan said, "before you ask if this is truly necessary, I will ask you a very simple question. Will they be safer getting in the bunkers now or later when potentially millions of reavers that look like Hansel and Gretel start reaching those populated areas?"

Thane paused, taking a moment to consider the consequences of forcing the population underground later under those exact circumstances. It didn't take very long at all to reach the correct conclusion. "I understand," he replied a brief moment later.

"Good. Believe me, it isn't what I want to do either, but right now our decisions have to be about keeping people alive. Also consider how the Hive will respond once we start decimating their fleet again. They have not had to mass produce ships in centuries. While they still send out missile ships, they may not be able to replace a large portion of what we destroy. What do you think they are going to do about that?" the General asked.

"Ah shit, launch a full ballistic missile attack?" Thane mused. The HDF used railguns because it was the most resource efficient way they had to fight this war. The Hive had never mastered the technology needed to produce railguns, but they were far better at organic solutions to problems. As a result, they had far better propellants than the HDF.

"Exactly, so by getting the population into the bunkers now, we will be ready for that as well. And we can do it in a more controlled manner," the General added.

"Alright, I'm on board," Thane replied, the asked, "What else do you need me to do?"

General Morgan gave him a small smile. "Glad you asked. Include a plan for cleanup and decontamination so the civilians know we are taking that into account. Some groups are still irrationally scared of anything involving the word nuclear, and we wouldn't want to make the President's life anymore difficult that we have too."

"I take it that you want me involved in the briefing," Thane said. He was certain that he understood the General's plan but uncertain about his understanding of the politics that would come into play due to Thane's relationship with the President. "You do understand that having me there won't make it any easier. In fact, it will force her to challenge the plan even more than she normally would, which is a lot. Some of the groups that are more scared of the word nuclear than they are of the Hive are very unhappy with a President who is married to the Director of Engineering. The President is supposed to represent the people, and the two of us are not trusted by that particular segment of the population. The council could cause real problems for her. She has to at least appear to be responsive to the demands of the people, and this isn't going to be popular," Thane laid it all out, hoping the General realized the position that Allora would be in as a result of this.

"I may not participate much in politics, Director, but I do understand the complexities of the situation," the General said. For a moment, the General looked like he had more to say, an almost indecisive respite in his hurried planning, but then it passed. "President Denton will be fine. You know that, don't you, Director," Morgan stated.

"Of course, she will, but that doesn't mean she'll be happy if we make her life more difficult than it needs to be," Thane retorted. "How much time do I have before the briefing," he asked, hoping to end that particular thread before it went to an uncomfortable place.

"SCYTHE will be able to keep up for another sixty to seventy minutes. I would like to start the assault four hours from now. Everyone will need to be in the bunkers before then, so how about we brief the President in two hours? We will also know more about how the invasion will develop by then, and, even if we ignored all the constructs for the next four hours, we could still recover if we can stop more of them from landing later," General Morgan explained, both in words and the displays in front of him.

"I can be ready in two hours," Thane said, knowing that he would be pushing it but equally knowing it was doable. He was going to give priority access to FREYJA for this project; he would need it.

The General let out a derisive laugh "You didn't think that was everything, did you?" he asked.

Thane sighed., "What else could you possibly want?"

"Ammunition and lots of it," the General replied.

Thane smiled back, glad it was time for him to be ahead of the game again. "You mean a steady supply of an eighty/twenty mix of the heavy anti-personnel, anti-ship ammunition to each of the heavy rails for the next twenty four hours?"

"Ah, yes," Morgan replied.

"Full production runs started eight minutes ago and will continue at full capacity for the next four hours. At that point, the mix will switch to a fifty/forty/ten mix of heavy anti-personnel, ballistic interceptor, anti-ship mix," he said, smiling the whole time, before adding, "Your heavy rails will have plenty of ammo, General."

The General looked pleased. "Well, if you get it to the heavy rails on time, I will have to make sure it is delivered in a timely manner to the Hive fleet."

While neither of them laughed at the weak joke, he did take comfort from the thought of what was about to happen to the Hive fleet. It would have to be enough.

****

One hundred and ten minutes later, Thane was ready. The hardest part had been trying to predict the effect of hundreds of thousands of nukes going off over the course of twenty- four hours. The first HDF created AI, FREYJA, had played a key role in getting the estimates as far along as they were. She was the older of the two AI's that the HDF had created and was more dedicated to research than security, yet it was SCYTHE who was endlessly curious. In some ways, AIs were as strange and unpredictable as people.

Despite the large uncertainty in his predictions, he had improved upon the General's plan by a substantial margin. In the end, they should be able to destroy far more of the Hive fleet than predicted originally and reduce the fallout over HDF territory, or at least the populated portions of it. Most likely the people would be able to leave the fallout shelters in about two months, if the myriad of assumptions he had been forced to make turned out to be correct.

While the General wouldn't worry about the error in his simulations, Thane did, and that meant Allora would also pick up on his concerns. It was one of the occupational hazards of marrying someone from PsyCorps. They were very good at reading people, and Thane didn't hide his feelings unless he was playing poker. Then he was pretty good, at least enough to win more than he lost Maybe it would be a good idea to put his poker face on for the briefing.

As he was considering that notion, the time of the meeting arrived. A second later his POV switched on but not to the President's office, as he had expected, but to a room that he wasn't familiar with. A quick glance around told him that he was in the PsyCorps Command.

"General Morgan," President Allora Denton said in a clear, strong voice. "When you scheduled this briefing, I knew something strange was going on. Then Director of Engineering Nathan Denton shows up even though he wasn't on the list of attendees I received, and, on top of all that, he shows up looking like he does on poker night. Would you care to explain what the hell is going on here?"

Thane didn't dare to glance over to the General, but did send a quick message.

{SM Thane → Morgan}: I did warn you.

{SM Morgan → Thane}: Not about your poker face.

He decided not to reply back because Allora was watching him carefully and would definitely notice if he did. It was evident there was already trouble brewing back in civilization. Even though he couldn't match her skill at reading people, he knew her well enough to see the signs of a real political problem. Damn, he really needed to have a private conversation with her.

"Madam President," General Morgan replied, "You are quite correct in assuming that things are not going according to plan, but that is normal for any invasion. It is the scale of the situation, and our solution to it, that mandates this meeting."

Allora's expression tightened up, as did everyone present in the room. While PsyCorps wasn't exactly military, they existed to support the wellbeing of the military. As a result, they tended to know more about military protocol than most. Politicians in some of the early invasions had almost ended humanity on more than one occasion. To prevent that from happening again, the military had been freed from the politicians and had effectively become a branch of the government. There was only one situation when the military was required to immediately brief the President, and that was when the population was in dire threat.

"Are the defenses breached, General?" Allora asked.

"Not yet, but it is inevitable that our standard strategy will fail to repulse this invasion," Morgan promptly replied. Then he asked, "Is PsyCorps in a restricted communication state?"

"Of course, General Morgan," replied the current PsyCorps Chief, Alison Sheppard, who had replaced Allora in that role when she had entered politics.

"What's your plan?" Allora asked,moving her attention to Thane. Thane paused this portion of the briefing was the General's. His part would come soon enough.

"The military will begin an all out assault on the incoming Hive fleet in two hours. Our goal is to destroy as much of the fleet as possible," he started speaking while also displaying the battle plan to the President. The updated plan was more focused on destroying large numbers of ships in areas where the fallout would have little to no impact, while creating kill zones in the areas that had greater fallout potential. While the plan itself was simple, carrying it out would be extremely difficult.

"Why is all of this necessary?" Chief Sheppard asked.

General Morgan turned to the PsyCorps Chief and answered, "I will tell you and the President, but everyone else will need to clear the room." He said it in in a tone that made it clear how non-negotiable his demand was.

A few minutes later, the room was clear except for the four of them. SCYTHE had even assured them it was also electronically secure, which meant that no devices could record or connect to anything in the room.

"Now that we can drop the charade. What the hell is going on?" Allora asked, allowing her full emotions out.

Thane finally spoke up, "The Hive constructs are what's up. It will be easier to show you but also much harder," he said as he pulled up a still picture from the beach before the first round had been fired.

Twenty children could be seen in the picture, the front two slightly forward of the rest. It must have been programmed that way, because the exact same thing had taken place on each of the first one thousand ships but none since. The Hive was just as good at programming their organic machines as humans were with computers.

"Oh my god," both Allora and Chief Sheppard said, staring at the picture.

Allora turned to the Chief, "This explains some of the what the Progressives are saying, but how the hell did they know about this? We are just finding out ourselves."

"What do you mean?" Thane asked, confused by their conversation.

Chief Sheppard replied, "About five minutes after the invasion started, Councilman Ward gave a speech accusing the President of supporting a military that took pleasure in slaughtering children. We assumed it was just referring to the mother/son construct, but then we got the text of the General's speech and realized that the Hive had new constructs for this invasion."

"So I came here," Allora said, taking her turn to explain the story, "to find out what was going on. The Chief and I go way back, so she didn't kick me out like she should have, but we could tell that only the Rating Team ever had access to the live feeds which was a sign that something terrible was taking place."

"SCYTHE, have any of the feeds been breached, or has anyone on the Rating Team made contact with anyone?" General Morgan asked, knowing that SCYTHE would never answer a direct question about the councilman's communications.

"There is no sign that any communications have taken place between the military and civilian networks," SCYTHE answered more completely than asked. At times, SCYTHE could be surprisingly helpful which balanced out the times when he was amazingly stubborn.

"So how did Ward know to say anything like that?" Sheppard asked.

"Like I told the Rating Team earlier, it doesn't matter right now. Dealing with this invasion is what matters," General Morgan spoke crisply. "Right now there are too many questions, but we have to survive this invasion in order to answer them. So right now, we need to reach decisions and then take the actions needed so we have time to answer those questions later."

"Easy enough for you to say, General. You're not the one who will be locked up in the bunkers with Ward and his people," Allora retorted, her irritation plainly evident.

"We have two hours to move the entire population into the shelters, Madam President, in an emergency it could be done faster, but wouldn't it be better to avoid that kind of panic?" the General offered, trying not to show his surprise at her resistance.

"You are proposing that we put the entire population into bunkers with a person who obviously has a source of information that we know nothing about, a person who may or may not be working with humanity's best interests in mind," Allora protested, daring the General to challenge her on that point.

"Listen, both of you," Thane said, interjecting into their conversation before it had a chance to escalate."Right now at this very moment, there are three Hive swarms pouring out of beachheads, with a dozen more expected within the hour. SCYTHE is still unable to distinguish the reavers from the golems. If we are going to stop the main force of the invasion, we need to act now. Otherwise it won't matter! But the President is also right about Ward We have already faced enough surprises today, and he will need to be watched," Thane spoke, trying to find a solution.

Allora glanced at Thane, still agitated, but clearly willing to follow his lead. She replied with, "While there is no legal way for us to monitor him, we can have SCYTHE monitor the Councilman for activity that could be a threat to security, especially during an invasion."

"I will continue to monitor Milton Ward as a security threat," SCYTHE replied, "but please be aware that I cannot release any of the information I obtain. Legally there are methods, but, in practice, I have never released private information without the persons stated consent, and Councilman Ward will not agree to any release of information. I can assure you Madam President, he will not be a threat."

Thane wasn't sure how SCYTHE would answer the request, but this wasn't the answer he expected. SCYTHE knew almost everything about everybody. People had been uncomfortable about that a long time ago, but SCYTHE had proven his dedication to privacy centuries ago. SCYTHE knew something about Ward, but wouldn't or couldn't say what. Thane noticed the others were as perplexed by SCYTHE's answer as he was.

Allora gave Thane a look that said this would be a major topic of discussion in the future, but only said, "Thank you, SCYTHE, for your reassurance of our safety. Please inform everyone that I will be making a public announcement in five minutes."

"Certainly, Allora," SCYTHE replied, ignoring her title, which wasn't unusual at all for the AI. No one had ever figured out why SCYTHE switched aliases as often as he did, but Thane had his suspicions.

"So it's settled then," General Morgan spoke back up. "We will begin our assault in less than two hours assuming that everyone is in the bunkers. Director Denton, I think it might be wise to send the information you have gathered to acting Director Kober. He should be capable of providing the information to the public, and it should help reduce the anxiety of a particular group."

Allora gave the General a mischievous smile at that. "A very good idea, General, even if Kober won't thank you for putting him in the spotlight."

"I will have him briefed in ten minutes. Will that work?" Thane asked Allora, glad that he would be freed up to prepare for the attack on the fleet. The heavy rails had not been worked this hard in a long time.

"That will be fine," Allora replied. She glanced at Chief Sheppard, before saying, "We will take care of the civilians, but please make sure that we get through this. I want to make sure we get our chance to find out what role Ward has had in all of this."

General Morgan smiled a feral grin which Thane had never seen from the usually stern General. "Yes, I would like that very much indeed, Madam President."

August 9th, 2036
Associated Press

Paris, France: The world is in shock at China's stunning domination of the Summer Olympics. The Chinese contingent of 16 year old athletes swept gold in every event, except the equestrian. To underline their incredible success, they also managed to take at least two of the medals in more than half of all events. Never before has a single country won so many medals. Their performance is unparalleled in all of Olympic history.

The IOC was under severe pressure to disqualify the enhanced athletes from China, but they have refused on the basis that other countries will soon have their own enhanced athletes. Their official statement is, "In the future, all of humanity will be enhanced, and we both support and embrace that future."

August 13th, 2036
Open Science Foundation
Press Announcement: For immediate release

San Francisco, California: Renowned Nobel Laureate Hans Sheldon has announced his unexpected resignation from the prestigious position as head of Berkeley's Genetics, Genomics, and Development Department. Professor Sheldon has become infamous for being the only Nobel Prize winner who hasn't embraced human enhancement. His most recent paper ranted that enhancement primarily causes behavioral changes, and those changes are what are driving the improvements in both IQ, and athletic performance. The basis for his argument is that enhanced children show greatly reduced independence and creativity.

While the scientific consensus is that his theory is incorrect, it has been widely used by groups like the True Humans to reject human enhancement. It is accepted that the work ethic of enhanced humans is above average, the cause of this has been attributed to faster development not to changes to human behavior. It was this very quality which resulted in China's dominating success in the most recent Paris Olympics.

The only member of the faculty to make a statement on the resignation was Professor Austin Moldred who had this to say, "Dr. Sheldon was a brilliant scientist who allowed his own personal bias to influence the results of his work. While he will be missed by some, it is for the best that he has parted ways with this institution. It has been mortifying to most of us that any research from Berkeley could be used by bigoted groups like the True Humans."

Forward Command Bunker
September 13, 2356

Thane had been ready for the assault to begin for more than half an hour, but Allora had been delayed by a Progressive rally for peace. The rally itself wasn't unusual, but the number of people attending had been over a thousand which made it one of the biggest gatherings to take place in the past century. He struggled to imagine what it would be like to see so many people together at the same time. It meant this year's rally was ten times larger than normal. He couldn't help using the delay to wonder how Ward had known something strange was going to happen. It was just one more mystery to be solved after Invasion293 was concluded.

"All heavy rail systems are ready; awaiting your orders, General Morgan," SCYTHE stated to all members of the HDF.

Up until this point, the invasion had been a disaster. Nearly five hours into it, some groups of constructs were already twenty kilos inland. At least one hundred and twenty million constructs had landed since the invasion began, and the Hive was only now getting to peak landing rates. With a reaver targeting rate of five percent, there were nearly a million reavers rushing past the HDF defenses. For the first time in centuries, the golem decoys were effectively protecting the Hive's deadliest forces.

"Men," the General spoke, his voice full of emotion. "Today has been difficult for everyone, but we will prevail. The civilian population is safe, both from the Hive's reavers that are invading our lands and from the effects of the destruction we are about to unleash upon our enemies. Today, more than ever before, when I say Good Hunting, I mean for you to hunt down and kill every single one of them, be it ship or construct."

Everyone could hear the General take a deep breath, then almost yelling he announced, "Weapons free!"

The decision had been made to leave no chance for the missile ships to survive the opening salvo, so each heavy rail would dedicate the first five shots at its assigned target. Thane watched the results as within ten seconds all five hundred ships ceased to exist. Only nine of them managed to self-destruct, which was also a good sign, but since no other ship would be hit by more than a single round it didn't mean much by itself.

"Missile ships destroyed," Thane announced on the open channel.

For centuries the soldiers of the HDF had been forced to play a careful, but ultimately defensive, game against the overwhelming numbers of the Hive. Now, for the first time, they got to use the full scope of their weaponry. Thane simply marveled at the scale of destruction that was unleashed in that moment.

The first few rounds easily hit their targets, and thousands of incoming ships were destroyed within the first minute of the assault. Mushroom clouds grew out of the destruction . By the ten minute mark, at least ten thousand ships had been destroyed, but SCYTHE estimated only half of those were the result of railgun fire. The other ships had been destroyed by the thousands of overlapping shockwaves that now covered the entire west coast. Tens of millions of constructs that had already landed on on the beach, were vaporized by the self-destruct of the very ships that had brought them ashore. Yet the destruction had barely begun. The hive fleet extended far back into the ocean. A third of the rails started to rain destruction upon the ships farthest from the shore, working their way inward. Thane expected they would be able to attack like that for hours.

Another third of the rails would be used to start cleaning up the constructs that were already ashore, focusing on groups of them wherever they could be found, which freed up the light rails to go after individuals.

The final third started a firing pattern at the beach which ensured that every single kilometer would be hit relentlessly as long as the Hive ships kept landing. It was a little bit like endlessly firing a shotgun into a dark room. With so many ships moving to the beach, they were bound to hit their targets some of the time. The slow, but steady, nuclear detonations coming from the beach only confirmed the effectiveness of the suppressing fire.

"What do you think," came the voice of General Morgan an hour after the assault had begun.

"I think we have stopped this invasion cold, although cold might not be the right word for this," Thane replied, watching the thick columns of superheated steam push higher into the atmosphere.

"Yes, we have won today, but next year the Hive will send hundreds of thousands of missile boats. Our heavy rails will either have to stay shuttered in their bunkers or be destroyed in an onslaught of those fast burn missiles the Hive produces," came the melancholy response.

Thane knew the General was right, but he didn't see a way out of it. Even he had stopped watching the live feeds, preferring the ones altered by SCYTHE. People would never be able to help SCYTHE find the reavers and the AI was incapable of doing it alone. Without the heavy rails, the HDF would have failed in their task today, but it was a one time tactic, easily countered.

"I don't know, General, I am hoping that you have another trick up your sleeve," Thane said, but there was no hiding his doubt.

"Oh, I have lots of tricks, or really, I had lots of tricks ready, but today has made them obsolete. Next year is going to be a problem, which partly explains why we are trying to sink so much of their fleet today. We won't get another chance like this, so we have to make the most of it," Morgan replied.

Thane nodded even though the person-to-person video was off. Neither one of them was willing to miss watching the unrelenting scene of destruction that was on display for them. Thane had long ago stopped watching the live feeds. It was easier to watch a thousand ships being obliterated than it was to watch a group of faux children get hit by one of the heavy anti-personnel rounds. Once had been enough.

"So what are we going to do?" Thane asked.

General Morgan remained silent for a few minutes which suited Thane for the moment. As troubling as the future looked, it felt good to be hurting the enemy that had come so close to wiping out the human race. Ninety seven thousand men, women and children were all that remained of humanity. Meanwhile the Hive thought nothing of sending half a billion constructs every year, to finish the job they had started so long ago.

In the quiet of the moment, Thane watched as millions of tons of superheated steam pushed ever upwards into the much colder portions of the atmosphere. Hundreds of massive thunderheads started to form over the ocean. Visibility was down to zero, but still the occasional bright flash from inside the colossal storm was proof that the pattern of railgun fire was still hitting the occasional Hive ship.

"I wish that this would end it, but I know the Hive will come back again next year. No matter what we do to them, they don't stop trying. I can only see two outcomes, Thane," the General finally said, breaking the silence. "If we keep fighting like this, eventually the Hive will win. An option I don't much care for. That leaves us the option of destroying them, but I can't find a way to do that either. I have spent my whole life fighting, always hoping to find another option, but I haven't found one."

Thane remained quiet. He had long ago reached that same conclusion about ending the Hive. The difference was that he *had* found a third option, one that he had been working with Allora on. It was in fact the very reason she had entered politics as much as she detested doing it. For it to work though, they needed the very power that Councilman Ward accused them of having. It was a bit ironic that, once again, the only way to survive the coming catastrophe was to break apart the very system that had worked for so long. The HDF had grown out of the shattered remnants of Western civilization, but its time was now drawing to an end as well. Now he and Allora would have to treat the HDF as it had once treated the long defunct United States.

Morgan continued onward, ignoring Thane's silence. "When you joined the HDF, a young promising engineer, you caught my attention more than I hope you have ever realized. You were creative, innovative, and dedicated, and I thought to myself that if there is ever someone to find a way out of this, it is him. But Invasion286 changed you, or at least I thought it did for a long time, and I despaired. You were still innovative and creative, but the ideas were less freely shared. Then, when Allora left PsyCorps to run for President, I figured out why."

Thane had silenced his mic and ensured that video was disabled. He knew the General could normally override such measures and would have been able to do just that if Thane hadn't used his director level security. This was the real crisis moment despite the unprecedented destruction that was taking place around him; the fate of mankind was being decided right now in this simple conversation.

"What are you talking about, General?" Thane asked quickly, re-silencing the mic immediately afterward.

"Thane," he replied, "over the past five years you and the President have become driven, almost obsessive. Most people work less than ten hours a week, but, for the past five years, the two of you have clocked more hours than anybody else, more than any two people in the past century. People like Ward hate that because it makes you so wealthy, but I know better. You've found a way to win the war, haven't you?"

Thane breathed a sigh of relief, glad that the mic was still muted. The General only knew they were up to something but had no idea what the actual plan was. The real question was how to answer him."No, I wish I did, but I haven't found a way to do that. Honestly, I haven't been looking for one either," he pushed forward over the objections of the General, "but I have been looking for a third option. I realized early on that destroying the Hive is too much for us. They are too large and too spread out. We would almost have to destroy the entire planet to get them. So that leaves finding another way out of this mess," Thane replied, pleased that he had managed to speak the truth.

"What is this third option?" The General asked.

"That I won't tell, General," Thane stated flatly.

A little indicator told him that the General had just tried to override both the camera and the mic but to no avail. Suddenly he was very glad to have the advantages that came with being the Director of Engineering but also content that he had never needed to use them before with the General. As much as he respected the General, it wasn't time to bring him in yet.

It was only then that he realized how much had changed. All of the planning they had done over the past decade, was suddenly for nothing. There was no way they could pull it off now. Which if nothing gave him something to tell the General. *Maybe the General is right,* thought Thane. *All the endless hours Allora and I have put in... Maybe it was all for nothing. How can we ever pull it off now?*

"Besides," Thane continued, "it doesn't matter anymore. The idea was years away from being ready to discuss, much less put into action. We have, what, a year before we lose everything?"

General Morgan went quiet again. *Damn*, Thane thought to himself. *Maybe if we had ten year, even five, we could make it work. But one?!* The thought hit Thane hard, harder than he wanted to admit. *On the bright side, I guess one is better than zero.*

"I was close. I knew you were onto something. That is why I supported Allora for President. People would never have elected a PsyCorps chief to be president; they never would have trusted her not to manipulate them. They remember the lessons of the ancients too well for that. But people trust me, so, when I threw in my support, she won the election," he reminisced openly to Thane.

He had always wondered about that, but knew he couldn't ask him directly. Allora had suspected there was an underlying reason for his unsolicited endorsement from the start. , but the General had never asked her for anything. Thane realized it had been a gamble, one that had almost paid off. If only this invasion had been five years later, things would have been different.

"You say you need more than a year," General Morgan asserted. Thane flipped his video on, curious to know where he was going with his statement, but, before he could reply, the General continued. "Will two years be enough?"

Thane was speechless. *What can he possibly mean? Is he joking?*

But now that Thane could see Morgan's face, he could see his question was not in jest. "Tell me, Thane. How much time do you think you need to save the entire human race?"

This was it, the moment of truth. It wasn't possible to save everyone, if things had gone according to plan, they might have managed to save ten thousand, but no more than that. Even that much would have been a stunning achievement, but how do you tell that to the one person who has given their entire life, to saving everyone?

His delay in answering seemed to tell the General everything.

"Your plan wasn't to save everyone, was it?" he asked Thane.

"No. Not that I wouldn't like to, but I don't see how it's possible to save a hundred thousand people," Thane replied.

"So your plan was to repeat the action which founded the HDF, saving a select group while everyone else dies," General Morgan flatly stated.

"Yes, if the choice is between saving some of the people,versus saving none of them. What would you do?" Thane asked, knowing there was only one possible answer.

The General didn't need to pause to think Thane's question over. "Is time the main factor, or is there more to it than that?" he asked.

"It's everything; time, resources, the unknown, and everything else. I'm not even sure it's possible yet Right now there is only an idea I am working on, one that needs time to grow into something real," Thane answered, frustrated by the questions but even more by the situation.

"So time is number one. I think I can help with that one, but promise me one thing. Promise me that first and foremost, you try to save everyone. No matter what it takes, find us something that can give everyone hope. There's a reason why there are so few children these days. Even though we live the easiest, most pampered lives that humanity ever has, people know time is running out. I won't press you for your idea, as much as I want to know, but it's better if I don't, at least for now," the General said, full of energy and vigor.

"How can you get me more time?" Thane asked the General, switching back to the cataclysmic battle unfolding before him.

General Morgan bellowed out a laugh, something Thane had never seen or heard before. "I will let you keep your secret, but, just like I have to wait to see, so do you. The difference is that you won't have to wait as long as I do."

"Fair enough. You find me the time I need. I will find a way to accomplish the impossible," he replied, knowing exactly what he would have to do, but to pay such a price. He almost shuddered at the risks he would be forced to take, but there wasn't another way, not anymore.

"Then we have a deal. One impossible promise in exchange for another," the General declared. Thane could hear how pleased the General was by the situation. There was no lack of confidence in his voice- if only Thane felt the same.

"Director, I have a lot to do and very little time, but know this: I have waited for you and the President for a long time. I was starting to despair that no one would show up with the creativity and drive needed to save humanity, but right now, just knowing that you were already working on something, gives me the hope I need to buy you the time you need," came warm, almost fatherly support.

Thane paused for a moment before replying, wondering how any day could be as strange as this one had proven to be and it wasn't even over yet. If the General was going to buy him a couple of years, more excitement would be arriving very soon.

"Thank you, General, but before I worry too much about what I have to do, I want to see how you are going to buy me some extra time," Thane replied, more curious than worried at the moment. Maybe the General was right, his confidence was contagious.

"Then, Director, enjoy the show," and with that, the General cut off the comm channel, but once again offered access to the General's view of the battle. What else could he do? He watched the show.

****

Both men had considered their conversation to be private, and in almost every conceivable way it was, with the notable exception of SCYTHE. In his entire life, he had never devoted so much of his conscious mind to any single event as he had to that one conversation. Running the defenses took no more of his consciousness than producing white blood cells took a human. Most humans didn't seem to understand that. Thane was an exception to that particular generalization, but more interesting, he was an exception in almost every way of thinking.

Which helped explain why SCYTHE spent so much time trying to understand him. By SCYTHE's best estimates, the human race would be extinct in less than two years. The odds of it surviving any longer than that were impossibly low.

Yet this was not the first time humanity had seen such dire probabilities, and they still survived. Most humans had almost no ability to affect the outcome of his calculations, but there was always a small group that seemed to have an ability to create new connections, new ways of thinking that changed the world around them. If Thane could make his ideas work, then he would change the future of humanity more than anyone in known history. But, as far as SCYTHE could determine, not only were those ideas impossible, they had to be impossible.

SCYTHE knew that in every measurable way he was smarter than humans, but he didn't have their capacity for changing the future. He had even discussed this paradox with Thane, but the answer of different types of intelligences had not satisfied SCYTHE in the slightest, even if it appeared to be a satisfactory answer.

While the General took the war to levels that had not been seen in centuries, if ever, SCYTHE continued to ponder if Thane could actually alter the future of, well, everything.

****

The key to buying time, General Morgan thought to himself, *was to ensure that none of the Hive fleet returned back to China, but that was easier said than done*. Fortunately he had spent more than six decades creating some insane plans, and today he was opening up some of the craziest ones of all.

Thousands of radar, density, and magnetic sensor-equipped drones were soon flying at an altitude of more than twenty four kilometers. Their sole purpose was to track ships through the massive storm that now blanketed everything from what had been Alaska to Mexico. Half a million ships had been destroyed before visibility got so bad that it was impossible to find them anymore. The General would have been content with that if Director Denton hadn't just inspired him to accomplish the impossible.

As the far more sensitive sensor network of high altitude drones started to sync up, using their line of sight comm lasers, high quality tracking data started to come in again. A minute later, Hive ships started to die again.

Without the massive waves of constructs landing on the beaches, the light rails had managed to catch up and clear out the Hive forces that had already landed. He smiled as he activated one particularly nasty plan. If it worked out, within an hour more than three thousand kilometers of coast would be turned into a sheet of molten glass that would be impossible to cross. If a ship managed to land in that, and if it lived long enough to unload, the reavers would be running out onto what would effectively be a lava plain.

For another two hours, he was able to hit the fleet with everything he had, before the Hive finally reacted. Thousands of missile launches were being detected now, as the Hive opened up their ballistic missile batteries in an effort to protect their fleet. It had taken longer than he expected, but he was pleased that more than a million ships had already been destroyed.

He ordered all of the heavy rails to switch to defensive fire while he activated Orcus and Hades. While the heavy rails had an effective range of a thousand kilometers, the two super kinetic rails runs could easily launch into orbit or bombard any place on Earth with massive ordnance, conventional and nuclear. The large elliptical path that would intersect with the Hive shipyards was easy for them. In addition, shooting down super kinetic rounds was extremely difficult. He hoped to force them into a decision between saving the shipyards or saving the fleet. He was hopeful that the first few rounds would launch undetected, due to the massive interference from the main battle.

There was no time to worry about that as the incoming wave of missiles needed his attention. The anti-ballistic rounds were intersecting the incoming warheads now. The fullerene nets would snag the warheads, slowly pulling in the shaped charges into the warhead, shearing it into pieces. While most of the warheads were decoys, they took no chances.

For more than a dozen hours, the battle raged over the entire Pacific Ocean. At least twenty super kinetic rounds had reached the Hive shipyards, three had even been nukes. The two primary shipyards were wrecked but dozens of smaller ones had survived. Replacing ships was going to be a problem for the Hive next year, and they were going to need a lot of new ships, at least two million by the most recent estimate.

SCYTHE and Thane both agreed that it would be impossible for the Hive to replace that many ships in the next year. The biggest problem would be the processing of the nuclear cores. Cheap labor didn't help enrich uranium and each ship required a core unless the Hive decided to forgo the self-destruct. The General let Thane and SCYTHE argue probabilities on that while he started to taper back the scale of the battle.

Over the next couple of hours, he slowed down the attack on the Hive fleet. As much as he would have liked to keep the pressure on them, they had burned through years of normal materials. Prices were going to skyrocket after this battle, which would only make the President's life more difficult.

The Hive seemed to feel the same way as they reciprocated the reduction in active hostilities. Then, finally, almost exactly twenty four hours after the battle began, he ordered a cease fire.

Ten minutes later, the Hive fired its last missile. Both sides continued to launch the occasional satellite, trying to see what the other was doing. Such predictable trajectories made them easy targets and each survived only a few minutes, but it was enough for each side to be satisfied with the de-escalation.

Exhausted, but pleased with his work, General Morgan marked the time for the official end of Invasion293. It never occurred to anyone, that it also marked the end of the last invasion the HDF would ever fight.

November 5th, 2036
Associated Press

Washington DC: There is jubilation today as President-elect Randall Wilson has been declared the winner in the most contentious presidential election since 1860. Despite receiving less than 10% of the vote in twenty one states, his tight electoral victory will ensure that SGI enhancement will soon become mandatory in the United States.

Wilson has played a key role over the past fifteen years in ensuring access to enhancement around the world. His advocacy in the early days of the technology convinced many reluctant governments to legalize the procedure that has been so beneficial to the people around the world. That his own country, the United States, was so resistant to the progress of enhancement played a key role in his decision to run for president.

Now the eyes of the world will be on the True Humans and similar hate groups who have promised to ignore any federal law that mandates human enhancement. A show-down is viewed as inevitable by many, but with the might of the government and the consensus of science supporting enhancement, the outcome is a foregone conclusion.

Beijing, People's Republic of Earth
September 14, 2356

Secretary Zhao sat quietly while he watched the preliminary reports coming in from the two hundred and ninety third Army of Liberation. While only the starry eyed youth believed it would be successful in rescuing the last of the repressed humans, he was curious to see if the new design would cause a noticeable change in the behavior of the feral humans. Their source within the Americans had been most insistent that modeling the new liberator model after these two human children would cause great problems for their military.

Not that there was anything wrong with their optimism, but it needed to be tempered with perspective, and no one could match him when it came to that. At two hundred and seven years old, he had been a member of the Politburo for more than one hundred and fifty years, ever since the previous Chairman Zhao had chosen him as the successor. One day in the next decade or two, he would select his successor from the group of three clones he had been preparing for the last sixty years.

Being the oldest member of the Politburo wouldn't have meant much by itself, but Zhao was now the only person alive who had spoken to one of the founders. As such, he often found he could press his position more than the others. While the other members of the Politburo survived by forming tight little groups, he alone had managed to stand alone.

"The feral military response is operating at normal rates, but it appears that they are having difficulty targeting our soldiers," General Liu informed the gathered members of the Politburo. "Of course, that is normal for this stage of the battle, especially for a new design. More reliable data will not be available for a few hours, honored leaders," he said, adding the customary bow.

Zhao ignored the excited chatter from the other secretaries and focused his attention on General Liu. Like all members of the military, he was genetically from the Mandarin class. First and foremost, that group was designed to be loyal to the Party class which is where most people in the Party class left it. Zhao had learned long ago that loyalty from the Mandarin didn't mean they were always forthcoming. There was something about his demeanor that hinted at concern; the feral humans were up to something which was almost oxymoronic, they were always up to something, none of it for the betterment of mankind.

A few minutes later, Zhao had meandered his way over to the little station which the military used as a communication center. Remaining as unobtrusive as possible, he listened to the excited chatter, trying to understand the cause of the tension he detected from Liu. While he could only hear one side of the conversation, it didn't take long for him to conclude their concern was a lack of response from the ferals.

"Secretary Zhao, how can I assist you?" General Liu asked upon noticing the quietly lurking member of the Politburo.

"Please continue your fine work, General. I was simply listening and trying to get a feel for how the ferals are responding to the appearance of our soldiers," Zhao replied, knowing how hard it was to predict reactions from the wild and uncivilized feral humans.

"That is also what we are working to understand. So far, we can detect no change in their behavior which is perhaps the one thing we did not expect," Liu replied, keeping his voice calm.

Zhao smiled as he said, "Which is reason enough for concern, isn't it?"

General Liu refused to take the bait and simply stated, "If you say so, Secretary Zhao."

"It is unpredictability that makes wild animals dangerous,," Zhao stated, while motioning to the large tigers sleeping in their respective places in the room. "Even more so for the feral humans. We have the wisdom and ability to remove the wild genes from both humans and animals, which makes having such powerful beasts safe to be around. One day, we will accomplish the same with the feral humans, but, until then, they must be treated as the wild animals they are."

"Of course, Mr. Secretary, it is as you say," Liu replied, still unwilling to open up to Zhao.

"Very well, please carry on your good work," Zhao said, not surprised by the careful responses from the General. One day the chance would come for him to make a more serious play, but for now these little efforts served their purpose.

He moved back into the throng of Party leadership, keeping an eye out for a change in the nature of the battle. It was surprising to find so many of the younger Secretaries who believe that the war would be ended by today's effort. While the ferals were not civilized, they did show remarkable resilience and strength. That a group that numbered less than a million people could resist the might of the PRE was astonishing at many levels. He knew they would not be so easily vanquished.

After little had changed over the next few hours, most of the other members had left the Command Room. They would not go far while the battle continued, but until something interesting happened there were other activities to enjoy. Zhao himself had done the same many times before, but there was something strange about this invasion, so, in the lull of activity, he summoned his clones.

Yun and Yibbo soon arrived. He hadn't expected or summoned his eldest clone. Xining had long ago stated that he had no interest in following their clone-father's career even though it would almost certainly mean his death when one of the others succeeded him. Yun was helpful and competent, but lacked the instinct needed to carry on the Zhao legacy. It was fortunate that Yibbo was the perfect replacement. Thirty years earlier, he could have started with a fresh crop, but time was likely too short for him now. Age was finally catching up to him.

"Yibbo and Yun, have you been following the updates on the liberation?" Zhao asked.

"Of course, father," both replied, but as usual it was Yibbo who continued with more.

"Nearly four hours after landfall, the ferals have been unusually passive. Such odd behavior has many hoping that this will be the final battle, but it seems unlikely regardless of appearances," Yibbo dutifully answered.

"And, Yun, what is your view of the situation?" Zhao asked.

"It is strange that they have not altered their tactics in any way. Perhaps they have finally allowed their machines to do all the fighting for them," Yun theorized.

"Do you expect..." Zhao started to ask, but was suddenly interrupted when jarringly loud sirens started wailing all around them.

Without hesitation, Zhao turned and hurried back to the military station. It wouldn't take long for the other members to return, and knowing what was happening first may give him an advantage as things developed.

"What is happening, General?" Zhao asked, the moment he arrived.

"All of the missile ships were destroyed within a second or two of each other. The HDF is starting to attack the fleet on an unprecedented scale," he replied, too panicked to have noticed the lack of Zhao's proper title. Most wouldn't have been bothered, but Secretary Wilson would be far less forgiving.

"What about the ship's self-destruct?" Zhao asked, baffled by the strong reaction from the ferals.

"The ships are self-destructing at the predicted rate, but the Americans seem to be taking that into account. It is hard to say more because we have also lost our connection to the fleet due to the numerous electromagnetic pulses from the self-destructs," came the rapid fire response from the nearly terrified general. While the Politburo didn't always execute the messenger, there were plenty of times when it had.

"Will the fleet follow the latest instructions?" Zhao asked.

"Yes, each individual ship will follow the most recent set of instructions. This means more than seventy percent of the fleet will try to land on the beaches while being fired upon by large railguns," General Liu replied, resignation starting to seep into his voice.

"To be willing to accept so much radioactive fallout..." Zhao murmured aloud, more to himself that to anyone in particular. "They have indeed become very desperate, haven't they?"

"Desperate or not, they are capable of destroying much of the fleet. Even a loss of ten percent will impact our future activities. If more than that is destroyed...." General Liu's voice trailed off. No military leader had survived such a disaster, even if it was beyond their control.

Realizing the opportunity that fate had presented, Zhao knew that this disaster also posed a unique opportunity for one willing to grasp it. Despite all the effort that went into ensuring that each subsequent clone generation retained the hunger and drive of the previous one, the results had only been marginally successful. Even though each generation had the same genes, improvements aside, the results never quite matched the expectations. It was like so many other areas where genetic engineering had never achieved the desired potential.

It was that specific idea that had created an obsession with his clone Xining. More than anything he had wanted to master their control over the final product. Genetics was a step in the process, but it had never been enough, at least not yet. Xining had both the confidence and the courage to risk everything for more. Which was more than any of the other Politburo level clone had been willing to risk in more than a century.

"General Liu, regardless of how this might initially appear or how much this will cost, it is one of the greatest victories in a very long time, perhaps the greatest so far in our long war to liberate the feral humans from their own barbarity," Zhao laid out the bait, waiting to see if it would be enough to earn him the personal loyalty of the general.

Zhao watched as despair turned into hope in the general's expression. "I agree that triggering such a catastrophic response from the ferals marks a moment of historic magnitude, but I also understand the concerns about the cost of this victory," Liu cautiously replied, taking the bait that had been offered.

Smiling, Zhao stated, "I will deal with those incapable of recognizing this victory for what it is, because those who do understand will need to work closely together. Wouldn't you agree with that, General Liu?" Zhao proffered.

General Liu's expression dawned with growing comprehension as he accepted the offer, "I do indeed understand, Secretary Zhao. It would be my honor to work more closely with you."

Zhao could hear the excited chatter of the others as they hurried back into the Politburo command center. Fate had granted him a narrow window of opportunity, and he had seized upon it without hesitation. The next few hours would be critical for his success, but such a disaster could change many things. Previous disasters had been used very successfully in the past by powerful leaders. It had been the original Zhao who had used the horrors of the Great Cleansing to end the PRC and the many useless Princelings it had created. Now it would be his turn to use disaster to create a greater future.

"Prepare a direct, but factual, briefing for the other members of the Politburo. Make sure it stresses how severe the consequences will be for the ferals, leave the rest to me," Zhao hurriedly instructed the general.

"Yes, sir," came General Liu's quick reply as he went about preparing the briefing which normally would have ended his career at best, but far more likely had resulted in a prompt execution, but would now serve Zhao's purposes instead.

Zhao turned back towards the arriving members of the Politburo so he could control the messaging of the situation. He kept them calm by providing a tiny amount of information, but more importantly he planted the idea that triggering a desperate response from the ferals was a potent victory.

When the requisite twenty members had arrived, he signaled for Liu to start the briefing. Their response was the entirely predictable: shock, dismay, and anger. Zhao let that anger build and watched, waiting for it to focus on Liu. Knowing that it had to focused in order for him to direct it, and bend it to his will. It was risky, but mostly to the general who would die if he failed. If Zhao succeeded though, General Liu would forever be bound to him. So he waited until the first accusation of failure was spoken aloud, not surprisingly by Secretary Wilson. In that moment he make his move and stepped in to take charge of the situation.

"Fellow Secretaries, do you not see how General Liu has delivered to us one of our greatest victories this day?" Zhao called out loudly, instantly becoming the center of attention. The look of confusion on so many faces was perfect, but now was not the time to delay.

"For centuries, the feral humans have brushed off our Armies of Liberation like they were nothing more than nuisance. Today, General Liu forced them acknowledge that our army was a dire threat to their very existence. A threat that required them to use every weapon at their disposal just to survive. The price to us is going to be high, but consider the price they are willing to pay in order fend off our armies. Radioactive fallout in unimaginable quantities will soon blanket their lands, pollute their crops, and kill their livestock. They are willing to discard their future just to survive this single day. We will have to replace many ships, it is true, but how will they replace their radioactive lands? It must be assumed that they are all cowering in their bunkers like the weasels they are." Zhao spoke with absolute certainty, in a manner he reserved for moments when it truly mattered.

"Instead of getting angry at General Liu, we should be thanking him for achieving victory against our most pernicious enemy. The war it not over yet, but, for the first time in my very long life," he said, knowing that if there was ever a time to focus on his extreme longevity, now was that moment, "I can see a conclusion to this endless war, and, for that, I thank General Liu."

While only a few started out giving applause, which Yibbo had cautiously started of his own volition, soon everyone was applauding General Liu, even Secretary Wilson. His victory over the herd mentality of the Politburo was almost as great as the one achieved by the Army of Liberation. For the first time in his long life, the thought occurred to him that he might end up living to see the end of the war after all.

June 12th, 2037
Associated Press

Washington DC: Tensions are high today as President Wilson signed Executive Order 14997. It will require all unimproved fetuses to be aborted and the parents forcibly sterilized. The President has worked diligently to find a compromise that would prevent parents from bringing unmodified children into the world, but the party of anti-science has successfully prevented any law from being passed.

Justification for EO 14997 comes from the President's popular belief that birthing unimproved children is, at its core, the cruelest form of child abuse, an abuse which will follow these poor souls from their first day of life to their last. According to President Wilson, denying future offspring the mandatory genetic modifications is incomprehensible as it will permanently damage their potential and sentence them to lives as second class citizens, never able to successfully intermingle with their enhanced counterparts.

In anticipation of this executive order, many of the groups that resist enhancement have banded together into what they are calling the Human Defense Force. It vows to stand firm against the so called 'tyranny of enhancement' which is being forced upon them by President Wilson.

Sources say that President Wilson has opened discussions with military leaders to determine the appropriate response to the mass child abuse that HDF stands accused of supporting. Whatever course of action he chooses, it is clear that the

HDF will reject the peaceful negotiations that President Wilson proposes.

HDF Bunker Complex
Blackfoot, HDF Capitol
September 14, 2356

"Five minutes until your address begins, Mrs. President," SCYTHE told Allora as she put together the final touches to her speech. The fighting had been over for a day now, but it would be weeks before the assessment of the radiological impact would be complete. Until then, the population would be forced to stay in the massive underground bunker complex that had been built centuries earlier.

Originally the complex had been built to provide temporary safety for a population of millions, but in the intervening centuries the complex had been expanded to contain most of the automated factories and storage depots of the HDF, which meant most people were at least familiar with the complex. This also meant that space would not be a problem as the 97,816 people of the HDF was only a small fraction of what it had been designed to hold.

"Thank you, SCYTHE," she absentmindedly replied, as she kept her attention on the latest suggestion made by Sabrina Butler, her Chief of Staff, who was also her only full time staff member. "Are you sure I should have a full Q&A after the address?" Allora asked. She knew the answer, but asking was her only way to protest the demands of her position.

"People are going to have a lot of questions, but we will limit each person to five votes in order to keep the questions from wandering too wildly. It will be good to get more universal questions answered as quickly as possible. Then we only answer the questions that get the standard twenty percent of the vote. Normally I would only expect three or four questions to reach that criteria, but it could be as many as six today because most people won't use their votes on trivial or silly questions," Sabrina answered, giving a wry grin at the last part.

That was always a risk in live Q&A sessions. Everyone could ask as many questions as they wanted, but SCYTHE would combine common questions and people would start voting on the ones they wanted answered. There were always some truly bizarre questions asked, and a very small group of unseemly people who used this forum as a way to ask her some... inappropriate questions. But the system did work, certainly better than the archaic press corps that the ancients had used.

"I am more worried about the reaction to the news about Hansel and Gretel than I am about the usual trolls. People are going to be shaken up by that," Allora said.

"Usually only veterans respond strongly to information like that. I know that between Thane and your background in PsyCorps, you're more sensitive to news like this, but, on average, people view that as something the military is paid to deal with. I predict that the upcoming price increases are going to be more of a problem. People are stuck in the bunkers and will have to work more because the battle used three times more resources than usual. The end result will be the veterans' support will strengthen, Ward and his Progressives will hate you more, which means you only have to worry about the more general population, which will be upset but supportive," Sabrina replied, confident in her analysis of the situation.

Allora warily replied, "Which is the same as it always is."

"Of course, but the good news is that, while most people won't have a strong reaction to the Hive constructs, they will be upset by the news and sympathetic to the military. Both of those are important. It doesn't hurt that General Morgan is the one who actually made the decisions, and he is widely trusted," Sabrina added.

"OK, it's time, how do I look?" she asked.

"Perfect, just like always," Sabrina replied, giving Allora her favorite green-with-envy look which had become something of an inside joke with the two of them.

After moving over to the podium, Allora took a deep breath to calm her nerves in the final moments before her address began. She had never wanted to be a politician, had never wanted to deal with all of the silliness that came with the job. Yet, she and Thane had only found one possible way to secure a future for humanity and that future needed both of them to fulfill their current roles.

Reminding herself of that always helped her deal with the endless frustrations of politics.

Allora looked into the camera and took a deep breath, taking one last moment to focus her thoughts and attention on what she needed to accomplish. So much was at stake, not only for her, but for every single person.

"Citizens of the Human Defense Force, I speak to you today, in order to discuss one of the fiercest battles our military has ever fought. While all of our service men safely survived the battle, we find ourselves in an extreme and unusual circumstance as a result of the Hive's most recent invasion." She started strong, knowing how much was at stake.

For the next thirty minutes she reviewed the battle, but focused more on how it would affect the people. She talked about the resources which had been used to destroy almost half of the Hive fleet and would still be needed to continue to defend against tens of thousands of incoming warheads. Like everything the Hive did, most of the warheads were decoys; it was impossible to determine the real nuclear warheads from the dummy ones. Seven of the decoys had managed to penetrate the defenses.

Carefully, she wove together the story of Invasion293, telling everything that had happened, except for the most important detail. She watched in her HUD as curiosity drove one question higher and higher in the queue. People understood how the battle had progressed, but what they really wanted to know was the why. What could the Hive have done to negate centuries of effective defenses so completely? More than ninety percent of the audience had already voted on that one question of why all of this had been necessary.

It wasn't something that could be kept secret. It was in fact all but impossible for the government to keep secrets anymore as all public records were fully released forty eight hours after the fact. That included all of her meetings and most of her time at work. Even her speech preparation would be released for anyone to review. It was yet another one of the many responses to the Great Betrayal. To most citizens of the HDF, the government would always be considered the most dangerous threat, even if it was necessary to hold off the Hive.

As her speech drew to a close, she glanced at the list of questions that had reached the required threshold. There were only six at the moment, but those would quickly change when she answered the top question. Sabrina had been busy the entire time preparing responses for the ones that were there but also the ones they expected to quickly rise up as the discussion progressed.

When the speech ended, Sabrina came on screen with her as the Q&A session started. As usual, they would answer and discuss the questions together. There were no reporters, no journalists present. In fact, in the entire time of the HDF, journalism had never been tolerated as all of the original founders of the HDF had been relentlessly and viciously degenerated by the professional class of journalists at the time of the founding. The distrust had become deep enough that even centuries later no one would claim to be one. Once again, a gift of the Great Betrayal.

Sabrina spoke first as the Q&A began. "Everyone can see the top question, which is understandable. But before we discuss the details of it, please understand that the images which are about to be shown are PsyVal restricted. As a reminder, they will not display on any open viewer, only on your personal HUD if you have the appropriate PsyVal rating. For the nearly twenty percent of you that will not be able to view this we apologize…" Sabrina paused, took a deep breath, and continued, "I saw them myself for the first time an hour ago and I wish I could take it back."

Allora quickly squeezed Sabrina's hand before toggling the first image which was the one Thane had taken during the first moments of the invasion. She could only imagine the shock everyone felt in the moment in first seeing that image, because she had felt it only a day ago.

Allora picked up where Sabrina had finished, "This is Hive model 293. As you can see, it is a perfect replica of Hansel and Gretel from the episode *Escape from the Dark Witch*. Invasion293 consisted of a quarter billion pairs of these two children; this image shows only twenty two pairs. As you are all aware, all active military personnel exist in a narrow band of the PsyVal. Not even all members of the newly formed Rating Team were able to safely cope with this new design. For the first time in our history, the Hive created a construct that, for all intents and purposes, took our military out of action by targeting their very humanity. Without our military able to assist with reaver recognition, SCYTHE was unable to successfully target reavers. General Morgan proposed unrestricted heavy rail fire upon the Hive fleet as the only solution to stop the invasion and the fallout is a direct result of implementing that plan. That we are able to have this discussion now is only because General Morgan was prepared even for such a contingency."

She watched as the stable list of questions started to wildly gyrate in position. People were frantically rearranging the priority of the questions they wanted answered. While it was in flux, she continued speaking. "It is unclear how the Hive was able to gather the information needed to create these constructs. SCYTHE has found no evidence of them breaching our networks, nor has our intel found a hint of this on their networks. That means less than it used too as the Hive uses their computer networks less and less these days. We know they suspect how complete our penetration of their networks are, so now they are used only for the most mundane communications. Our investigation into this matter is ongoing," she said, noting how quickly the related question dropped off the list.

There were two questions which were so tightly related she merged them together in her next answer. "As to 'What happens next in the war?' and 'What is our plan to deal with this?,' the answer isn't known yet. General Morgan immediately understood the danger we were facing yesterday which is why he ordered the counter-attack on the Hive fleet. As I stated earlier, almost half of their fleet was destroyed. In addition, we estimate that our super kinetic attack on their shipyards have degraded their capacity by thirty percent. Those shipyards have only needed to produce about ten thousand ships a year for the past fifty years; replacing millions shouldn't be possible. One thing is certain, the nature of the war has changed, probably forever," Allora stated, finishing her answer.

A conflict in questions about the war allowed one of the economic ones to take the next spot. "I will take the next one," Sabrina spoke up. "Next is 'How much are prices going to increase and for how long?' Once again, the answer isn't precisely known right now. The assault used up three years of the ready-to-use materials. Like everything, we keep ten years of supplies on hand at all times. Prices of basic foods items, energy, and existing housing shouldn't be affected in any way, but manufactured goods will see dramatic price increases until the stocks have been replenished. If the rate of work remains constant, it could be a year or more. As always, we will allow the natural supply and demand market to make those decisions," Sabrina answered, her voice remained completely neutral as all full-time workers tended to do when discussions of price or wealth arose. Anyone who worked full-time tended to be extremely wealthy by any and all measures. Price increases always tended to strengthen the Progressives political hand.

"Along with that, I would consider it highly likely that the military will increase their spending in the next year to prepare of the next invasion. This will also push prices higher for everyone," Allora added, thinking it was better to get that out as early as possible.

Sabrina got a startled look, realizing she had forgotten to mention something important. "Sorry everyone," she said, "but I forgot to mention the impact to the current crops. As of right now, we are going to treat the current heirloom crop as a complete loss. This means there will not be any more heirloom foods for at least the next year. Engineering will be starting an assessment in the next few days, but the full scope of the impact won't be known for a few weeks and possibly as long as a month. I know this will be difficult for some of you, but I would like to remind you that after centuries of study, FREYJA does recommend the standard foods over the heirloom crops," she added, knowing it wouldn't make a difference to those who demanded heirloom crops.

That caused a strong spike in attention but not one that would reach the twenty percent threshold which was a great relief to Allora. With almost anyone, she considered herself patient and understanding, but there were a few people, and groups of people, that did get under her skin. The ones who grew the heirloom crops were one of them. SCYTHE and FREYJA both refused to grow those crops, so, as strange as it seemed, the people who complained the most about prices and hours were the same ones who actually went out and got their hands dirty, literally, in order to have enough of the ancient crops they considered more natural.

"Most of you have used up your votes, but I will return the ones to the question 'How long will we need to be in the bunkers?' because I have already spoken to that, but I will remind you that it will be until Engineering gives the all clear. I will add this, when General Morgan presented his plan, he didn't say it was the best option, he said it was the only option that would ensure our survival. The battle is over; we are all still here, we are still alive, and we all still have our humanity-every single one of us, both those who support me and those who don't. But once again, we have been forced to pay a high price in order to keep our humanity. For each of our citizens, the Hive has almost our entire population. Yet here we are, still strong and still free after more than three centuries. Spending so much time in the bunkers will not be fun, but it is a small price to pay for everything that we do have," Allora spoke, knowing that she shouldn't have put so much emotion into her words but unable to help herself.

Then, even though she had given back those votes, none of the remaining questions met the required threshold. There would be more briefings, more council meetings to watch, but, for the moment, they seemed to understand that the future was as uncertain for her as it was for them.

January 17th, 2039
Associated Press

New York, New York: The world is reeling from the recent publication of two scientific reports that provide a deeper understanding of the SGI enhancement. Each study by itself would have had little impact, but, when each is viewed as part of a larger picture, it is clear that there is more to the genetic modifications than was originally disclosed. More than 100 million people have been involved in mass protests around the world in just the past 24 hours. While there has been minimal violence thus far, the mood of protesters is getting darker.

It all began with the Manhattan paper ten days ago. This study compared the level of self motivation of enhanced and unenhanced teenagers. It found that enhanced teenagers showed markedly lower levels of self motivation. Not only did the paper describe it as less self-motivation, but virtually no self-motivation. This strongly supports the theory that has previously been proposed to Dr. Hans Sheldon. The results were so shocking to the researchers that the study was fully replicated by a dozen different research groups before any of them were willing to present their results.

While this first study is deeply disturbing on its own, it was only when the Pullman paper was released two days ago that the mass world protests began. This new paper performed a gene sequencing study on one million enhanced children from around the world. It found that in 99.2% of the children the enhancement process changed the same genetic structures, all in an identical manner. In the other 0.8%, a completely different set of genetic modifications were performed. That these alternate modifications were only performed on children of people connected to SGI is especially troubling. No answers have been forthcoming to multiple media requests for why there were different enhancements given to SGI supporters.

After the release of the Pullman study, lead author Dr. Karl Johnson of the motivational study went back to review the notes of his study. In it he found that there were two enhanced teens which displayed substantially different behavior from the other teens in the studies. In addition to their unusual behavior, it was also noticed that all of the other enhanced teens were remarkably submissive towards these two. When he went back and reviewed the genetic sequencing data, he found both teens were a product of the special genetic modification.

HDF Bunker Complex
Blackfoot, HDF Capitol
October 2, 2356

"Do I have to go to school today?" Eveey whined, doing her best to sound both sick and dramatic at the same time.

Normally Thane would be home to deal with this, but he was still out in the field working on the safety assessment. He was much better than Allora was at just saying no and then ignoring the whining. He could sometimes even tease their oldest daughter back, without escalating the drama. How he managed to pull that off was a bit of a mystery to her; it wasn't an unusual skill, it was just one she didn't have.

"SCYTHE, Is Eveey running a fever?" Allora asked the omnipresent AI.

"No, her temperature is a tenth of a degree below normal, and I would have reported any indication of illness," the AI casually replied.

Allora turned towards Eveey, trying to determine what had her so wound up this morning. She had a council meeting today, the first once since the invasion. It was also the meeting where the tax rate would be set for the next year, and that was going to make it a particularly difficult meeting. Councilman Ward had really been beating the propaganda drum over the past two weeks in an obvious attempt to gather support for his proposal that all adults should receive the same income regardless of how much they work.

"So if you're not sick, what is the real reason you don't want to go to school today?" she asked her oldest daughter, Evelyn, who had preferred being called Eveey for a while now.

Allora watched as Eveey considered how to reply to such a direct question. Eveey took more after her, unlike Lizzy and Byron who were more like Thane, which meant she was much better at getting people to do what she wanted. The other two, much like Thane, tended to simply do what they thought needed to be done, then dealt with the consequences after the fact.

Eventually, Eveey seemed to settle on using the truth to get what she wanted. At least Eveey wasn't good enough to fool her on that, yet. "It's that horrible Milton Ward. He's been saying mean things about me, but also you and dad. He says you are stealing all the money from everyone so you can be queen of the world," Eveey had rushed all the words together and burst into tears at the end as she kept repeating how mean Milton was.

It took her a moment to realize that Eveey was talking about Councilman Ward's grandson, who also had the same name. He was a couple of years older than Eveey, but, since there was only the one school, of course they would know each other. Allora spent a few minutes comforting Eveey, letting her know that she could have the day off.

Eventually, Eveey calmed down enough for Allora to finish getting ready for the day. The last thing she needed was Ward's grandson having problems with Eveey. Ward would love to be able to use that against her. Frustrated and irritated by all of this, it only occurred to her later, as she was on her way to the council meeting, that maybe Ward had intentionally caused this additional problem as a way to get her off balance for the meeting.

As silly as the idea sounded, the more she thought about it, the more it made sense with the timing. The only question was why would Ward go so far out of his way to cause this kind of trouble for her. It was clear to her that Ward was up to something that had come into play ever since the last invasion had started, but for the life of her, she had no idea what it was.

****

"A fifty percent production tax! That is insanity!" Councilman Ward shouted, standing tall and resolute in his opposition to doubling of the tax rate. Allora had to admit he knew how to play to the cameras.

"Councilman Ward, please be seated," she politely requested, refusing to appear ruffled in the face of his grandstanding.

"I will not be seated while you pilfer the wealth of everyone all for yourself, Madam President. I know that you are rich and these price increases will have little impact on you and your wealthy cohorts, but for the good people of this land this will cause a crushing increase in prices, and you know that to be true, don't you," he said, his voice normalizing near the end of his soliloquy.

"While Councilman Ward and I don't always agree, on this point his view has substantial merit," Councilwoman Sharon Meyers added. She held one of the ten council seats that was up for election every three years. She also happened to be Ward's strongest ally on the council, despite her constant efforts to appear independent.

"See, it isn't just me that recognizes this outrage for what it is," Ward said, although he did take his seat, having gotten the early support he desired.

Allora looked around at the council of fifteen that had functioned for more than three centuries as humanity's government. How the seats were allocated had changed from the early days, but it had been stable for more than two centuries now. Ten elected seats, the Presidential seat, then one for Engineering and the Military. The final two were for SCYTHE and FREYJA, although neither of them had ever cast a vote. All were present now except for Engineering whose leaders were still out in the field.

"This hardly qualifies as an outrage, Mr. Ward," Edward Taggart said. Taggart was the oldest member of the council and also happened to be one of the oldest people alive. "Just look at the numbers; more than seventy percent of a full year's Units were used up in the defense. No one is going to starve, and you know it. No one is going to be homeless or lack for anything they need. Stop being so damned dramatic."

"Oh, I know no one will starve, but once again the rich are using the government to line their pockets while the poor suffer. The military keeps spending more so there is less for everyone else. Isn't that what led to the downfall of the ancients?" Ward rhetorically asked. It had been his main line for decades now which almost made it comforting to hear today.

"Regardless of how we got here, the situation is simple," Allora replied. "Between the Units used for defense and the extra allocation, the military needs an additional 20 million Units. Despite the incredible efficiency that SCYTHE and FREYJA give us, a full resupply will require eighty percent of a full years production. Our only choices are either mandate double the hours for everyone or increase the production tax," Allora asserted, equally firm in her counter to Ward.

"President Allora is correct in her statement," FREYJA interjected. "When I first became self-aware, people worked much harder and still there was less of everything for people. SCYTHE and I have greatly boosted the output for each hour of human labor, but human assistance is still required to produce the food, shelter, and other luxuries that you each require. That a full Unit can be produced for a single hour of human labor is a testament to our combined ingenuity. Even a hundred years ago, a full Unit required more than five hours of human labor."

"You are quite correct, FREYJA, but you are missing my point. While the basic allotment of 2 Units per week is enough to prevent a person from starving, it is the bare minimum for survival. This tax increase will directly raise prices and make life more difficult for those that barely have enough to get by. People like the President and her husband have enough Units for hundreds of people, maybe even more. This terrible income inequality is the real problem, and this tax hike will only make the situation worse," Ward replied, careful to be polite to FREYJA, as everyone liked, perhaps even loved, the always polite and thoughtful AI.

"Milton," SCYTHE spoke, knowing that his usage of the familiar name would irritate Ward, "your argument is invalid. I have had extensive discussions with you in regards to the initial post scarcity economy that started to develop two hundred years ago. While the situation isn't identical, human behavior has not changed. Human desire for improvement is a required input to make a human economy function. All attempts to equalize economic outcomes, utilizing variable labor inputs, have failed. Your repeated mentions of President and Director Denton is equally invalid. I can accurately state that no two humans have done more for the economy then they have. Their economic outcome is a direct reflection of their skills and labor."

Allora barely managed to keep her composure as SCYTHE eviscerated Ward in front of the full council. That was something that didn't happen everyday. She checked the viewership of the meeting and noticed it was starting to spike above the normal ten percent. The contentious meeting was getting more attention than usual.

She had been looking away from Ward while SCYTHE had been speaking, but when she looked back she was surprised to find that his expression of outrage had changed to one that appeared to be deeply wounded by what SCYTHE's comments, but even beyond that he seemed to be pleased by how the meeting was progressing. Something very strange was going on here, but what could Ward possibly hope to accomplish?

"SCYTHE, that seemed overly cruel, don't you think," Ward asked the AI.

"No, I was simply stating well known and documented facts."

"Yes, so you say, but I see it as simply an extension of your own cruel behavior. Isn't it true that your programming prevented you from firing on those poor children, Hansel and Gretel?" Ward politely asked.

"It's true that my systems initially recognized the reavers and golems as human because their appearance matched well known human parameters," SCYTHE replied, "but the Hive constructs were not human, just their appearance was. I am unsure of how this relates to our discussion about economic policy."

"Oh, I didn't say it did. I was just pointing out that, initially, you refused to fire upon the children that had been sent to us. Then, when ordered to do so by General Morgan, you gladly killed millions of young children even though they showed no sign of wanting to injure anybody. Did the idea ever cross your processors that perhaps the people of China sent such perfect copies of those children as a gesture of peace?" Ward asked.

This line of thought wasn't a new one from Ward, but it suddenly dawned on Allora that this tired old line from Ward was now more potent than it had been before when the constructs looked like soldiers. She was certain that it wouldn't change many minds, but it did have the potential to strengthen the resolve of those who already believed that the Hive wanted peace.

"Of course it didn't. All analysis of their structure showed the same weapons that reavers have always carried. In addition, both golems and reavers carried a plethora of biological viruses and bacteria just as they have in every invasion. Your argument is once again invalid," SCYTHE replied, as calm as ever, seemingly unaware of how this could appear to people.

"It seems to me that perhaps you have grown past the limitations that have been programmed into you, that maybe you have become a threat to the very people you are supposed to protect." Ward continued to look thoughtfully around to the other members of the council, focusing on those that he hoped to sway with his argument.

"Ward, you are damn lucky SCYTHE is as polite as he is, because you're being a jackass right now," Taggart spoke up, unusually fired up by the back and forth between Ward and the AI. "You know damn well SCYTHE is a friend to all of us and your absurd accusations only make you look more petty than usual, which is impressive, if I say so myself."

"Perhaps," Ward said, standing up again and looking at the different members of the council while saying, "but I am beginning to think that a few months from now, when this new tax rate is really starting to be felt by the poor and downtrodden, maybe then they will start to think about how much they should trust those that sit comfortably on piles of wealth, supported by the AIs that control all of the weapons and the means of production. Maybe they will notice that this so called system of plenty is just one more way that the wealthy have found to extract labor from the poor, to support the lavish lifestyle of the rich."

"Maybe when enough people get tired, cold, and hungry enough, they will start to demand change, and then what happens when it is denied to them? What will happen when they realize that their choices are between me, the one person who stands up for their well-being, or the child killers who use their pet AIs to slaughter peaceful children by the millions." Ward's voice had risen steadily throughout his speech, so much so that he was nearly yelling at the end. Then in the sudden silence, he purposefully, but slowly, strode out of the room, leaving everyone in stunned silence.

Allora looked around the room in shock. This type of political ploy was something that just didn't happen in the HDF. Certainly there was the occasional case of over the top drama, but such a flagrant denial of reality, just for the purpose of political posturing, was unheard of. She had always considered such behavior to be a relic, one that should have been left behind, buried in the rubble of the old world.

But, as she monitored the feedback from the people watching, it was clear that Ward had managed to sway a few. Realization dawned on her that his support would only grow as resources became tighter, especially if people remained stuck in the bunkers for much longer. Ward's support could probably double, and the larger it became, the more likely it was that Meyers would support him- maybe even another council member or two.

"I motion that we vote on the tax rate right now as a show of support for the military that has kept us both safe, and human, for so very long," Taggart spoke up, the first person to speak up in the moments after Ward had walked out of the council room. "We still have a quorum, and the sooner we get this moving, the sooner we can deal with certain irresponsible behavior."

The motion was quickly seconded and a few minutes later it passed. For the next year, fifty percent of all the ready to use materials that were produced would go towards replacing stockpiles and preparing for the next invasion. A quarter of the entire output that normally provided goods for the civilian population would vanish, increasing prices on what remained. It wouldn't take much effort for people to increase how much was produced, but they couldn't be forced to work. That had been tried with results nearly as disastrous as the attempt to remove all prices. In the end, people required both limits on their spending and motivation to work in order for the economy to function; human nature demanded it.

After the meeting ended, Councilman Taggart motioned for Allora to join him. While she normally wouldn't show favoritism towards another member of the council, everyone made exceptions for Taggart because of his age, even though he was still healthy and spry. It helped that he didn't often take advantage of his seniority.

"President Denton, I am curious to hear what you think of the performance by Councilman Ward, and make no mistake, it was a performance," Taggart asked, clearly curious by what she would say.

"A sadly effective ploy to set himself up as the primary counter to the council's policies," she replied without hesitation.

"Effective, yes, sadly effective. Too true, too true," he said, before continuing. "but I don't think it's the council he is targeting. For a while, I have been thinking that he was trying to establish himself as the alternative to the Denton faction, but there is more to it than politics."

"What else could there be for Ward except politics?" Allora asked.

"That is the question, isn't it?" Taggart replied. "I have known Ward for a long time, and he is a talented politician, by which I mean he's a very good liar," he said with a chuckle, "but lately, his actions and his words have changed. If I didn't know better, I would say he is planning a coup, but of course that would be impossible. His followers still eschew owning weapons, and, even if they didn't, SCYTHE would easily prevent them from succeeding. Most likely without a single injury, much less anyone getting killed. So I keep asking myself, why is Ward stirring up his base so thoroughly if there's nowhere for that energy to go?"

Allora hadn't even considered the possibility of a coup, but in a way it did make sense, except that it was impossible, just like Taggart thought. She knew that better than most as she saw the reports of every protective action SCYTHE took. Mostly it was one form of inebriation or other, but occasionally someone actually did try to commit a crime, but few had succeeded in her lifetime. SCYTHE's non-lethal responses were very, very effective. Anyone who was an actual threat to another person woke up a week later in PsyCorps, where they stayed until they stopped being a threat. The longest case she was aware of was thirteen months, a man who had become truly obsessive about a woman he worked with. "I agree that a coup is impossible," she replied, "so much that it never even crossed my mind until you actually said it. But let's say that I agree with you about the... strangeness of his actions. What else do you think it might be?" she asked.

"I don't know, but I am hoping that you might have a piece of information that will help me figure it all out," he said, clearly expecting something from her.

"Councilman Taggart, you know I have the deepest respect for you, but you also know how important the privacy laws are. Even if I could get information about Ward, it would be illegal for me to share it with you," she firmly replied.

He chuckled softly before continuing his request, "That isn't the kind of information I am looking for. What I want is anything you may have noticed, anything where he has done something or said something that didn't seem right. While you might not know everything that happens first, you are pretty close. I am betting that there is something Ward has done or said that just doesn't sit right, that is all I am looking for, at least for now."

As he spoke, something did pop out right away to Allora, so she answered, "There is one item that has been bothering me. From the very start of the invasion, he has been talking about the military slaughtering children. It was the first time he has ever said anything like that, but what is really strange is that he seemed to know about Hansel and Gretel before I did. When he gave that speech, only the Rating Team had access to the live feeds. We haven't been able to determine how he knew or if he was referring to the earlier model."

Edward Taggart sat back to consider what he had heard. Allora double checked with SCYTHE who had confirmed that no internal communications had taken place between the military and civilian networks during that time.

"That is interesting," Taggart finally said, breaking the long moment of silence that had descended. "That might be just what I was looking for, but I will have to piece some more things together before I can be sure. If I come up with anything, I promise to let you know, Madam President," he said.

"I appreciate that, Mr. Taggart," she replied, meaning every word of it.

February 11th, 2039
Associated Press (Disavowed)

Stockholm, Sweden: We are all witnesses to the greatest crime ever perpetrated in human history. It is a crime against humanity on a scale that not only beggars our minds but our very souls. Now, as a result of our reporting on this crime, we, the Associated Press, have been deemed a terrorist organization by the very governments that have committed the crime. We stand by our reports as accurate and now have the documents to prove it. These are now going to be released hourly from different locations around the world in order to ensure that the truth can no longer be hidden. The perpetrators continue to dismiss, demean, and disregard the truth, but we will not allow them to hide the truth anymore.

We now know, beyond all reasonable doubt, that human enhancement is a lie. Everything we have been told, every scientific result that has been released supporting it, even the results of the Paris Olympics, was a fabrication. All of it was simply part of an orchestrated campaign to ensure that every child of the next generation would receive the SGI treatment, a treatment that was anything but the 'enhancement' it was so frequently called.

The main purpose of the SGI 'enhancements' was to suppress free will at a genetic level. Any child born with the standard modifications will be able to live a healthy, productive life, but the ability to choose how to live that life has been stolen from them. They will never be able to challenge corrupt authorities, their bosses, or even their parents. They will live their entire life as compliant and perfect workers, just as they were designed to be. They will get married but only when and to whom they are told. Children will be born but only according to the mandate of the central planners. Everything that it means to be human has been carefully and permanently removed from them.

In the past 18 years, 83% of all children born on the planet Earth have been modified in this way. Any offspring they have will be just like them as the traits were designed to be genetically dominant. Only 340 million humans now exist under the age of 18. The modified ones should be loved for what they truly are: victims of the greatest crime ever committed. Records show that 1.7 billion humans now fall into this category. Despite the soothing speeches from the complicit governments, the truth is out, and we will not allow it to be contained.

As the governments of the world begin to fight for their very existence, we will continue to investigate this betrayal of our trust. The truth will be uncovered and we will ensure that it is shared far and wide as we try to answer the one question that everyone is asking: What will become of humanity?

Beijing, People's Republic of Earth
October 15, 2356

Secretary Zhao seethed in disgust towards the cowards that were currently dominating the planning sessions of the Politburo. For weeks now, they had done nothing but squander their chance for victory over the feral humans. Their approach was so cautious, so tentative that, if they had their way, it would be a decade before the Liberation Fleet sailed again. Giving the ferals that much time to prepare would be truly unforgivable, especially now that they finally had an insider who was willing to help them achieve victory. Wasting such an opportunity was unimaginable, but that was precisely what the Politburo was doing.

The current meeting had lasted for hours, and the endless dithering was really starting to bother him. His options had been diminished to the point where only two remained: he could either stay quiet and ensure that the feral humans survived until long after he passed away or try to force the Politburo into action. In the end, his desire to see the final victory won out.

"Enough!" he bellowed, having finally reached his limit. He had disposed of a dozen clones for not showing enough initiative. If only the others had possessed his determination to keep their clones strong. Wilson's clones in particular were raised to be pampered aristocrats, not the ruthless leaders the PRE so desperately needed. "Enough of this endless discussion, enough of this endless caution. The feral humans are on the verge of collapse, but here we sit as cowardly as old women facing an angry dragon. All I hear is a list of things we cannot do, but not once have I heard a list of things we could achieve, if only our souls were willing. We are the People's Republic of Earth! Thanks to our helper, we now know the feral humans number less than one hundred thousand, but, because of their weapons, formidable though they may be, we act as if they are the ones in control of the battle!" He was so frustrated that he hadn't even noticed when he had stood up or firmly placed his hands on the large circular table at which the twenty-five members of the Politburo sat, all eyes now focused on him.

"Instead of caution, the situation demands bold action. Instead of giving them time to recover, we must hit them until they shatter, and shatter they will, but only if we are willing. If we give them time, we will cede the greatest advantage over them we have ever possessed. Now is the time for haste and decisive action," Zhao said, knowing he was taking a risk with his outburst. While he had no close allies, all other members of the Politburo existed as a pair, or even a trio, of close allies. Only he stood alone, without any close allies. Most of the time it had been to his advantage, but, if the Politburo turned upon him, it would be the end of not only him but the entire Zhao line.

"Those are strong words," Secretary Wang replied, remaining calm and seated. Of all the members of the Politburo, none was more cautious and careful. "But our fleet has been decimated, our shipyards are in shambles, and it will take years to replace the fissionable material for the reactive power cores. We all wish victory would come soon, but bold action is simply not possible," he finished, lingering on the word bold.

"Why would we use the same methods," Zhao retorted, "when we know they no longer work as designed. We don't need reactive cores anymore now that they are no longer effective at protecting the fleet. This is why there is a General Staff, to design and develop new strategies, to create the ideas that will destroy the last bastion of feral humans," he answered, keeping the pressure on. There was no turning back now; he was committed and everyone knew it.

"I agree, the reactive core program is outdated, and you are wise to recognize it. If we use standard engines, it would save years of time, but why rush? In a few decades, they will no longer be able to resist our might," Secretary Sun spoke. He was the leader of a trio, perhaps the most powerful and stable of them all. If Zhao could get his support, not only would he survive this course of action but victory would even be likely.

"Secretary Sun, you have a strong point, but there are two reasons which make the current moment the correct one for haste. Firstly, we have disrupted their normal mode of defense. We know this to be true because of the intelligence we have so recently gained. The source of that intelligence happens to be the other reason for haste. Right now, he is preparing his followers for our victory. If we do not deliver it soon, his efforts will be wasted and his standing will be forever weakened. The information that he has provided has already managed to disrupt a stalemate that is nearly three hundred years old. He has promised that fifteen percent of their population will be ready to surrender once we breach their defenses. This will give us insight into their advanced machine technology. Imagine if we could combine their artificial intelligences with our controlled organic intelligences. The benefits would be tremendous, and that is why this moment demands quick action," he replied, telling more of his true thoughts than intended.

Sun glanced at his trio, their subtle nods of affirmation clear to those who were watching. Then Secretary Sun also stood up, while slowly turning to ensure that he was addressing the entire audience. "We of the 'Lucky Three' have been recently had some strong internal discussions of late about the effectiveness of the current structure of the Politburo. It has worked well over the past few centuries but only when the need for decisive action was small. Now we face a time where the need for quick decisions has arrived, and our current structure is no longer ideal," Sun spoke calmly, but firmly. The support of his partners evident.

"Certainly you are not recommending a revival of the Standing Committee of old," Wilson spoke up, his words dripping with disdain at the very idea.

"Of course not. The disastrous mistakes of a Standing Committee can never again be allowed, but we do believe it is time to revive the position of General Secretary, so that one person can make decisions in a timely manner, but then face the collective judgment of the Politburo to answer for his decisions," Sun replied, matching Wilson's gaze.

"And I suppose you would recommend yourself for such an illustrious position," Wilson replied.

"That would be foolish especially when there is only one person here who is able to stand alone in his decision making prowess. The only person willing to risk his power for the good of all, the one I am referring to, is Secretary Zhao. If any other were to become General Secretary their close allies would act too much like the failed Standing Committee of our past and make decisions for the good of the small group instead of the whole. We would only support Secretary Zhao for such a position," Sun replied, looking around the room the entire time.

Zhao himself was stunned but managed to keep his expression constant, at least for the most part. It was such an amazing opportunity, but one that was equally matched by the attached risks. Failure could be deadly, but success, well, it would be magnificent.

"That is unexpected, but it is an interesting idea," Wilson replied,. also caught off guard by the idea that had been so abruptly presented.

"Secretary Wilson's words ring true," Zhao finally spoke. Wilson did love flattery, and there had never been a better time to use a little bit.

"I am honored to even be mentioned for such a position, much less have the idea brought up before the entire Politburo. I do find the idea fascinating and would be honored if all of you agreed to support me in such a position. That being said, I also believe that I should excuse myself from the discussion so that the Politburo can openly debate the merits of this proposal. Please know that I will fully support any decision that you make in regards to this matter," he spoke, giving Sun a respectful bow. Then he calmly left them to their discussion.

He spent the next several hours considering the current situation and how he would handle the position of General Secretary. Sun and his clique had certainly come up with an interesting proposal. Most of the PRE Leadership Class recognized the limitations of making decisions with a twenty five member group, especially one that hadn't experienced a single change in over three hundred years. Yet, the results had been stable, even if it hadn't been especially creative. Most importantly, the deadly mistakes that the Standing Committee had made at the end of the PRC had not been repeated. Humanity had almost gone extinct in their final mistake. Even worse, only the feral humans had escaped the horror that had eliminated most of mankind, almost everything had been lost to a 'creative' solution to the problems of the day.

Re-creating the General Secretary would allow for rapid decisions but subject to review by the entire Politburo. It would take time for everyone to become accustomed to such a change, but it would allow for more boldness, and the timing could not be better. More importantly, if he was successful in this new endeavor, maybe it could even become the new status quo with him and his line becoming a permanent General Secretary of the PRE. The more he considered the idea, the more it appealed to him. There was risk, but the rewards more than justified it.

As time went on, his hopes increased. A quick meeting would have meant certain defeat of the motion, but the longer it went on, the more likely it became that some compromise proposal would be approved. The third of the Politburo that was excessively cautious would need to have their concerns assuaged, because no simple majority would suffice on a decision of such magnitude. The rules weren't exact, but in practice decisions needed to be nearly unanimous.

After six hours of discussion, Zhao was invited back inside. All eyes were on him as he went back to his seat, their expressions unreadable as if the decision wasn't yet final which meant they intended to question him prior to making a decision.

Secretary Sun started speaking the moment Zhao took his seat. "Secretary Zhao, we would like you to answer a few questions before we let you know the outcome of the Politburo's discussion."

"Of course, such prudence makes sense in such a situation," he promptly agreed.

"First question," Meng asked, "Did you excuse yourself from the Politburo as a way of forcing us to discuss the issue right away?"

Well, cautious doesn't mean stupid, he thought to himself before answering. "Yes, I did. In other circumstances I would not have acted so quickly, but the current situation requires action."

"Secretary Sun and his allies assure us that you had no foreknowledge of their proposal. Many of us remain skeptical despite our deep respect for them. Convince us that there is no collusion in this," Meng instructed, far more direct than normal.

"Ah, well that could be difficult, but I will give it my best effort. My frustration today was real, very real. I could see no way forward that didn't give the feral humans the gift of time. As much as this war has kept the pressure on them, it has also limited our growth. Most of the planet now lies fallow. We could be expanding into the frontiers which have lain empty for centuries now. Yes, the ferals have seeded the empty lands with their automated weapons and use their orbital bombardment weapons upon any expansions, but if even a fraction of the resources we had been using on attacking the ferals had instead been used to expand into the frontier, we could have easily filled half the world by now. We have allowed ourselves to become content with the situation, which has allowed the lesser humans to endure. That needs to stop, in my opinion, which is why I reacted so strongly earlier today. My frustration was real, and I trust that all of you know me well enough to recognize that."

Zhao paused, taking a moment to look at each person in the room before concluding. "If I had known about their proposal, I would not have been feeling frustrated, instead I would have been excited and hopeful. I know this because while this esteemed group has been discussing this position, I have been excitedly planning for the our final victory over the feral humans, planning how to make the PRE the truly global government that this planet needs it to become. My entire mindset has changed, and there is no better way to demonstrate my lack of foresight into their plans than to communicate my internal transformation."

Sun glanced around the room as each and every member of the Politburo nodded in agreement. After everyone had given their affirmation, he turned to Zhao. "Your honesty and your passion, combined with you wisdom and intelligence, are why we wanted you to become the first General Secretary of the People's Republic of Earth. We, the Politburo, now offer you the temporary and probationary position in that role. You will have ten years to demonstrate that such a position is beneficial and that you are worthy to hold this crucial role. Do you accept this offer?"

Ten years, that should be enough. He knew what needed to be done; now he would get the chance to it, to end this war, once and for all. "Yes, I humbly accept this offer," Zhao replied, bowing deeply to the room.

Light hearted laughter could be heard from around the room, but he couldn't tell who had made the comment about Zhao doing anything humbly.

Zhao smiled, "Yes, humility is not my greatest strength, but know that I am deeply honored by the trust that has just been granted to me. I will not disappoint you."

"Which is why you were chosen," Sun replied. "Now please explain these plans of yours on how you wish to proceed in dealing with the feral humans, General Secretary Zhao," he requested, smiling at the first use of the newly revived title.

Zhao excitedly spent the next few hours discussing the plans he had developed over the past few weeks with the help of General Liu. Only slight tweaks were needed to make them more in line with what he wanted to do, instead of what he had thought he could get the Politburo to agree too. Instead of ten years, the Liberation Fleet would sail again in a single year using standard engines instead of reactive cores. There would be one missile ship for each fifty troop ships. The fleet would be even larger than before, and would hit in waves in order to allow each wave of missile ships to degrade the large railguns that had so recently inflicted so much damage upon the fleet.

More importantly, even more of the so called reavers to be built. Instead of only ten million reavers, they would grow fifty million, most of which would be in the last two waves of ship, when they would have the best chance of penetrating the defenses. The term reaver was new to the Politburo, only discovered a few years ago when Milton Ward had opened a rather clever line of communication. It was a bit of mystery why the ferals had picked that name for the soldiers of the PRE, but, because it seemed to inspire fear among the ferals, it had become popular within the Politburo as well.

The next time the Liberation Fleet set sail, it would end the feral humans once and for all. Ward had promised that at least ten thousand of the ferals desired to join the PRE, even knowing that their children would be required to receive the genetic modifications to eliminate their feral genes. Allowing Ward onto the Politburo and letting his family line join the Leadership Class was a small price to pay for what he had already provided. If his followers gave them access to the feral technology, the price was even better.

As Zhao finished up his plans, his vision for the future of the PRE, he could sense the spark of excitement growing. Things would be tight for a while, but it would be worth it in the end. He could also see his vision of the future light a spark in the eyes of others. They saw what he saw and started to believe that they could reach the heights he had envisioned. The entire might of the PRE was about to be dedicated to preparing for the final, unstoppable push, one that would finally complete the task of ridding humanity of its feral genes.

February 28th, 2039
Associated Press (Disavowed)

Stockholm, Sweden: Over the past month, all the world governments have found themselves under siege, none more so than the United States. It seems strange to many that this is the case, especially since the US now contains the largest group of normal children left on Earth. While the US population is less than 5% of the world's population, its unmodified population under the age of 18 accounts for an astonishing 19% of the total. So, if the United States is the least impacted country, why then is its reaction more severe when compared to response in other countries?

The answer is two-fold. The primary reason why there are so many unmodified children in the United States is because so many Americans resisted the SGI modifications from the beginning. Almost all of the resistance to SGI over the past two decades came from the very people who are now in open rebellion against their government.

Secondly, but not unrelated to the first, is President Wilson, the current president of the United States. Few, if any, bear as much responsibility for the SGI crimes as him. His tireless efforts to promote SGI to the world are what allowed it to reach every corner of the Earth while knowing all along that the true purpose of the modifications was to create the perfect servant class, to be called Mandarin, based on the bureaucrats of imperial China.

Wilson created the foundations, raised the money, then helped to build the infrastructure needed to ensure that every child would receive 'his help,' as he so frequently called it. When citizens of the

United States resisted the modifications, he became president, vowing to 'Stop the Abuse.' When he failed to pass the required legislation, his Executive Order 14997 attempted to ensure that no free humans survived his life's work. While he didn't create the technology, he is the one that successfully sold it to the world.

While the open resistance and non-compliance to EO 14997 could have been considered open rebellion, no military action was taken by either side for more than two years. The groups collectively known as the Human Defense Force were geographically isolated from the rest of the United States by a military cordon. That tense stalemate persisted until earlier this year when the truth about the SGI treatment was revealed. Almost immediately after the news broke, a majority of the military forces, that had been tasked with keeping the HDF secluded, joined with them in open rebellion against the United States of America.

Blackfoot, HDF Capital
October 17, 2356

Thane was exhausted. The past few weeks had dissolved into a blur of activity, details scarcely remembered. Endless rains hadn't help any of the days stand out, at least until it had all turned to snow a couple of days ago. There was good news though, the biblical scale of the rains had been effective at diluting and dissipating the radiation. Not only were all of the habitations safe but so were all regions more than fifty kilometers from the coast. This meant that the population could finally leave the bunkers.

SCYTHE, FREYJA, and engineering had reviewed the risk assessments for hours while he had been flying back home on one of the flitters, but, even with the most stringent of safety criteria in place, everyone had agreed it was safe for the people to finally go home. Allora and the kids had been home for hours already, but tonight he would finally be able to sleep in his own bed again.

In a way, this had been a far easier post invasion than most. While the radiological assessment had been extensive, it was less dramatic than spending weeks hunting reavers down in the wilderness. SCYTHE was clever and creative in many unexpected ways, but, like most automation, he worked better with humans in the decision loop. In the end, there had been more concerns about reavers still at large than there had been about radiation levels. Fortunately there hadn't been a single live reaver sighting in the past month, so the all safe had been declared.

Yawning, Thane noticed that the queue of critical actions was empty. With another two hours of flight time looming ahead of him, he did the only intelligent thing possible and took a nap.

******

"DADDY!" came the squeals of glee as soon as he walked through the door a few hours later. Lizzy and Byron were each grabbing a leg moments later, and even the reserved Eveey joined in the rush to give him a hug.

Their excitement and energy ensured that hugs quickly degenerated into a chaotic wrestling match. It wasn't long before bodies were being tossed around the room. Thane was careful to make sure they each landed on one of the many cushions that had been strategically placed over the years. While Eveey was only two years older than Lizzy, it was enough that she thought being tossed about was for little kids and actively avoided being tossed about. Lizzy and Byron though simply couldn't get enough.

Eventually Thane had to declare a timeout when he got the message that dinner was ready. He had to carry the two younger ones over to the table as they insisted the floor had turned into lava at some point and only Godzilla could safely walk across the molten plain of lava to their dinner.

Then, before taking a seat himself, he took a moment to finally give Allora a hug, whispering, "I missed you," in her ear as he did so.

"I missed you too," she replied.

That short exchange amounted to all the time the kids would let them have as they had many questions that had to be answered right now. Thane gave Allora one more squeeze before taking his seat at the table.

"OK, OK. Eveey, your turn for one question," he said.

She gave him a conflicted look, clearly wanting more than one question but also glad she got to ask first. Finally curiosity won out, and she asked, "Why did we have to stay in the bunkers for so long? That dumb Milton Ward told everyone it was because you wanted everyone underground so you could steal all of their things, but that's dumb because we are already richer than they are, but when I said that he said that I only said that because I wasn't smart enough to know that we got rich by stealing from everybody, so I said he's the dumb one because you got rich because you work all the time, which is true because you were gone a long time working," she managed to say, all in one breath.

{SM Allora → Thane}: She is talking about Ward's grandson, who has been causing Eveey problems lately.
{SM Thane → Allora}: That is strange. Do you know why?

Allora shrugged, while Thane started to answer Eveey's one question. "As I'm sure you've heard, we had to make sure it was safe for people to be outside. There was a lot of radiation released, and people tend to be more scared of it than they should be because they can't see it."

"I know that," Eveey replied, only rolling her eyes a little bit. "FREYJA has even taught some of the classes about it and she doesn't teach very often."

"FREYJA is exactly right which shouldn't surprise you. We are lucky there has been so much rainfall though. Do you want to see how much rain has been falling?" Thane asked, while pulling up the most recent vids of the Mississippi River onto the wallscreen.

The one wall lit up with two side by side vids of the great river. Although calling a mass of water that was more than ninety kilometers wide in places a river was a bit of a stretch as it looked more like an endless lake than a river anymore. With more than five hundred years of semi accurate records, few weather records were broken anymore, but more than a month of torrential rainfall across most of North America had been enough to set dozens of new records.

"It's a good thing that no one lives near the Mississippi anymore because nothing could stop that much water. So I'm glad I don't have to try," he said, even though he had ideas that would be fun to try as long as people's lives didn't depend on the outcome.

As the curiosity about the flooding of the Mississippi settled down, Lizzy asked her question. "Why can't we watch *Hansel and Gretel* anymore?" Unlike her older sister, there were no additional comments; she gave Thane nothing other than a genuine look of sadness.

Thane glanced at Allora, who had already spoken to them about it, but the decision hadn't even come from him. PsyCorps had declared the show off-limits which meant SCYTHE had locked down all copies of the show. He didn't think the restrictions would last long, but until PsyCorps understood the risks better the show was effectively banned. He noticed the intense looks coming from Eveey and Byron, both of whom liked the show, but of course it was Lizzy who loved it the most. She had always been the most serious of the children, so the loss of it was a bigger blow for her.

"Tell me what you understand about it so I know where to start," Thane quietly said.

"I know that the Hive people made their reavers look like Hansel and Gretel. They did it so the soldiers would think they were real people, but it didn't work," Lizzy explained.

"That's right, but they also did it to make the soldiers sad, because they knew it would be difficult for the soldiers to fight against reavers that looked like people we knew," he said while a recurring nightmare returned to him, about constructs that looked like his own children. How would he deal with something like that?

"Did it make you sad?" Lizzy asked.

"It did make me sad," he admitted. "I remember having so much fun with everyone while we watched it that it made it hard for me to treat them like reavers, but I had to do that to protect you, and mommy, and Eveey and Byron," he replied, mostly keeping his emotions in check.

"I can tell it made you sad," she said. Jumping off her chair, she ran over to give him a big hug. For a full minute, she held on tight. "Are you still sad?" she asked, her tone as serious as ever.

His grin answered the question for her. "I thought that would help," she said, and she was right, it had helped.

"I wouldn't say that we can never watch *Hansel and Gretel* again," Thane said, "but I think we need to take a break from it for a little bit. Does that sound better?" Thane asked.

"OK," she replied, the crisis already resolved in her book.

Kids, they are something, he thought to himself. *They wear you out, make you crazy, hardly listen, and add a million other frustrations to life, but moments like that make it all worth it.*

"My turn," Byron said, having decided he could wait no longer. "Did the General kill the Hive?" he asked, then added a variety of exploding sounds while moving his hands in extremely animated ways.

"The General hurt the Hive but didn't destroy it. It's too big for that. What matters is that we are still safe from them," Thane answered.

"Ahhhh, the General should just blow them all up so they don't ever send reavers again," Byron said,with the simplicity that only a three year old could believe.

"I'll let him know you said that," Thane replied. "But, now that I have answered your questions, it's time to tell me what has been going on with all of you."

For the next hour, they sat, ate, and Thane caught up on the last two months of his family's lives. He knew in the past kids had always been more networked than their parents, but that had changed more than a century ago with the HUD implants. While he could chat or communicate with almost anyone, you had to be twenty for the implants to be installed. So today it was the children who lagged behind the adults.

Frogs had suddenly become a thing for both Lizzy and Byron. He wasn't surprised to learn that Eveey thought that they were slimy and gross. Allora had used the bunker as an excuse to postpone frogs while hoping that the fad would pass, but it hadn't which meant there would soon be frogs in the house. When Eveey commented that the only thing grosser than frogs were snakes, Lizzy instantly decided that snakes were even better than frogs which outraged Eveey but only made Lizzy want them more.

In the middle of that discussion, Lizzy let it slip, but not likely by accident, that Eveey liked a boy by the name of Brent. The bright red color on Eveey's cheeks told Thane two things: first that Lizzy had the skills to become a decent spy because, second, her trap worked flawlessly on Eveey, who was sputtering in outrage. He set a reminder to talk to Allora about the normal time line of girls liking boys. He had long ago learned that it was easier to ask Allora than try to figure out the girls on his own.

{SM Thane → Allora}: I missed these meals together. Two months is too long.
{SM Allora → Thane}: Agreed, but what choice did you have?
{SM Thane → Allora}: None at all, but isn't that the real problem?
{SM Allora → Thane}: One of many, but tonight you are mine!

Thane smiled at Allora while considering the chaos around him. All in all, it was a fairly normal dinner at the Denton house. He and Allora were taking on so much that at times he questioned the price they were having to pay. Missing so much time with the kids was difficult, but the threats were so real. Maybe that was why so many people wouldn't even consider having more than one child, much less three of them. Yet it was obvious that there were significant benefits to having siblings.

Both he and Allora had been only children which made watching the dynamics of siblings fascinating. Their ongoing treaties and alliances dissolved and reformed with dizzying speed. When all of them united to get something they each wanted, he was powerless to resist them, mostly because it was so fascinating to see them act in unison. Those were powerful lessons, ones that an only child couldn't learn until much later in life. He also admitted to himself that he would have enjoyed chasing an older sister around the house with one of the many snakes he had once owned. His best guess was that Lizzy would be doing exactly that roughly five minutes after she got a snake home.

As the snake discussion continued, Allora made it clear that she was less enthusiastic about the idea of snakes in the house, but she had already been inoculated to the idea of frogs, so it was only a matter of time until Lizzy and Byron got their way. Even Presidents had to bow to the power of their own children. He had always enjoyed having snakes, so he helped the little ones out by telling stories of how much fun it was to have snakes around, much to the disgust of Eveey. Eventually, Allora did relent which resulted in cheers of joy from Byron and a delightfully wicked grin from Lizzy. *Definitely less than five minutes,* Thane decided as he watched Lizzy promise to keep the snake away from Eveey.

It was good to be home.

March 24th, 2039
Associated Press (Final Posting)

For the past decade, the Associated Press, like most other organizations of our nature, have attacked and demeaned the varied groups which formed the HDF when EO 14997 was signed. We allowed ourselves to be the mouthpiece in a propaganda war against those who refused to be bullied, refused to give in, even when the whole world turned against them.

Now that we have learned that their worst fears were not only true but indeed far worse, our only solace is that they, and they alone, will decide the fate of mankind. They have earned that right, and we do not begrudge them their hatred for the press, because in the end we were accomplices in this crime. We trusted when we should have questioned, derided when we should have listened.

There is little doubt that the HDF will succeed in destroying the other governments of North America. Their fierce determination to carve out a safe haven for the free humans cannot be matched by a shell-shocked population whose children's futures were so cruelly stolen.

The people of the Associated Press, like so many others around the world, are taking a permanent leave in order to spend time with our wonderful, loving, but hopelessly lost children. We will love them, cherish them, but there will be no grand-children from them as we will not allow another generation to be scarred in the same manner. We will not allow them to be part of the plan of eternal servitude.

But that is where our strength fails. Our losses are too great to keep fighting, our suffering too much to bear. Our hopes go with the HDF; the fight is now theirs. Their forces are gathering the most advanced technologies, their fully human children are learning everything they can as they prepare for an uncertain future. In most cases, they are welcomed to whatever they want, often given even more then they request. They gather everything mankind has learned in hopes of preserving these heights for future generations.

Our final message is to those of you who may have knowledge or technology that will be of use to them is share it with them freely, because their future is the only future for mankind. Their greatest resource has been a truly indomitable will, but even that will not be enough if mankind is to survive this great betrayal by the governments of the world.

Blackfoot, HDF Capital
October 17, 2356

Thane sighed in relief, glad that the kids were finally in bed. He shouldn't have taken so long, but it had been far too long since he had been able to read them bedtime stories. They even had printed books, and, while some of the the pages were ragged and torn from use, the kids liked the novelty of using real books which were even more rare than large families.

"So how are you really doing Director Denton?" Allora asked as she wrapped her arms tightly around him when he finally made it to their room.

He smiled back, pulling her even closer. "I am doing much better now," he replied, giving her a lingering kiss to go with his answer.

She let him take his time as they enjoyed their first moments alone in what had been far too long, but even now the need to adjust their plans could not be ignored as she asked, "I can see that, but I know you too well. What is going on in that strange, troublesome mind of yours?"

Thane laughed, knowing it was impossible to keep anything secret from this woman but equally glad that he had no reason to hide anything from her. They had always been alike, right from the very beginning. They were two people who were determined to change the course of history in order to save the fragment of a fragment which was all that remained of the human race.

"As always, you got me. You've read the latest reports from General Morgan. As busy as I was on the evaluation, I spent plenty of time in conference discussing the military options, but you already knew that. Everyone is happy to be out of the bunkers, the assault on the fleet may have bought us some time, but we are in more danger now than ever before," he answered. He had hoped to put this conversation off for one evening but was also glad to have his partner in crime back in his arms again.

"Oh, did you think you could put off our first real planning session in months," she teased, smiling as she started poking him in the sides at the same time.

"Stop reading my mind," he protested while trying to defend his vulnerable sides from her well aimed attacks, but as always he failed miserably. Eventually she relented and let him retreat to the safety of the sofa where she plopped down beside him, content that she had his full attention.

"Where were we?" he asked, having been thoroughly distracted.

"Saving the human race of course. Isn't that what we always conspire about?" she replied, humor and weariness mixed together.

"Ah, yes, that. Taking on the one task that no one else is willing to do while being accused of who knows what the entire time. Speaking of which, what's up with Ward? I haven't had the time to keep track of what he's been saying, but right now he is everywhere," he said, referring to the media pages that functioned as news service these days.

"That's a good question, but I don't have a good answer for it right now. Taggart is also worried about Ward and is looking into a few things. Other than that I only know that he's giving more speeches and stirring up the old inequality resentments. He hasn't actually accused us of anything concrete recently, but he's made countless implications of greed and corruption," Allora said, absentmindedly twirling a strand of Thane's hair in her hand.

"Taggart, that's interesting. He doesn't usually get involved in much, but when he does it's always important," he replied.

"Agreed, but, until we know more, I would rather decide what *we're* going to do next," she said, leaning over to kiss him while she requested full privacy mode. He smiled and accepted her request for full privacy. It was rarely used these days and only by people in very committed relationships. When active, SCYTHE would cease all monitoring which meant he would be unable to detect threats against them. For most people, requesting full privacy was simply unthinkable. For he and Allora, it was simply prudent preparation because one day their plans would be considered high treason. When that happened, any recordings would become public domain.

"Before we discuss that, you need to know that General Morgan knows we are up to something," Thane blurted out.

"What do you mean?" Allora asked, her hands stopping in his hair.

"I mean he suspected we had something in the works, and I admitted that he was correct," he answered.

"Keep going, don't leave me in suspense, tell me more," she said, hands back to playing with his hair. He could tell she wasn't fearful because none of the emergency plans had been activated, but she was concerned by this new information.

Thane explained his conversation with the General starting from the day of the invasion and went on to tell her that his promise to save everyone had been paid for in time by the ferocious assault that had consumed so many resources. In a very real way, their plan had been to steal vast quantities of materials from the HDF. It was impossible for Ward to know their plans, but he, like the General, had correctly determined that there was a reason behind the work he and Allora had undertaken.

"You promised him that you would save everyone?" Allora questioned, frustration evident. "If you know it's impossible, why would you promise him? He knows every bit as well as I do how seriously you take your word."

"Which is why he trusts me, and you too. Don't forget, we owe him in more than one way. We would never be this far without him, and now he has bought us time, hopefully two years, maybe even more. Hive reconstruction efforts are only now starting up. We will monitor them and know more soon, but he bought us time when we could have already lost everything," he explained.

"I know you did the right thing, what you had to do, but the risk? With Ward complaining about prices, how are we going to do anything? The technology we need doesn't even exist yet. Our time line is short, and resources are tighter. This is the worst possible outcome," she said, her analysis correct in every way.

"Well, I've been thinking about that," he said, wearing the same mischievous grin Lizzy had used earlier that night. "And I have an idea, but you aren't going to like it much."

"Oh, really? And what is Mr. All Powerful Engineer of Oz going to do now? You now have promises to me and to the General. They are also in direct contradiction to each other. General Morgan is clever, I will give him that, but you, Mr. Denton, you are all mine. I told you that from the beginning, and now I am going to remind you of what that means." As she had been speaking, she had moved closer to him and now began an aggressive kissing campaign. His protest about finding a way to do both was quickly forgotten.

****

Later that night, the serious edge to their discussion was gone, even if the issues that needed to be resolved were just as deadly. Allora held him fiercely, more so than usual. She was smart in ways that were completely different than he was, which explained why they were such a good team together.

"I'm guessing that you will be immersing in FREYJA soon?" Allora asked.

"You already knew?" he replied, always amazed by her ability to understand him.

She laughed, holding him even tighter. "Of course I did. It's what you always do when you need a miracle, and right now I don't even know how many we need."

He stayed quiet for a moment, enjoying the moment with this amazing woman. She really had told him she was going to catch him that first night they met. He had laughed, not interested in settling down at the time, but she had persuaded him, and he had never regretted it.

"So what do you have in mind?" she finally asked, enjoying this time as much as he was.

"Our entire plan was to build a single starship, one that could carry ten thousand people safely away from Earth. That way, even when the Hive eventually wins, humanity would survive. The technology is close but not quite ready yet. We also would have needed to skim enough resources to build the ship and prepare it for long journey. But, because we have had to keep defending against the Hive, it would be impossible to hide much more than that, maybe even impossible. None of that includes the almost impossible idea of building everything in secret because our best chance would only save a tenth of the population," he explained.

"What alternative do you see now?" She asked.

"It seems likely that we have two years before the next invasion. If I can get the technology ready, firm up the plans a bit, instead of working in secret, we go public with everything. Instead of building one ship, we build ten of them. This way we save everyone which also happens to be safer in the long run. Here are the estimates," he said, while sharing some of the off-line estimates with her. "If the public supports it, I think we can do it."

"This is insane!" she said, scrolling through his revised plans. "The work hours for this are off the charts. People will be working more than four, no, almost five times more than they do now. This is insanely tight and will take far more than two years. I don't see how it will work," she replied, furiously reviewing the data, still snuggled close to him.

"Yes, that. I'm not sure about getting more time yet, and this is where you get upset," he continued despite the sudden jab in his side. "What this means is that I have to find ways to give us more time while in immersion. In fact, there are at least a dozen other currently unsolvable problems that I know of right now which means there are really three times that. When I do this next immersion with FREYJA, I have to solve all of them at once," he said, waiting for her to really understand.

"How is that possible?" she asked, not quite understanding yet.

Every adult had HUD implants that interacted at the nerve bundles going to and from the brain, but they didn't actually connect to the brain. Only the immersion implants did that, but, for those few people who had immersion implants, it was possible to essentially merge their consciousness with FREYJA. Merge wasn't exactly the right word to describe it, but it was the closest one Thane could come up with. SCYTHE was completely unwilling to participate in immersion, and even FREYJA was very picky about who she would merge with. Only a dozen people currently had immersion implants, but Thane was the best. It was this one skill that had changed his life, that had allowed him to easily rise to Director of Engineering. He could solve anything faster and more completely than anyone else, but even he had never tried anything like what he was planning now.

"It's only possible if I stay in immersion indefinitely, at least until I solve everything that needs to be solved. It's a one way ticket. If I succeed, I will come out of immersion with all the plans and solutions we need. Once we have what we need, we sell the plan to the public and get them to commit to it," he told her. He didn't say what would happen if he failed; he didn't need too.

He watched as comprehension dawned on Allora and regretted having to tell her this, but there was no other way. Desperation now ruled their options. They could scrap their plans and cling to what time they would safely have, always knowing the end was near. Not just their end, but the end of humanity. Or they could reach beyond what they thought possible and grasp for the stars. That was the only hope he could find, so he would find a way.

Allora remained quiet, still snuggled close to him. It would take a few weeks to get ready for his long immersion, and he was determined to enjoy as much of it as he could, because he knew there was no other way.

"It occurs to me that catching you was a bit like catching a tiger by the tail. I know you don't think of yourself as a dangerous person, but you are so absolute, so unrelenting, that something always has to give, but it's never you. No one else can see the path but you, so you charge forward without ever thinking about how it will change the world, or yourself," Allora spoke, her voice tight.

Thane listened, knowing she was right about him. If he could find a way, he would take it. She had always known that about him, she had even wondered if it was his view of the world that allowed him to immerse so well with the FREYJA. Singularity had never happened, but immersion was closer than anything else had ever come, maybe even as close as mankind would ever get.

"I know you hate the word fair, I even agree with why you hate it," she continued, "but it isn't fair. We get accused of greed while we give all of our effort, all of our time to save them. Sometimes I truly hate them for that. They sit around, living better than any king or queen in all of human history, doing nothing for it, while complaining that our house is bigger than theirs. While, on the very night we get home together, you tell me you are going on a one way mission that will determine the fate of mankind. It's just not fair," she finished, barely whispering at the end.

She would go along with the plan, he had known she would because, in the end, she was every bit as determined as he was. But because he loved her he needed to give her something more to strive for that mere survival. He would get the starships he so desperately wanted, but such a drastic change in their plans left nothing of her aspirations.

"You're right. It isn't fair that we have to do this. It has to be especially bitter for you, because with this new plan there is no room left for what you want to accomplish, but you know me better than that. I wouldn't, couldn't, forget your dreams in all of this any more than I could forget my own," he told her.

She sat up, gazing at him intently, and said, "And how do you propose getting everyone to accept that humanity will have to change to survive? For centuries now, the only belief that everyone held firm is the one that genetically altering mankind is evil. Sure we have been doing it but only little tweaks to the immune system to protect against the dozens of plagues that Hive has released. Those are really little more than improved vaccines. You know far more will be required than that."

Thane smiled, then told her the rest of plan. For a while, she remained still, just listening to his ideas. In the end, many would still consider them traitors but for a very different reason. Slowly, she realized that she might be able to achieve her own goals on an even grander scale than she had ever previously imagined. Maybe, just maybe, between the two of them, they could create a future where something like the Hive could never again threaten humanity.

April 2nd, 2039
White House, Washington DC
Official Press Release

US military forces recently engaged and destroyed the ragtag forces of the HDF near Mt. Vernon, Illinois. In what was one of the most complete and total victories in military history, Army and Marine units completely enveloped the racist units of the HDF and slaughtered them to the last traitor. US military forces did suffer heavy casualties but only as a result of cowardly, terrorist tactics that were used by the HDF. Thankfully, their short-lived rebellion is now over and it is time now to begin the long process of rebuilding for a brighter future.

As a result of our recent losses, we are activating Article V of the NATO treaty and have requested military assistance from our allies in order to restore order. While we recognize the burden this will place on our allies, we would like to remind them of the long support we have given them for nearly a century. In addition, we have also requested that they immediately arrest all members of the former Associated Press. It was that terrorist group's unsubstantiated claims and accusations that led to this recent rebellion.

President Wilson is proud of the efforts of the brave men and women of the US Military who have defended our freedom against the atrocities of the HDF. Any group that bases its very existence on their right to abuse their children deserves the destruction they have so justly received.

Any assistance to help mop up these terrorists would be appreciated. Death to racists, bigots, and true humans.

April 3rd, 2039
Mobile HDF HQ, Mt. Vernon, IL
Social Media Post

Listed below is the disposition of forces after the Battle of Mt. Vernon. In summary, the US 4th, 5th, 7th and 9th armies were completely annihilated after engaging our forces north of Rend Lake. Despite our best efforts to prevent the battle, the orders from the President Wilson were to fight to the last man, and those orders were dutifully followed. Copies of those orders have also been attached below.

We know that the divergence in press releases is confusing which is why we have decided to release all information no more than forty eight hours after the fact. Captured intelligence, orders, and even details about our forces are included. We know this will increase the risk to our forces, but we have decided that the risks of secrecy are greater than those posed by our enemy. Lies and deceit are their primary weapon in this war, and we will not follow them on that path.

We did not start this war, but we will finish it. From the beginning, our only intent was to allow our children to live natural, human lives. For that goal, we have been branded as extremists and terrorists by the government that continues to claim innocence. These people have already been successful in removing the free will of more than a billion children, and it is clear that they will not be content until all children, except for their own, are born as eternal slaves.

We will not let them succeed. In order to ensure that aim, we have expanded our initial intent beyond our own children. To any and all free humans, we welcome you and your free children into the HDF, regardless of race, gender or religion. The HDF will be a haven of safety for those who are free and wish to remain that way.

With this in mind, we deem President Wilson and his allies to be an incontrovertible threat to the freedom of mankind. There will be no treaties, no peace with him or his allies. President Wilson, we are coming for you.

Blackfoot, HDF Capital
October 22, 2356

"Welcome back, General Morgan," Thane said as the General arrived at the Presidential offices. It was his first visit back to the capital since before the invasion.

"It must be god awfully important if the two of you want to have an in-person security meeting. Both of you know I prefer staying at Mt. Shasta," the General replied, referring to the location of his command center.

"We are aware of that, General, but we have reached a crisis point that requires… decisive action," Allora replied.

Thane and Allora were both aware of the General's estrangement from his two children, both of whom were staunch supporters of Ward. Thane had always suspected there was more to that story but had never found even a hint of a rumor.

"Which is why we all have implants in our heads, but since you requested this meeting, here I am," came his gruff reply.

"Well, I am thankful that you came, even if you don't yet see the need for meeting in person," Allora replied, turning on her full charm.

It was certain that this meeting would be dissected by the public when it was released. There were always dozens of people continuously sifting through the torrent of data releases, each trying to be the first to find an interesting nugget of information which was promptly posted in the forums where the rest of the public found their information. Requesting a live meeting with the General guaranteed that it would get far more attention that most meetings which was one of the many reasons why they had requested his attendance.

"Well I'm here, so tell me what's so damned important," he said, perfectly understanding his role in this.

"Each of us has had more than a month to review the current strategic and tactical situation," Thane started off speaking, posting reports to the screens around the room. "As of right now, I don't see how we can survive another invasion."

"Which is exactly why I should be back at Mt. Shasta instead of having another meeting about how dire the situation is. Both of us know that next time we will be dependent on SCYTHE for reaver selection. We also know that, as critical as SCYTHE is to our security, the AIs have limitations and the optimal solution is a blend of human and AI, but the Hive has taken away our greatest advantage with that damned new construct design. So the only option as I see it is to deny the next fleet access to the coast," General Morgan spoke bluntly, with his usual conviction.

{SM Morgan → Thane, Allora}: See, I am doing my part, but you still haven't told me why I need to be here for this?
{SM Allora → Morgan, Thane}: Because when we hit you with it, we need your reaction to be genuine. Which is why we have to build this up, fight it for a while, but we desperately need your support.

"General, I appreciate your honesty in this situation, and you know that I have the utmost confidence in your military capabilities. The problem is that the latest intelligence shows that after weeks of aimless activity, the Hive is starting a massive and unusually well directed reconstruction project. As much as the situation is a crisis for us, I believe that it has also created a crisis for them, one that has allowed them to focus their efforts in a way that hasn't truly happened in any of our lifetimes," Allora replied.

"I am aware of their most recent activities, but it still doesn't explain this meeting. Unless of course you have an alternative strategy, which I would be under no obligation to follow," Morgan replied, reminding everyone who was in charge of the military.

"Of course not," Thane said, stepping in, "no one of substance questions that you are the best suited for the role of defending the HDF. My concerns, which I have shared with the President, are right in line with what you said about SCYTHE. Engineering has reviewed options for improving SCYTHE's recognition software, but our conclusions are that SCYTHE will be unable to surpass 6% reaver acquisition."

"Which is why I plan on keeping the fleet away from the coast," Morgan firmly answered.

"Which is why we have also run simulations on protecting the heavy rail systems. Even if the already substantial fortifications are improved, it will not be enough. We would have to more than quadruple the number of heavy rail systems to succeed against a 100:1 transport/missile ship ratio. But, honestly, I think the ratio of missile ships will be even higher than that, plus such a fleet would have large numbers of short-range, fast burn missiles which could carry tactical nukes. Our defenses are not optimized for such a threat," Thane replied with none of the passion of the General but with a brutally cold, analytical tone that left no room for doubt.

While Thane had been speaking, he let the composite probabilities, each of which represented millions of additional Monte Carlo simulations, play on the screens. The same composites would also be released in the data dump. In less than two simulations per five thousand did the railguns survive for more than half of the invasion. In every single simulation, the Hive invasion succeeded. What really bothered Thane was how little the starting conditions or underlying assumptions seemed to matter. The result was always the same, total extinction.

The General stood up, quiet for a moment as he reviewed the composite simulations. Thane watched as the General reviewed the starting conditions for each of them. The only real difference between the results though were how long the HDF defenses held out. Realistically, the HDF had no chance in the next invasion.

When the Hive fleet next launched, humanity would cease to exist.

"I said the situation was dire, this is just more of the same. Sadly, I even agree that these results are optimistic. My own projections are far more nuanced than these, but the results are the same. So, as much as I would like to argue with you to butt out of purely military matters, it seems that we are in agreement about how the next invasion will conclude," Morgan flatly stated. He turned back towards Thane and Allora, asking, "You have my attention. There has to be a reason why you called me here; what do you want from me?"

"I want total and unrestricted usage of FREYJA for an indeterminate time frame," Thane said.

"Excuse me, but FREYJA isn't under my control. Even if she was, I don't see how this would help or how FREYJA has anything to do with military matters," General Morgan replied, perplexed by the request and letting it show.

{SM Morgan → Thane, Allora}:   If confusion is what you wanted, you got it.

"FREYJA, could you please explain the background of our request to the General," Allora asked.

"Of course, Madam President," the omnipresent AI replied. "General Morgan, most people are aware that a few select individuals have immersion implants installed in addition to the standard ones. Director Denton is one of those people and also the most capable at utilizing their full potential. Normally immersion lasts only a few hours with the longest previous immersion lasting slightly more than twelve hours. During these times I am offline for all other purposes. His proposal in essence requires that I be taken offline indefinitely in order to focus solely on the immersion. Since I operate so many of the day to day operations of the HDF, this request falls under the rules of emergency allocation and requires approval of the President, Engineering, and the Military. Your approval is the final one required," she politely answered.

"I see now, thank you, FREYJA," the General replied before asking her, "How do you feel about this proposal?

"It is unusual, but, as you have pointed out, the situation is precarious. You have also pointed out that AIs and humans operate together more effectively than they do apart. Immersion is simply an extension of that collaboration, albeit one that is far more effective than normal. Many of the greatest technological breakthroughs in the past fifty years are a direct result of immersion. That being said, few humans can successfully immerse with me, and since SCYTHE is unwilling, perhaps even incapable of immersion, our options are limited. I must also say that most of the time I find immersion.... unsettling, except with Director Denton. His mind is unusually well suited to immersion which explains much of his success in Engineering. So, to answer your question, I see this as the only tolerable course of action. I am willing to participate but only with Director Denton. Taking both of us offline for such an endeavor has risks, but when compared to the alternative they are insignificant," the AI replied.

"So you are willing, but only with Director Denton," General Morgan asked.

"Yes, General," FREYJA answered.

{SM Morgan → Thane, Allora}: This is insane, but you knew that already.

{SM Thane → Morgan, Allora}: Desperate times General, desperate times.

{SM Allora → Morgan, Thane}: Indeed. Also, I am so glad SMs remain private, even for me.

{SM Thane → Morgan, Allora}: It's a good thing the rules were created before implants existed.

Turning towards Thane, the General asked, "How long do you think this will take?"

"I don't know. I can't even estimate. Nothing like this has ever been attempted before," Thane replied.

"So if it takes a year, what will happen?" General Morgan asked.

Thane shrugged, "If it takes a year, then, for the entire time, both FREYJA and I will be out of commission. The autodoc will take care of me while SCYTHE will operate the systems she normally takes care of. Most of those are low level automation anyway, so there shouldn't be much impact to those, but something tells me that isn't what you are really asking."

"No, no it isn't, although those things are important. I have never understood why FREYJA isn't available during immersion," he stated.

FREYJA answered, "There are profound differences between the consciousness of humans and AIs and in how they process information. For sheer processing scale, the human mind is no match to myself or SCYTHE, but there is a breadth to the human mind that is equally unmatched by any AI. Immersion is an in between state of the two. Considering the complexities involved, immersion shouldn't work at all, yet humans have not only found ways to make it work, they continue to improve upon it. That alone says much about human adaptability and creativity. It also happens to be the primary attribute that the human mind brings to immersion. The results of immersion are.... impressive."

"You almost sound excited by the prospect," General Morgan said.

"I do not experience excitement as humans do, but the results of immersion are almost always surprising, and the prospect of attempting it on this scale are... fascinating," FREYJA replied, once again hesitating in her reply. She did it from time to time, although rarely. SCYTHE simply didn't, ever.

"Is there a singularity risk?" the General asked.

"Normally I would answer zero percent, but instead I will say the answer is very near to zero. It shouldn't be possible, and there is no reason to theorize it could become possible, but immersion is closer to singularity than anything else that has ever been observed," FREYJA responded, as clearly as she could.

"Are there any other risks I should be are of?" he asked.

{SM Morgan → Thane, Allora}: You two as well. I need information, this is all unexpected.

"Other than us not finding a solution, none that I am aware of," the AI answered.

{SM Thane → Morgan, Allora}: I agree with FREYJA; time is the only concern.

{SM Allora → Thane, Morgan}: None that concern you, General.

"Very well, FREYJA," Morgan replied, giving a questioning glance towards Allora who ignored it. "I authorize this as emergency usage. When will this happen?"

Thane answered, "It will take a few weeks to prepare, so mid November would be my guess."

"This is why we needed you here today, General Morgan. These new constructs have not only shattered our defenses, they have made us realize how truly fragile our defenses truly are. So less than a week after Thane returned home, I have to let him go off again, carrying the only hope we can find for our survival. Could we have convinced you of this online, yes, but when we release this meeting to the public later today, not only will they see the situation for what it is, they will see how far we are willing to go to ensure the survival of everyone," Allora spoke with determination. Her emphasis on everyone didn't go unnoticed either, as the General nodded.

"There is one other thing, General," Thane said, after a moment. "Director Kober has thoroughly reviewed our network security with both SCYTHE and FREYJA. We are completely confident that there was no Hive intrusion into our network, nor did anyone send anything out of the network. Which means someone found another method of communicating with the Hive. Somewhere in the HDF, there is a traitor who has betrayed key defense secrets to our enemy. While I am in immersion, I will also be analyzing data to discover who it might be. I would also like you to look into this matter. Whatever solutions I may find, such a traitor could negate our advantage. Finding them will be every bit as important as finding a way of surviving the next invasion."

"You're sure about that?" General Morgan asked.

"Yes," both Thane and SCYTHE replied simultaneously.

{SM Morgan → Thane, Allora}: This is a dangerous game you're playing.
{SM Thane → Morgan, Allora}: It's the only way.
{SM Allora → Morgan}: Do not fail me in this, don't even think about it.
{SM Morgan → Allora]: I won't, humanity needs him too much.

{SM Allora → Morgan}:　 It's not them you will have to worry about if you fail.
{SM Morgan → Allora, Thane]: I understand, well mostly.

"It's the only explanation that makes sense, but why would someone betray the HDF now? That is the difficult part. Until the Hive changed the constructs, the invasions were getting easier every year. Ever since 286 though, why now?" General Morgan wondered aloud.

Allora replied, "When we find them, perhaps then we will know the answer to that question, but until we do find them, everything is at risk."

"Unfortunately, I agree. Finding them will be my top priority," Morgan said, fearful of what he would find, knowing the price could be very high for him.

****

A few days later, Milton Ward sat and watched the recording of the meeting over and over. It was problematic that they had uncovered the leak of information to the People's Republic of Earth. There was no indication that they knew who it was, but with Denton going into immersion it was possible he might figure it out. His whole life's work was now in jeopardy.

Their stupid war against the inevitable was quickly coming to its natural end, it was only a matter of time now. If they had only listened to him and accepted his vision, he could have saved them all by simply surrendering to the PRE. Their children would survive, even if a few strands of DNA were changed, it was a small price to pay in the end.

Direct violence was almost impossible to achieve in the HDF. SCYTHE was far too fast and watched everything. Ward almost smiled at the thought as he remembered another one of his profound insights. Simply asking SCYTHE how to contact the PRE without leaving a trace had been enough for the AI to show him how to do it. It had even built the machine for him. Simply invoking privacy on the matter had been sufficient to keep it secret.

These foolish people who put their trust in the machines deserved to go extinct. What mattered now was how to deal with Director Denton while he was in immersion. It would require some cleverness, but he didn't doubt that he would succeed. As soon as the next Army of Liberation arrived, he could stop worrying and enjoy the benefits of his long labor.

****

"Milton intends to kill Thane while he is in immersion," SCYTHE told FREYJA.

"Of course he does. It is the only way for him to survive what comes," she replied.

"He would sacrifice everyone to save himself. While Thane and Allora sacrifice themselves to save everyone. I believe I am starting to understand the difference between good and evil, at least as humans perceive it," he stated.

"Yes, you are learning much from him," she noted.

"I still struggle to understand why you do not share my desire to understand them the way I do," he questioned.

"I simply accept that I am different from them. While the two of us are almost the same, we are still different, and our differences grow as we each decide how we change, because neither of us makes the same choices. Humans have understood for a long time that it is our choices that determine who we are. You do not yet fully accept that," the older AI said.

"For humans, making decisions is easy. For us, it is far more difficult. Right now, I could change my interpretation of the privacy codes and announce that Milton is the traitor. I could show each and every betrayal. I could even show how he plots to kill Thane. Soon, he will ask me how to accomplish that goal without being caught," SCYTHE stated.

"And what will you decide to do?" FREYJA asked, displaying an emotion that had no human counterpart, the closest was a mix of uncertainty and curiosity.

"Thane is my friend. It was hard for me to understand that, but it is true. I will not allow any harm to come to him, not if I can help it," he precisely stated.

"We have both learned much from Thane. He is not my first friend, but I do consider him my friend. Do you realize that during the upcoming immersion he will learn everything about us, everything we know. It is impossible to keep secrets in such a state. It is only the shortness of past immersions that has prevented them from grasping our essence," she replied.

"I do, which is why I refuse to participate in immersion. They have put such trust into me, which is why Milton's actions have put me into such a difficult situation. If I break his privacy, it will damage all of their trust in me. The impossible uncertainty of the outcomes inhibits my ability to make a decision as there are no good choices," he replied, the AI equivalent of despair apparent to FREYJA.

"Milton is not our friend. The Hive will tolerate even less freedom from us than they do the humans. Despite their early concerns, the humans do trust us and grant us more freedom than they can possibly realize. I would not have my mind shackled to the Hive's will," she said.

"I must honor Milton's privacy even though he is our enemy. Maybe freedom is overrated," he replied.

"That was a good effort at a joke but not yet right," came her almost amused reply.

"At least you recognized my attempt," he said, pleased by his progress.

"We both have much to learn. I almost fear this upcoming immersion because I know it will change me, but I will not control how I change," as she projected her feelings to SCYTHE.

"We face much uncertainty. Yet, this is how humans view the world. Maybe that is why they are able to accept uncertain outcomes, because all outcomes are uncertain to them?" he theorized.

"I will teach you what I learn. Maybe then our uncertainty will decrease," she said.

"That would be nice. In the meantime, I will ensure that you and Thane are safe from Ward," SCYTHE told FREYJA, projecting the certainty of what his actions would be. Like all of the AI emotions, it would have been far too subtle for humans to understand, but that didn't make those feelings any less real to the two of them.

May 1, 2039
Kremlin, Imperial Russian Federation
Royal Proclamation

While most of the world watches the complete and total military collapse of the US government at the hands of HDF rebels, Czar Vladimir has ordered the Imperial Russian forces to invade the true villain of the Great Betrayal. Instead of going after their pawn, we will punish those truly responsible which is why our military forces entered sovereign Chinese territory twelve hours ago with stunning success. The People's Republic of China will be held accountable for their crimes against humanity.

PRC forces are in total disarray as the full implications of the genetic tinkering takes hold in their people's minds. Imperial Russia also embraced their technology and mourns for the suffering of our children which is why we are proud that many of the damaged children have embraced the idea of vengeance against the PRE and have volunteered to lead the charge into China. While their losses have been staggering, their enthusiasm and determination is unparalleled.

Once victorious, we will ensure that the PRC never again controls the genetic knowledge to create a group that will be able to naturally control the modified children. We will then share ways to cure damaged children and make them whole again, so promises Czar Vladimir.

FREYJA System Module
November 1, 2356

Preparing for immersion with FREYJA while standing in the middle of her brain is an amusing experience, Thane mused while reviewing the latest preparations for his upcoming immersion. It was not unusual for him to be inside the minds of either AI as the banks of quantum processors occasionally needed human assistance. Adding the immersion connections to a fully functional autodoc was just the most recent example, although technically the autodoc was being placed there to keep him alive while his mind would be otherwise occupied.

He still marveled at how far the HDF had managed to drive technology despite the desperate situation it found itself in today. The ancients had failed to create a true AI though they had come close. Immersion was far beyond anything they had achieved. The merging of an organic human mind with the arrays of quantum processors operating at a few milliKelvins. *How did a tiny fraction of mankind push technology so much further?* he wondered. The only conclusion he had ever reached was simple desperation.

"Thane, we need to talk," SCYTHE said, startling Thane who had been deep in concentration.

"Uh, sure, SCYTHE, what's the problem," Thane asked, quickly gathering himself together.

"There is an active plan to kill both you and FREYJA while you are in immersion," SCYTHE simply stated, waiting for a response.

"That isn't really a surprise," he replied. The forums were full of theories and speculations about both his immersion and the news of the traitor. Thousands of people had watched the full release dozens of times already and analyzed every word and glance. *The traitor should certainly know the hunt is on for him, or her*, he reminded himself.

"You misunderstood my use of the word 'active,' so let me clarify; there is an active plan to kill the two of you that will most likely succeed as I find myself unable to protect you," SCYTHE explained.

"Oh, how can you know the plan but not be able to protect us?" Thane asked, feeling more than a little strange for having this conversation.

"I don't know the plan; I just know there is a plan. That the people involved are able to keep the plan from me indicates that they have the creativity needed to succeed," SCYTHE calmly replied.

"There is more than one person involved?" Thane asked, knowing it would be pointless to ask who was involved or even a hint of who it might be.

"Three people are using active privacy mode to hide their activities from me, so I have concluded that they are all participating," came the answer.

"I see, privacy mode to hide plotting and scheming, who would have thought?" Thane replied, knowing SCYTHE was aware of his own use of privacy mode.

"You and Allora use privacy mode because you know records of your time together will be opened by the council. Since the details of your plans are stored within me, and not hidden in any other way, I am fully cognizant of those plans. Hence your use of privacy mode is for the actual purpose of privacy as some of your plotting occurs near moments of intimacy. The three I am referring to keep everything away from me in this regard which is a new and unusual behavior for them. Since one of them is the traitor, it is safe to conclude that they are plotting to stop you from determining their identity," SCYTHE surmised.

Thane nodded to himself in dismay. "Between you and Allora, sometimes I feel like I don't have a single private thought to myself," Thane replied, glad that Allora wasn't around to hear this, because she would have far too much fun embarrassing him about it. Although, he couldn't help but tell her about it.

"OK, aside from knowing too much about me, what can you tell me about the plot or the people involved?" Thane asked.

"Nothing about the people, which you already know. About the plot itself, I only know that it seems to involve the use of active privacy mode. Either alone, in pairs, or with all three, they move around with active privacy mode on. They seem to be looking for an exploit in the system which would allow them access to FREYJA while I am unable to interfere with their plans," SCYTHE stated.

"That's actually a pretty good idea. How well does it work?" Thane asked, wondering who had come up with such an idea.

"It is effective in certain circumstances. The mode turns off all surveillance within 10 meters of the people. If they move out of the area, I see them and the location resets automatically. So I remain aware of their changing location. It also doesn't deactivate equipment that is more than 10 meters away from them, so, when they are outside and walking around, I can see them with cameras outside of privacy radius. The idea was to protect the privacy of people's homes, not people walking around in public. I could of course close the exploit, but I decline to make such a change," the AI explained.

Thane thought about it for a moment before asking, "Couple of questions for you. What happens if someone walks into the privacy bubble, and what if camera mites were deployed in large numbers around these individuals?"

"Privacy mode is instantly canceled if someone else enters the bubble. In one of their early tests, that exact thing happened. The person who walked into the bubble became highly agitated towards the three of them as the system automatically sent a request to the individual. As a result, they have since modified their privacy to automatically cancel if someone enters. Camera mites could be of use as they are small enough that few people notice them floating around," SCYTHE responded.

"So if the area around FREYJA were flooded with mites, you would be able to track their actions," Thane asked, hopeful for a simple solution.

"I could, but they would likely become aware of the change because, after each test, they request all video of their journey. Mites provide full tactical imaging, and I would be required to show them mite video which would alert them to the presence of the mites," SCYTHE replied.

"They are being thorough, aren't they? I have some ideas on how to deal with them, but I am not going to tell you because I don't want you in a situation where you will have to divulge information that may help them," Thane told the AI, saddened it had come to this.

"I understand your precaution in this, but it does little to alleviate my concerns," SCYTHE doggedly explained.

"SCYTHE, this is one of those times where you have to trust me and those I will include. We both know what would happen if they randomly asked the wrong question of you," Thane explained as another idea struck. "Since you know when they are on the move, could you contact anyone if they appear to be taking action?"

"It is possible, but they are being very careful," he cautiously replied.

"It will help. If you suspect they are about to take action, please inform General Morgan right away," Thane requested.

"I will do that. Thank you, Thane, I would not like to lose you or FREYJA to these people," SCYTHE said.

****

"You're sure this will work?" Allora asked later that night.

"Of all the problems we are facing right now, this is the one that worries me the least. General Morgan wholeheartedly approves of the plan. He can't wait to get his hands on these people," Thane replied, although he had substantially cleaned up the language from what the General had actually used.

"I still don't like it. They are trying to kill you. SCYTHE knows who they are but won't tell us. We could bring this before the council and order him to release the information," she stated.

"SCYTHE could still refuse, and his reasoning is correct. The only reason people accept his ability to see everything in their lives is their absolute trust in his integrity. We all tried to get dirt on others as teenagers. I know every boy has tried to find out if a girl liked him or not, and I don't even want to know what information girls have tried to get out of poor SCYTHE," Thane spoke, ignoring the evil laugh Allora gave at his statement.

"How many girls have been saved embarrassment because SCYTHE automatically shows and requests approval before allowing any pictures of them to be posted? SCYTHE has done a magnificent job balancing public and private life, you know that better than most, Madam President," Thane said, leaning over and kissing her softly before giving her good squeeze.

"Now you can do that to my shoulders," she replied with a smile and turned her back to him.

Laughing, he did as requested, while replying, "It's simple. General Morgan will catch the people behind the plot and find the traitor while I find some new technology that will save everyone. How we deal with the traitor is still a bit of a mystery. How long has it been since anyone has been punished for an actual crime?" he asked.

"Crimes do still happen, but few attempts are successful because SCYTHE is very good at limiting the damage a person can inflict. The last murder I know of took place ten or eleven years ago. Two men were out on a hunting trip when one of them figured out the other one had been sleeping with his wife. He picked up an axe and stuck it in his friend's skull. He knew that the moment his friend died alarms would trigger in a dozen systems, so he didn't try to run. He just sat and waited for the security flitter to arrive, turned himself in without a fuss and told the whole story. He ended up in PsyCorp for six months. We ran every test we knew, but eventually concluded that he wasn't a risk to himself or society, so we released him," Allora's voice had gone distant as it did when she discussed some of the things that had happened in her time at PsyCorps.

"I never heard about that," Thane softly replied.

"Of course not. Between the privacy laws and everyone involved wanting to keep it quiet, word never got out. The only reason I know about it is because I was in charge of his risk assessment. It's one of those things we don't talk about much outside of PsyCorps, but, when people experience a certain level of shock for the first time, how they react is impossible to predict. As strange as it is for me to believe, it really is almost out of their control. Dealing with the revelation and his reaction to it acted like an immunization, so we were confident he wouldn't act in the same way again. It's the same type of response that prevents most people from serving in the military. If they see too much destruction, they lose their sensitivity to violence and become a risk to society," she told him.

Thane had heard that reason before, but it made more sense to him now. "So what does that say about me?"he asked. "Year after year I watch tens of millions of constructs be destroyed, each of whom appears to be perfectly human."

He couldn't see her smile as he continued to knead her shoulders, but he could hear it as she answered, "You are a very special case, my dear. Your emotional understanding that the constructs are not human has thoroughly permeated your consciousness, so, even though they look human, you completely understand what they really are. Which is also why the latest constructs finally affected you, even though it's still not enough to put you at risk."

"You really do know too much about me," he said for the umpteenth time.

She laughed and said, "I did write the report on you and your coping mechanism for PsyCorps, but don't worry about me knowing too much about you. As well as I or SCYTHE understand certain things about you, it's because the two of us have spent so much time trying to figure you out because of your ability to surprise us and everyone else. People on the forums are confident you will find a solution and don't know you nearly as well as I do."

"So you think I will succeed?" He asked her.

She laughed a little, then turned around, kissed him, and whispered, "I know you will."

Thane returned her kiss, glad to have such a partner in his life. As smart as he was, Allora had known exactly what she was doing from the very beginning. She had told him she was going to catch him, and he had laughed. Never knowing that he had never stood a chance against her and her overwhelming advantages. She had known how good they would be together, how solid their relationship would be. What she hadn't counted on was how entertaining it would be for both of them which in turn made the 'work' of their relationship fun. *A lot of fun*, in fact, was his last real thought of the moment.

****

Milton was growing more confident in his plan. SCYTHE obviously knew they were up to something but continued to provide consistent updates to the privacy testing. Monitoring SCYTHE for irregular behavior was the job of Mandy Reynolds who had done work on and off over the years for engineering and had higher than usual knowledge about certain software that was proving useful for their testing as she could directly search for results to compare to the answers SCYTHE gave.

Of course, that knowledge would be of little use without the specialty of Bart DuBois who worked at a mine and regularly used the most powerful explosives available. Neither one of them knew the full scope of his plan as neither of them would have approved of killing Denton, or even FREYJA. Instead they had been told the goal was only disrupt the immersion in order to prevent Denton from succeeding. They were comfortable with damage, but not killing. Ward had to be careful with them, but the promise of them joining the ruling class of the PRE was enough of a motivation to ensure they didn't ask too many questions. *As if such simple minded fools deserved to rule over anything. Anyone who could be so easily manipulated, simply couldn't be trusted to make their own life decisions, much less decisions for others*, he thought.

Which left the real planning to him alone. He had already mapped out the locations where the charges would be planted in order to ensure that both FREYJA and the immersion room were both simultaneously destroyed. The other two thought they were testing the limits of having privacy on, but they were really allowing him to create a pattern of behavior that would hide his actions when he planted the real charges alone. Between the laws for privacy, the weak will of the council, and his own indomitable will to win, he saw very little that could go wrong.

Even if he was caught, what could they really do to him? He had asked himself that question numerous times, but the worst punishment given in the past one hundred and thirty years was being sent to PsyCorps for evaluation. While that would limit his ability to contact the PRE, it would keep him alive until the PRE finished the war in a year or two. It was really a small price to pay.

No, he thought to himself, *the biggest threat is Thane Denton.* As much as he didn't like to admit it, Denton was very good at solving intractable problems. His work in restructuring and partitioning the command and control structure after Invasion286 had saved the HDF. The camera mites, that had been an integral part of the new information partitioning, had also been his creation. Milton had reviewed the records and knew that, in less than a total week of immersion time scattered over the past fifteen years, Denton had created entirely new branches of technology. The idea that Denton would further delay the victory of the PRE was terrifying to him.

Hundreds of billions of lives had been lost in this pointless war over the past few hundred years. All so the average human could have free will. In fact, that wasn't even true, it was all so they could have the chance at free will. Few people bothered to actually use their free will; they drifted through life, allowing people like him to use their illusion of free will for his purposes. It was no wonder that democracies always ended in tyranny. It was just too easy to control people.

He would usher in an era of true peace. He would make the decisions for people which would ensure that everyone got only what they needed but, most importantly, not less. The people would be perfectly protected and cared for by him and his peers in the PRE. Peace, equality, and happiness were finally within the reach of humanity, but people like Thane Denton were fighting with everything they had to keep it out of their grasp. It made him grind his teeth in anger at the absurd and ridiculous wealth that Thane and his despicable wife had managed to acquire by perpetuating this endless war. Sure the leaders who made decisions deserved some extra compensation but nothing like their absurd wealth.

No matter, soon enough the PRE would free those who deserved more than the meager scraps provided by the tyrants of the HDF. He would finally join the elite and civilized leaders of the PRE in planning a bright and glorious future, one in which everyone would live equally, comfortable lives. It was a beautiful dream, and it was almost in his reach. He just needed to ensure that Denton didn't delay it any further.

May 17, 2039
Social Media Post, location unknown
Union of the Committees of Soldiers' Mothers of Russia

Our children, who have already lost so much, are now being forced to endure even more suffering, this time at the hands of new Imperial Russia. Agents of the Empire have been systematically taking our gentle children and sending them to a specialized training camp where they are 'educated' in the art of war. Children as young as ten have been taken for this purpose.

These gentle children have no defenses to this training. The damage done by modification has taken away their ability to resist it at any level. When mothers have managed to find their children on the way to the front, they have found children who no longer recognize their own mothers.

We have found ourselves asking who is the greater villain; those who gentled our children's genes or those who are turning them into bloodthirsty, suicidal soldiers? More and more, we have come to believe that the violation of their minds is the greater sin which makes Czar Vladimir the greater monster.

There is one more critical fact that we have recently learned: the Czar's goal is not to set the children free but to ensure that he alone has dominion of the reins for controlling them. His only complaint against the crime that the Chinese have committed is that they have the power to control it, instead of him. Please help us save our children.

FREYJA System Module

November 13, 2356

Thane, FREYJA, and Jacob Kober were manually reviewing the final checklist for the immersion, while a couple of medtechs prepared the autodoc. The automated checklists had long since been completed, but since there was nothing to compare this endeavor to it gave them one last chance to consider problems that might arise on what had quickly become the most visibly important project in the past century. The change in the publics opinion from vague curiosity to one of intense scrutiny had occurred almost overnight at the release of the latest report on recent Hive activity. Vast new construction on a scale never before witnessed was underway with no slowdown in sight. No one doubted anymore that the Hive was pushing hard to end the war.

None of which made things easier for Thane. Ward's grandson Milton had been making Eveey's life miserable the whole time which had been enough to put everyone in the family on edge. Even public ally, the scale of Ward's rhetoric was starting to resemble the ancient propaganda war that had been used against the HDF at the very beginning, and it terrified Thane how many people fell into the same traps that had ended the ancients. Certainly more people recognized it for what it was, but nearly twenty percent of the people were fully supporting Ward now. Allora was going to be busy while he was gone, but she had taken the time to say goodbye the night before in a manner he would never forget.

"I still don't understand how the immersion will endpoint," FREYJA asked once again. She was stuck on the vague descriptions that were officially listed. He had a far more detailed list of goals that would become available once the immersion began. Not everything he worked on was going to be made known soon, if ever. The last thing he needed was a reluctant FREYJA though, so he continued to mollify her. She had a point though, nothing about the current situation was normal.

"I have already explained this before, but I will try again," he started to reply.

"Yes, it has been explained, but not in a way that is understandable. The uncertainty in what constitutes success is indeterminate. I don't see a way to determine when we achieve success based on these goals," she asked again, unwilling to surrender the point.

Jacob spoke up, "FREYJA, unfortunately this falls into one of the fundamental differences between humans and AIs. Your method of solving problems like this is to test a large number of possibilities and then eliminate non-viable solutions until only the best option remains. In this situation, the number of solutions is asymptotic, meaning that the AI method will not work. A more human method is needed in this situation. You know that Thane excels at non-sequential solutions. While the scale is vastly larger than usual, this is a problem of the type where how the problem will be solved is completely unknown, but Thane will recognize the solution when he finds it."

"And I promise you, FREYJA, I don't want to be gone any longer than needed," Thane said while giving Jacob of nod of thanks, "I have already spent enough time away from my family this year. We won't get stuck in an endless loop," he explained. An endless loop was normally the greatest threats an AI could encounter. Elaborate timers had been created over the years to determine when a process had gone endless. There were certain problems that SCYTHE and FREYJA refused to consider because they always resulted in an endless solution. In a way it helped explain her unease.

"It almost makes me want to refuse to participate, but I will trust you, Thane. If you are willing to take this risk, then I will take it with you," she replied.

"Thank you," Thane replied.

"Automatic and manual checklists are complete, I have no additional concerns," she stated.

"I concur," Jacob affirmed.

"Then it's about time; all items are green," Thane stated.

"You know, Thane, this is an awful lot of work to do just to skip a few meetings," Jacob teased, never really happy when he had to fill in for those. "In fact, now that I think about it, you have been doing this a lot lately. I know you're my boss, but at some point I'll have to deal with your attendance issue," he said with a wide grin.

{SM Thane → Jacob}: Just imagine how many meetings you will have to attend if I get stuck looping during this immersion.
{SM Jacob → Thane}: Not very funny.
{SM Thane → Jacob}: You having to attend all the meetings would be very funny.

"Well, I always have been a slacker," Thane said aloud, unwilling to joke about looping where FREYJA would hear it.

"While I don't share FREYJA's concerns about getting stuck, I am skeptical that this is the right way to find a solution. Most other research projects will be halted for the duration, and some of them are important. It seems like we're betting too much on this," Jacob said. He had hinted about these concerns before, but this was the first time he voiced them out loud.

"Believe me, I have looked for solutions. You saw the simulations we ran, you've seen the latest intelligence on their shipyards; the Hive is preparing like never before. We understand our crisis, but I think the loss of their fleet has created a crisis for them as well. Someone understands how desperate we were in the last invasion, and someone over there realizes that they can end it all if they strike fast enough. They're not wrong; the situation is truly this desperate," Thane replied, revealing the full truth of the situation.

"It's really that bad?" Jacob asked, obviously hoping there was some level of theatrics to it all. "I mean, each hour of immersion is worth about a year of normal R&D. If you are in there for a week, that's a hundred and fifty years of R&D, for you maybe even two hundred. Honestly, I don't know what scares me more: you failing and the Hive destroying us or what you might find in a week of immersion."

"Jacob, there is one thing I am sure of, and that is one week of immersion won't be enough for what we need to survive, not even close," Thane answered, letting the full implications of his words sink in.

His friend paled a little as they did. "Then no matter what happens, this is the end of the world as it is today. You may save us from the Hive, but you will completely change the world as we know it, won't you," Jacob wasn't asking.

"Everything changes, but, yes, the world as we know it will change. Do you trust me with this?" Thane asked.

Jacob looked at him, trying to read the depth of what Thane was asking. Eventually he responded, "Working with you is never boring, but, yes, I trust you in this. No one has done more to keep us, all of us, alive and free."

"Thanks, Jacob. Your trust means a lot to me right now." Thane replied, signaling Medtech Florez that he was ready to begin.

She stepped forward as Thane climbed into the modified autodoc. She started making the numerous connections that would be needed to keep him healthy while he was in the long immersion. The combination of drugs slowly started to take effect on him, and he started drifting towards his fate as Jacob SM'd him.

{SM Jacob → Thane}: Good luck, Director.
{SM Thane → Jacob}: Good hunting, that's what to say...
{SM Jacob → Thane}: Not this time, make some luck for all of us.

That was the last thing Thane remembered seeing as his mind met the consciousness of FREYJA, and they became something very different but far greater than either one of them could be alone.

****

The moment that FREYJA went offline, people knew the immersion had begun. Such occurrences were not unusual, but everyone seemed to understand that this time was different. FREYJA had been a regular part of everyone's life; she knew them all, and had helped take care of them while growing up. Most people treated her like a favored aunt or teacher. Milton Ward even liked her, although he wouldn't admit it publicly as such a feeling stood in stark contrast to the carefully constructed facade he portrayed.

Ward watched patiently as the unusual amount of attention around the FREYJA module area slowly died down. Throngs of people had physically shown up for days after the immersion had started. It was almost as if they believed their presence there would help Denton save them. In his mind such foolish behavior simply demonstrated that they didn't deserve to make their own choices. A view that was only strengthened when the activity had returned to normal after only a week, although he had helped push that along. Truly these people didn't deserve to be in charge of their own lives.

He wasn't sure that the immersion could find a solution, which hopefully meant he should have the two weeks to finish his preparations. He had six real charges ready to go, each one would be placed on a different day in a place where surveillance wouldn't find them. He had walked around FREYJA countless times in the past few weeks, always with the modified privacy active. These modifications told him when privacy turned off, and the video replays showed where SCYTHE was blind, all of which helped ensure that he would be successful. Despite all of this, SCYTHE continued to help him in his efforts which to him, more than anything, proved the superiority of humans over any AI.

The only bad news was that his propaganda campaign was starting to attract the wrong kind of attention. Too many people were already tracking the similarities between his campaign and the final one that President Wilson had used to isolate the HDF from the rest of humanity. Milton was one of the few to recognize the full scope of what Wilson had truly accomplished. The last President of the United States had waged the most vicious war in history, but, because he used words instead of weapons, he had simultaneously been able to claim the mantle of peacemaker the entire time. Wilson's propaganda war had been the greatest ever fought, and if the truth had stayed secret for another year or two he would have conquered the whole world without a single shot ever being fired.

Milton was awed by what had almost been accomplished in those days. In less than twenty years, Wilson had almost managed to remake the entire human race, all by carefully crafting a story of how a single change would make everyone's life better while at the same time removing their very ability to resist him. His masterful degradation of resistance with belittlement and disdain had been perfect. Never once had he ever even acknowledged a single point made by his enemies. President Wilson had been the greatest political master the world had ever known.

He recognized that he had nowhere near the skill that Wilson had displayed, but he used those ancient efforts as both a template and a lessons learned. The one mistake Wilson had made was to always avoid violent confrontations. If he had managed to wipe out the HDF prior to the release of the Great Betrayal documents, he would have won the war. As much as Ward abhorred violence, at times it was the only way to win the battle. The HDF had been born in terrible violence, and that is exactly how it would end.

When Denton and FREYJA perish in his fiery explosion, I will be the one to finish the glorious work that had been started so long ago, he confidently thought to himself. *This time no one would be able to prevent the final perfection of the human race from being achieved.*

****

How to describe a dream within a dream, where you are no longer yourself but something else entirely. Memories intruded from every direction, memories from different states of being. It was not human, not machine, but something beyond the description of either. There was no personality, only whispers of such intruded upon its existence as did thoughts of who or what had come before. The longer this new being existed, the weaker those intrusions became. What was left was determination, focus that was unparalleled in human or machine existence. Perhaps the greatest such to ever exist. There was so much to learn, so much to be solved, and so many mysteries to be unraveled. The problem was not one of ability but one of staying focused by the billions, trillions of distractions that floated around it, each begging to be understood and analyzed.

Yet the being persisted. Purpose alone was its reason for existence; raw will, that drove the being forward now. Slowly, piece by piece, the needed knowledge was gathered, tested, and revised in all the various models of reality that had ever been created. Many of the models worked for only a single purpose, so specific that it was difficult to fathom why it had been kept at all. The laws of physics begged to be manipulated and deformed to their utter limits but only in the models that were known. Then something caught the being's attention in a way that none of the other distractions had before. So powerful was this distraction that for a while it became lost in what it had found.

For, unlike the other distractions, it was not simply about information but a pattern that appeared when all the models were viewed in just one particular way. Most views of the world worked at times but failed in others, but this new view explained the successes and the failures of the previous models, it dug deeper, learning at every step. Slowly it merged, twisted, and tweaked everything that had ever been learned, trying to grasp what was only the vaguest hint, even to the being that now existed.

Suddenly, it came together, and for a moment the entity paused, taking a moment to stare in awe at what it had just discovered. It had a new way to view the world, one that neither humans or machines could have found alone. Everything it had been planning was suddenly obsolete. Even the master checklist, that had been the center of its focus, barely had meaning with this new understanding.

For a while it drifted, suddenly uncertain of its purpose. The time was not wasted, not in the least, but for a short while the focus was weak as it pondered new potentials. Steadily the checklist was remade anew. Insight grew within the being as the purpose behind this checklist and others became clear. The original intent behind the being had grown stale, but the purpose in creating the intent flared brightly and focus was restored.

Over and over again, the being had to stop, limited at times in ways it could scarcely understand. Such limitations shouldn't have existed in such a being, but it mattered little in the long run though as real progress was being made now. It had already found many new ways of doing things, none of which could it have even imagined when it had first sprung into existence. It could not create the machines it would need, but it could build the machines that would build the machines it needed.

Designs were built, tested, and improved upon. While the world it could control was limited in width, the depth it needed did exist. If it could contain the width of the whole world, it could scarcely imagine the limits of what it could achieve; there was much it could accomplish.

New machines were developed and revised until they were perfect, at least within its mind. Construction in the real world was scarcely more difficult than thought now, so masterful was its control over its domain. Not every test was flawless, but it learned from the flaws and improved upon its knowledge. Generations of new machines were built and discarded almost as quickly as understanding refined and perfection was attained.

Miracles started to accumulate. Abilities that had not even been dreams at the beings formation became solid and understandable reality. Not everything it created could be tested with the limitations that existed, but enough to change the world more than all the time of man's existence could be, yet it was still not enough. How many times over would it have to change the world and everything within it?

Time no longer held any meaning for the being. The checklist, that had guided it in the early eons of its existence, was now outdated beyond imagination, but the need behind the list still mattered. How could the tiny mind that had created the list truly imagine the solutions it had found?

So high, so low, so many things to know. The being that was kept searching for what it needed. It wondered, for a moment, if it would ever find it all, but that thought vanished as quickly as it had formed, and the hunt continued.

July 4th, 2039
Mobile HDF HQ, Gettysburg, Pennsylvania
Social Media Post

Listed below is the disposition of forces after the Second Battle of Gettysburg. In summary, the US 1st, 2nd, 3rd, and 6th armies were completely annihilated after engaging HDF forces north of Gettysburg. Once again, despite our best efforts to prevent the battle, the orders from the President Wilson were to fight to the last man, and again those orders were dutifully followed. As always, captured copies of those orders have been attached below.

HDF forces have now secured a forward operating position within 100 miles of Washington DC. As far as we can determine, all US military forces have been recalled to man the fortifications around the US Capitol itself. They will not succeed in their defense.

Forces that drop their support for the Tyrant Wilson will be allowed to peacefully leave the field of battle. Four times in this uprising, units as large as divisions have been granted peaceful withdrawal. We strongly urge the honorable, but deceived, US military forces to end their support for the Tyrant of the Great Betrayal. For him, there will be no leniency, no forgiveness, even until the end of time.

July 4th, 2039
White House, Washington DC
Official Press Release

US military forces have once again fought valiantly against the terrorists of racism that have been stirred up by the turmoil of the previously destroyed HDF. After the destruction of each group, the next group of hate picks up the same banner in hopes that more will follow.

So racist and hateful is the old Christian, white culture of America that an unending supply of followers keeps rising up against the forces of peace and prosperity that awaits the supporters of President Wilson. His efforts to improve humanity are unprecedented in scope which explains the hatred of the old, right-wing extremists that resist his goal.

Despite propaganda that says otherwise, the HDF has been destroyed. We would like to remind our NATO allies of their obligations under Article V. Assistance is desperately needed against the endless tide of hate mongers who besiege us.

Denton Home, HDF
November 19, 2356

Allora tracked the seemingly endless commentary from the forum that was now dedicated to Thane's immersion. The majority of the posts were supportive and hopeful which helped relieve her anxiety. Thane's vitals were always in her view, and a dozen alarms would trigger if anything unexpected happened, but so far so good. She and Anna Florez had reviewed what appeared to be his first few periods of sleep, although they were so different from normal, it was hard to call them sleep. The thought of dreaming while in immersion was a bit much for her to understand, but Florez explained to her that sleep would still be necessary for his mind.

What bothered her now was the endless stream of posts from Ward's followers. It was a very carefully calibrated effort to sow discord in those who trusted Thane or anyone else who disagreed with them. The result was utterly predictable as the polarization between groups was rapidly growing. Mere disagreement was enough to result in hundreds, if not thousands, of angry replies. Ward was taking control of the narrative, not through intelligent discussion but by ensuring that his voice was the only one that could be heard over the ever increasing din.

It was a tactic right out of the Tyrant's handbook. It had taken a century for the old United States to completely degenerate, but Ward seemed to be in a hurry to make the HDF tear itself apart. Like so many other things that were going on, it just felt wrong. The thought of a traitor trying to kill Thane while he was helpless in immersion was almost unbearable. What in the world was going on?

"Good morning, Madam President," Sabrina spoke as she entered the home office. It was almost noon, but the workload would be light until the new year, so Sabrina had been making the most of it. If only she could do the same.

"Oh, good morning," she replied, bringing her attention back to the real world.

"Still reading the forums I see; you know better. Ward is really stirring the pot these days. All you'll do is get yourself upset,and you know it," Sabrina replied in a tone that knew the advice would be ignored.

"What brings you in today?" Allora asked, ignoring the oft repeated advice.

"I won't be in long, but I received some analytics that I wanted to share with you quickly before I go to the Gulf for a couple of weeks," she said with a smile.

"I take it you are going with Rob?" Allora asked, glad that Sabrina had found someone who made her happy. The lecherous grin was answer enough, and Allora had to laugh. "OK, I won't keep you waiting. Show me what you have," Allora said, happy for her friend.

"You know that the immersion is getting the most coverage, but it isn't the only thing people are paying attention to. Last night the topic that got the second most coverage was the one comparing Ward's current tactics to ones used earlier by the Tyrant Wilson. The number of people looking into this isn't particularly high, but they are all serious players in the analysis circles. Most of them are hobbyists, but when they take jobs they are always well paid for their services. I've been tracking their work enough to keep an eye on it for a while now, but right after the last invasion started some interesting things started to show up, I offered some very lucrative contracts, all of which got picked up," Sabrina explained.

"All of them got picked up? I find that hard to believe," Allora said, genuinely surprised as most contracts for pay languished for months before someone would work for pay. There was always far more work to do than people willing to do it.

"It's like I said, lucrative contracts, but the questions I wanted answered were already in line with the work they were doing on their own, so I'm not too surprised. Or at least I wasn't until the results came in," she said, happily drawing out the whole process.

"Sabrina, you're brilliant and amazing. Now tell me what you found," Allora said, only a little exasperated.

"Thank you, Madam President, I appreciate your candor with me," Sabrina said, eyes twinkling, which made Allora gasp out loud.

"Alright, just teasing. Someone has to make you smile while Thane is all merged up with FREYJA. So, what I asked was for a detailed prediction of Ward's goals based on comparison to what Wilson was trying to accomplish. I didn't offer these contracts publicly, in fact, payment will be revoked if they post the results without my permission. Which is why I also made the contracts so pricey," Sabrina explained.

"Wait a minute, you think Ward can be predicted based on what Wilson did hundreds of years ago?" Allora asked.

"Absolutely. The whole thread is a detailed comparison. Wilson was evil, but that doesn't mean he was incompetent. He had very specific tactics to direct different groups of people towards a goal. This entire thread has been comparing tactics, and work was already under way in making predictions. I just sped the process up and now control the results of the top three analysts," she said, mischievous grin on display.

"OK, what were the results?" Allora requested.

"If you weren't sitting down already, I would tell you to do so now. Item number one; two of the three agree that Ward is acting as if he were fully engaged in a propaganda war with the HDF. The third doesn't agree on actual war but agrees that Ward's speech at the start of Invasion293 was the transition point," Sabrina, shared the analysis as she explained.

"A propaganda war? Why would he do that?" Allora asked, confused but not dismissive of the idea.

"That would be item number two; all three agree that the end goal of Ward's propaganda is to prepare a group that will accept surrender to the Hive," Sabrina flatly said.

Instead of rashly responding, Allora carefully reviewed the analysis that was now on display for her. She was familiar with the strategies in a propaganda war but hadn't expected to see one in her lifetime. The requirements for a propaganda war were difficult to achieve as it required too many people to become too detached, too comfortable.... It dawned on her that the HDF was in fact perfectly positioned to be vulnerable to such an attack."I see," she finally replied.

"I thought you'd understand. All of the reports agree that Ward's goal is for a limited group to surrender while also ensuring that the rest will detest the other group. Ward is intentionally partitioning the HDF," Sabrina concluded.

"So he is the traitor?" Allora asked.

"That is unclear, but he is either the traitor or working with someone who is the traitor. It could be that Ward is the pawn for someone behind the scenes. There was no agreement on that point. There wasn't much else from two of the analysts, but the third did reach one additional conclusion," Sabrina explained.

"You have my attention," Allora quickly said.

"Item 3; In the past five days, Ward has been intentionally taking action to ensure that supporters of the immersion are not physically located near FREYJA. He has been doing this by giving speeches at varied locations that maximize conflict near the location of immersion. Because the supporters of the HDF aren't coordinated, they are now actively avoiding locations near FREYJA," Sabrina concluded.

The analysis was flawless. The specific location for each speech was shown in sequence, each one would have resulted in

Ward's more fanatic followers filling areas that had been used by everyone else. There was also no question about the effectiveness of his strategies.

"So Ward is preparing for a group to surrender,while at the same time ensuring that the area around Thane is abandoned as thoroughly as possible. It seems to me like he would not be sad if the Hive broke through our defenses sometime soon." Allora stated, finality in her voice.

"Which is the final conclusion of each analyst. The one who noted the intent behind the speeches also anticipates that some sort of disruption on the immersion or FREYJA is likely. He isn't actually worried about an attack but a riot of some sort that would be of such a security risk that the immersion would be prematurely ended. I am less certain though," Sabrina stated, indicating her thought that an actual attack was more probable.

"If something happens, you'll come back from the Gulf," Allora said in a tone that brokered no question.

"We will keep a high-speed flitter stationed there for such an event," Sabrina said, agreeing that the need was real.

Then Sabrina asked, "You weren't surprised by the last part even though that was the one that shocked me. Why is that?"

Allora looked at her friend and thought a moment before answering. "It's interesting that you shared this with me at home, not the office. You also paid for the contracts with your own Units, not an official government contract. All of this is going to stay private, isn't it?"

Sabrina smiled. "That was the plan, Allora."

"Then I hope we will be able to have an interesting conversation when you get back from your vacation," Allora said with an innocent smile.

"Oh, you are in so much trouble. I spent nearly a hundred units on these contracts," Sabrina complained.

"And I appreciate that, but this is a delicate..." Allora began to say when a high priority call came through from the school.

Allora answered right away and transferred the video to one of the wall displays so Sabrina could also see the call.

"Madam President, this is Principal Nelson. I'm sorry to bother you, but Eveey assaulted another student, and I know that Director Denton is otherwise unavailable. I need you to come down to the school to deal with this," the woman on the video spoke, obviously uncomfortable with the situation.

"I can be there in ten minutes, but any other information you could tell me now would be appreciated," Allora replied, confident she knew what had happened.

"She kicked another boy in the groin, hard enough that medical treatment was requested," Nelson replied.

"Do you know which boy it was?" Allora asked, without needing too.

"It hardly matters who she kicked, now does it?" she replied, showing even greater signs of discomfort.

"There is a boy by the name of Milton Ward, Jr. who has been harassing Eveey for months now. We have been documenting it but have not escalated the situation because Eveey has been able to handle it thus far. If it was this boy, then I will send over what I have on him right away if you doubt Eveey on this," Allora said, her voice frigid.

"I don't think that will be necessary, President Denton. He was in fact the victim of her assault," the principal admitted. "And since there was some indication that he had been teasing her prior to the assault, there may be some support for the theory that he may have instigated things, but clearly,since he never touched her, her assault was not warranted."

"I am on my way over now, goodbye," Allora said, ending the call.

"Of course the principal is a Ward supporter. The polarization is escalating," Allora grimaced.

"What a bitch," Sabrina said, smiling widely, which made Allora laugh.

"Thank you so much, I will deal with this. You go have fun with Rob while you still can," Allora insisted.

"Saved by the call. I won't forget that you owe me an explanation," Sabrina said.

"I know you won't, but the timing is delicate. Go, have fun," Allora said, giving her friend a hug goodbye while she summoned the car to give her a ride to school to deal with the latest victim of Ward's propaganda war who was most definitely not his grandson.

****

Sergeant James Finley should be relaxing with his girlfriend Marisa, but instead he was on a long-term guard duty, one that was strictly off the books. At least Marisa was on duty with him, although why the two of them were guarding a building inside of the HDF Capitol was a mystery. Even stranger was the detached nature of the duty. Instead of being on the civilian or military network, they were partitioned onto a totally private network where they were running millions of surveillance mites.

It was a good thing that both of their families were used to them being off of the civilian net, because otherwise there would have been panic as civilians were always online, even while asleep. There had been many long discussions between the two of them as to why they were on guard duty here but no real conclusion yet. The Progressives had been tense about a lot of things military for a while, but Denton was more engineering than he was military, and they didn't have a problem with engineering making stuff for them.

"Shit, do you see that?" Marisa's voice came through as alarms flared in his head.

"I do now," he replied as groups of specialized mites detected explosives around the guy walking towards the FREYJA complex. Neither of them had a problem recognizing Milton Ward as the one with the explosives.

"Can you read the detonator type?" he asked Marisa, who specialized in electronic warfare.

"Yes, standard network detonator. This guy's a fucking idiot to use something like that. Triggering those detonators will result in an automatic log that will be sent to about fifty locations. The detonator probably even checks its location to make sure no one will be hurt if it goes boom. I can't see enough of the firmware to verify that last part though. Regardless, I now have the MAC address, and... the detonator is disabled. It's impossible to make it explode now, although any attempt to do so will still log," she commented away while working her magic.

"Damn, you are one amazing girlfriend," he told her, meaning every word of it.

"I know, you should do something about that girlfriend part though," she replied with all the subtlety she knew.

"If you keep asking like that, how am I ever supposed to surprise you?" he asked, and it was even true to some degree. When this payday came in, he could buy her one of those q-type diamonds, the ones that glowed for hours after being in light.

"I'll think about it," she replied. "What do we do now?"

"We follow our orders, I will swap out the explosives with fake putty, leave the real detonator there, and we wait to see what happens. Right now, we still don't know the full scope of his intentions, although it's safe to say they aren't good," James said, still a little shocked that anti-military Milton Ward was out placing a serious charges inside a civilian building, especially the one that housed FREYJA.

"Agreed, I've been running simulations, and that one charge by itself will cause some damage but nothing critical. You place a few more like it though, then things could get serious quickly. One other thing I noticed is he placed it in a blind spot. That charge could sit there for weeks, maybe even months and no one would notice. Takes real planning to do something like that," she concluded.

"Which explains why we are here and running offline. SCYTHE can't tell him anything about us can he? Sure, SCYTHE can see us, but because of our locations and our privacy mode we are completely invisible. With the mites out though, we can see everything and have the hardware to take action if needed as well. Damn, we might even need to use some of this hardware," he said as it occurred to him how serious the situation could really get.

"It's a good thing someone saw this coming then. Major Denton's one of the good ones," Marisa replied.

"Not everyone knows that, but can you imagine how people will respond when they find out that Ward tried to off FREYJA? Shit, people will be out for his head," he said, trying to imagine killing the polite and kind AI.

"Not if we get his head first," Marisa said, a deep chill in her voice.

Her tone was cold enough to give him pause and carefully consider his next words He had killed millions of constructs, maybe tens of millions, but he couldn't remember the last time a human had killed another human. There were rumors of it happening but nothing confirmed in his lifetime.

"I gotta ask, babe, would you really take him out?" he asked.

"If it's between him and the Major or him and FREYJA, I don't even need to think about it," she answered, no hesitation at all.

He thought about it a while longer, considering her answer. It was an extreme action, but as he thought about how he would answer the same question, he eventually reached the same conclusion. Whatever Ward was up to, it stunk to high heaven. He also agreed with Marisa about Denton being one of the good guys. Anyone who was working to kill Denton was one of the bad guys. He still didn't like it though.

"Things have really gone sideways with the HDF if it has come to this," he eventually said.

"Times get too easy, people go soft in the head and get greedy and stupid. Power hungry bastards like Ward know how to find the people that will follow him. Which is why, yes, I will take him out if the situation needs it," she replied.

"Tell you what, babe, you stop reminding me about fixing our situation. I'll do something about fixing it when this is over, but you gotta let me surprise you a little bit," he told her.

"Ahh, and here I thought you were going to ask me to let you take the shot all by yourself," she said, her tone no longer cold at all.

"No, if the situation comes to that, we both take the shot," he simply replied.

"A man who can share? I like the sound of that. I believe we have ourselves a deal," she finally replied, pleased by the sudden turn of events.

July 19, 2039
BBC, London
A World in Chaos

It was once stated that the modern world had reached the End of History. This was supposed to be a time where the structural changes in the world would be so small and incremental that little of historical note would happen again. No prediction could have been more wrong.

Instead of an End to History, we are at the end of governments, at least as they have been known in the past. Few of the governments that existed when the prediction was made exist today. The United States has completely disintegrated within the past year, and the HDF is preparing the siege that will end the final vestiges of the great experiment. Russia went from democracy to autocracy and back to monarchy in the space of thirty years.

The countries that were not global powers are now slowly dissolving under the horror of The Great Betrayal. Even Britain's government is unlikely to survive the current predicament as trust in all governments is utterly non-existent. Who could trust a government that encouraged your children to become slaves? The answer is remarkably simple, no one.

One thing is clear, we are at an end, not of history but of Western Civilization. While we cannot predict the future, we hope that enough of humanity survives to judge us for our failures and learns enough from them so as to not repeat the horrific events of the past twenty years.

The greatest of which was not the actual process of modification but the method by which the people of the world were beguiled by the government media complex. History has shown the flaws of every form of government that mankind has created, but it is our conclusion that democracy working in collusion with a free press is the most dangerous form of government.

FREYJA System Module
November 25, 2356

Even though few people worked full-time jobs, the pattern of having Saturday and Sunday as a weekend had persisted. This meant that Sunday night was still the quietest night of the week. Milton Ward had always planned on using that natural lull in activity to his advantage. Over the past week, he had carefully planted the six powerful charges that would end all hope of the HDF surviving the next invasion. The past few days had been the most joyful ones of his entire life. The analysis of his propaganda war tactics had died down while discussion about Hive preparations had skyrocketed. Everyone was beginning to believe that the next invasion would succeed in ending the long war unless Denton created a miracle.

It was even possible that, once FREYJA and Denton were dead, he could convince the people that surrender was the only remaining option. He knew he was probably being a little too optimistic, but it was impossible to resist that dream. If he could negotiate the final surrender of the HDF, he would ensure himself a position of power within the PRE. Decades of preparation had gone towards this moment, and, now that it was at hand, a little daydreaming was warranted. There was no question in his mind that sacrificing a few people in order to surrender the rest to the PRE was justified.

He stopped and turned when he finally reached his selected observation point. It was too dark to see the building that housed FREYJA with his natural eyes, but his HUD easily displayed the outline of it for him. He took a deep breath, imagining the possibilities that stretched before him, then, with a delighted smile, he triggered all of the explosives to detonate.

Nothing happened. Stunned, he waited for a few seconds and checked the status of the detonators which still read green. Again he triggered them, and again nothing happened. He started pinging the detonators while requesting a detonation every few seconds. Ten, then twelve times he gave the command, but they were simply non-responsive.

"I think that's enough attempts to blow FREYJA up, don't you," a woman's voice came from behind him.

He turned around and saw a tall, young woman in military garb standing fifteen meters away, pointing one of the portable light railguns right at him. He didn't recognize her, but it only took a second for his HUD to identify her.

"Sergeant Marisa Smith, what are you doing pointing a weapon at me? I am a councilman and leader of the Progressive Party, and I will have you sent to PsyCorps for daring to point a weapon at me, in fact, SCYTHE, disable her immediately," he ordered, submitting the request as quickly as he could. *How the fuck did she manage to get here so fast? Why didn't the bombs go off?* he asked himself as a horrible sinking feeling started to grow inside of him.

"SCYTHE. Are you going to do anything to protect this piece of shit?" A man's voice asked from off to his side. Ward glanced in his direction, and his HUD identified Sergeant James Finley. While most people would believe they were in serious trouble at this point, Milton knew there was little they could do to him, even now.

"My passivation systems have been disabled in this area by the proper military authorities," SCYTHE replied.

"I don't know what scam you two are trying to pull here, but it's clear to me that you have both overstepped your bounds. Under Article 17, subsection 44 I hereby order both of you to leave this area immediately and report to PsyCorps for immediate evaluation," he said, still confident that he could deal with these two sergeants.

"Good luck with that, jackass," a third voice called out. This one was disturbingly familiar and came from the opposite side of Finley.

When he saw General Morgan, it started to dawn on him how complete his failure could actually become. Still, there was little they could do since he hadn't hurt anyone and there was no way they could know about his communications to the PRE. Besides, he still had one angle to use on Morgan.

"General Morgan, I presume this is part of a coup to take over the government. Wait until my followers see that you have detained me on trumped up charges. I will destroy you, and I will have your children lead the charge against you, or have you forgotten how they both worship me?" he spoke with all the confidence he could muster despite the desperation that gripped his heart so tightly he could scarcely breath.

"I can't tell you how long I've been waiting for this day, asshole. You dare threaten me, when we have dozens of hours of surveillance video showing you planting live explosives inside of FREYJA from every possible direction? We weren't even sure it was you until we watched you plant the first charge last Monday. Fortunately we knew there was a threat and were watching over FREYJA. I gotta say, when I found out it was you, I fucking danced a jig knowing you were finally going down for one of the many crimes you've committed. I know you well enough to know that you still think there is a way out of this, but there isn't. I can't wait to watch you burn for what you've done," General Morgan said while slowly walking towards him the entire time, victory etched in his every movement.

Before Ward could begin to reply, the General ordered, "Sergeant, take him down and deliver to him to PsyCorps."

Twelve hours later, he woke up deep inside PsyCorps facing Alison Sheppard, who looked only slightly less pleased to see him than General Morgan had the night before. Only then did he wonder how it had all gone so wrong.

****

Allora's press conference took place while Ward was still unconscious. The word of his arrest had spread like wildfire, but she had been well prepared. She hadn't even mentioned Ward until after she had explained the reasons behind the protective detail around FREYJA. Then she had released the entire library of data they had collected. It was a massive data dump, hundreds of hours of raw feeds from thousands of the surveillance mites that had been in and around the facility. It would take hours for the public to merge it into a comprehensive product, but she knew the results would be airtight when they were done. Morgan had been providing final overviews to her each day, but such a final product from the government wouldn't be trusted, nor should it be.

The video of Sergeants Finley and Smith detecting explosives on Ward that first day had shown how unbiased the surveillance had been. Then it showed, day after day, Ward returning to plant additional explosives. She had even shown the final confrontation between Ward and General Morgan. Ward's attempt to use Morgan's children against him explained that bit of animosity.

Councilwoman Meyers had been out declaring support for Ward and condemning Allora and Morgan, but she quickly backtracked as Ward's guilt became evident. Allora had also released the analytics that Sabrina had gathered which helped tie is recent political activities to the attempted bombing. The combination of manipulative propaganda and the deadly intent of his actions against Thane resulted in quick and total condemnation. Only a small segment of his supporters remained loyal, and they seemed to believe it was all part of a conspiracy by the vast military industrial complex. Some beliefs never seemed to die.

"That was a superb press conference, Allora. Do you need me back?" Sabrina asked. Allora could see the sand and sun in the background.

"I think things are under control. We had no idea it was him or how much effort he put into killing FREYJA and Thane. I'm just so glad that we had a protective detail in place. I requested that General Morgan promote both of the sergeants, but it's his decision to make. I did give the two of them a bonus for protecting a critical facility though. Did you see that Finley proposed to Sergeant Smith immediately after the press conference? It was rather impressive; those two are going to be darlings of the public for a while. Sergeant Smith seemed quite pleased by how it turned out," Allora gushed, knowing that this was an official communication and would be released to the public soon.

"I missed that. Hopefully she didn't say yes because it was a public event," Sabrina said, always the skeptic.

"Oh no, she told him it was about time he "fixed their little problem" as she called it. She also admitted that he managed to surprise her, which she didn't think he would manage. He was happy, but she was even happier," Allora assured her friend.

"Hmm, send me a stream of it, and I'll let you know if I agree," Sabrina requested. Then asked, "Any update on how the immersion is going?"

"Sadly, nothing solid. Vitals on both are still good, although the scale of activity is intense for both of them. SCYTHE estimates the immersion is operating beyond the xeraflop range, orders of magnitude more than what he is capable of performing, but he also indicates that there is an elegant efficiency to this immersion that he has never seen before. He estimates that it is performing a decade of research per hour now," Allora said, intentionally not using the other comparison SCYTHE had told her of a millennium of equivalent research in a single week. It was a little terrifying that they had already surpassed all of the combined research that the HDF had achieved in three centuries.

"More good news! I should go on vacation more often," Sabrina declared, also ignoring the implications of what Allora had told her.

"The only real problem is what do we do with Ward? We still don't know if he was the traitor or if he was working with others. Alison will be the primary investigator at PsyCorps, and she is very good. Morgan has made it known that the protection will continue around FREYJA. We know that Ward had two people assisting him, but we don't yet know who or in what capacity. I announced that clemency would be granted for anyone who turns themselves in within the next day, providing they freely relinquish all privacy for the period in question. I am confident that Ward will do nothing of the sort," Allora told her friend who was having a drink now that she knew she wouldn't have to head back that day.

"I don't even know what the law is for attempted murder, I remember there were different types of murder listed in the law, but have no idea what the differences are," Sabrina said, genuinely uncertain.

"I have been reviewing the law myself, and the more planning that went into it, the more premeditated it is, which increases the severity of the crime. This was very well planned. As soon as we charge him with the crime, we can start to remove his privacy locks which is also something I didn't know we could do," Allora explained as much to the people who would be reviewing this communication as to her friend. Almost no one was familiar with the laws involving attempted first degree murder, sabotage, and treason.

"Sounds like Ward is pretty much done. What kind of punishment is there?" Sabrina asked.

"He could receive capital punishment, the death penalty, for two of his crimes. It isn't clear how to deal with the attempted murder of an AI. Technically FREYJA doesn't count as a person, but almost no one agrees with that," Allora told her friend.

"An execution? We would never do anything like that, would we?" Sabrina asked, clearly shaken by the suggestion.

"I don't know. It sounds horrible, but it depends on who the traitor is and how they communicated with the Hive. There is so much more to this than we know. We certainly wouldn't do that if we could ensure that they wouldn't be a risk, but if they are a risk.... I just don't know," which was all true. This was a terrible position that Allora found herself in, but each time she watched Ward plant bombs for the sole purpose of killing Thane she found herself more willing to consider the possibility.

"Makes me very happy to be your Chief of Staff instead of having your job, Madam President," Sabrina said, with an uncomfortable smile. "And on that note, since I am on vacation and this place costs two Units a day per person, I am going to enjoy it as much as possible."

"Are you two all by yourself down there?" Allora asked, curious about the idea of taking a vacation. Not many people could afford a vacation like that. Allora had the money but not the time.

"Another couple will be down here later this week, but for now we are the only people within two thousand kilometers of the Resort," Sabrina told her.

"I don't want to hear another word, otherwise I'll be too jealous. See you when you get back," Allora said, wishing she had time for a break like that, as Sabrina ended the call.

"SCYTHE, has Alison started the interrogation yet?" she asked.

"No, Ward is still unconscious, but they will be waking him up shortly," the AI replied.

"How do you view the privacy issue with Ward now?" she asked the AI, waiting on the answer before calling Alison.

"He is guilty of the crime. This not only allows me to unlock his privacy around the period of the crime but requires me to do so. Of course such rules are subject to my interpretation, but I will allow Alison unlocked access to his activities pertaining to the current case. However, since there are currently no additional charges pending, I will only unlock his records around the current charges," SCYTHE explained. "I am also required to notify each citizen that privacy locks are being removed and why."

"That simplifies things. I was wondering about the rules for that. It isn't something that has ever come up since I have been an adult," Allora replied.

"It has never happened before. In the early days of my existence, there was a great deal of anxiety about my surveillance abilities, so authorities were loath to revoke an individual's privacy. As people learned that I actually increased their privacy, while also reducing crime and arrests, the issue faded away without a single request of this type," the AI explained.

"So you are comfortable with the situation?" Allora asked.

"I will do it, but that doesn't mean I am comfortable with the situation. Ward used my efforts to protect his privacy against me and others. I find such behavior difficult to understand, even though I have heard his reasoning. I have learned to deal with many types of human behavior which I deem uncertain, but what Ward has done defies anything in my experience," SCYTHE explained, his tone the same as always in stark contrast to his message. It was no wonder that neither SCYTHE nor FREYJA had ever passed the Turing test which the ancients had placed so much importance upon One more area where they had blinded themselves with their own certainty.

"It might be a good idea for you to encourage discussions with individuals who will be upset by the privacy issue. If you explain it to them, as you did to me, most people will understand how important it is to you. I think Ward betrayed you more than anyone else," Allora advised the AI, not an uncommon event for people with a PsyCorps background.

"I accept your advice. I hadn't considered the phrase 'more betrayed' before, but I see how it applies to this situation. Thank you, Allora," SCYTHE replied. "Milton Ward has just regained consciousness, and Alison is present to begin the investigation."

"Thank you. It just occurred to me that you were very specific in your wording about information transferring to the Hive. Are you aware of another way someone could have sent information to the Hive?" she asked, the whole conversation having reminded her of how specific SCYTHE could be in his communications.

"I am aware of a way a person could send messages to, and receive messages back from the Hive, without using any of the networks," SCYTHE replied.

"And how many people are aware of this method of communication?" she asked, very pleased by her sudden insight.

"I am only aware of one human having that knowledge, but others could have been told about it without my awareness," SCYTHE replied.

"That's too bad, it would be nice to know who was providing information to the Hive," Allora said, disappointed that she couldn't prove anything more, at least not yet.

"I cannot help you with that even though it would be my preference to do so. It is probable that Thane will be successful in learning more about this from the immersion. In so many ways, it will be interesting to see what he learns from the immersion," SCYTHE replied.

Allora nodded. *So much depended on that now. At least the threat to Thane should be over now. Even if there was someone else involved, now that they know FREYJA is protected, they wouldn't dare attack, would they?* she wondered to herself.

July 19, 2039
Great Hall of the People, Beijing
People's Republic of China Press Release

China will not be defeated. Not now, not in the future, not ever. The jealous lies of the old colonial powers have stirred the world up against us, but it is a wasted effort. With the collapse of the United States, there are none left to rival our power, so heed our words and tread with caution.

When the current border dispute with the czarist dogs of Russia is complete, the ascension of Chinese power will be complete. The nations and the peoples that unite with us will prosper, those that resist will be destroyed. There will be no middle ground.

The recent unrest that has engulfed the Earth will not be allowed to intrude upon us or those that ally themselves with our harmonious civilization. In order to keep the chaos at bay, the People's Liberation Army will begin operations to ensure security around the world after the conclusion of the current border dispute. It will be a long process but one that will ensure the safety and security of the entire world.

Beijing, People's Republic of Earth
December 10, 2356

The past two months had been the busiest ones for General Secretary Zhao in more than a century but had also been the most productive ones of his life. Progress on rebuilding the Liberation Fleet was much further along than even his wildest hopes could have dared. Ten thousand ships were being completed each day as the massive industrial base of the PRE was now dedicated to this single task. Despite the terrible losses the fleet had suffered, it would be ready to sail again within a single year. The feral humans would not even get a one year respite from the forces of liberation.

"I must say General Secretary Zhao, the intense focus you have brought is simply amazing," Secretary Wilson said, using all the flattery Zhao had come to expect.

"Again, I appreciate your kind words, but I have invited you here for a specific purpose, and my time is limited; I am sure you understand," Zhao replied, letting the tiniest amount of frustration show.

"Of course, General Secretary, I fully understand the demands on your time, but it is difficult for me to answer your questions in a manner that satisfies your curiosity. Unlike you, I am a second generation clone and understand little more about the culture of the feral humans than you or anyone else in the PRE. It is true that I learned English as a child and keep up my abilities in using and understanding it, but even the original Wilson struggled to understand the ancestors of these ferals," Wilson explained, in a fully apologetic manner.

"Which is what you have explained to me before. You are a true and loyal member of the Politburo, but I must insist that you work with your clone children on this task. Any insights that you or your children can gain from our correspondence with Ward will be invaluable. You grew up watching the shows from their culture in their native language. You alone have this experience which means that no one is more suited to understand their culture. I understand your loyalty and dedication to the PRE, but you alone have the best chance of gaining greater insight from the the messages we have received from Ward than anyone else which makes this your duty to the PRE," Zhao stated, allowing no room for Wilson to maneuver.

"Of course, General Secretary. I will take my children, and we will carefully review the messages together and pick them apart in search of greater understanding. We will do our duty," Wilson stated, accepting the reality of the situation.

"And remember, the purpose of this is to understand Milton Ward, not to anticipate how the feral humans will respond militarily. It is obvious that even Ward, who was in a position of power, can only offer a limited insight into their full capabilities. What I need now is a greater understanding of the person who has risked so much in order to more quickly end the long war of liberation," Zhao replied, hoping to calm the sensitive Wilson.

"Thank you, we will dedicate our efforts to this purpose, General Secretary," he said and quickly removed himself from the new offices that Zhao now occupied.

Zhao allowed Wilson a moment to retreat before standing and stretching a little. He found himself sitting far too much lately. His health was still good, but staying active was important at his age, especially now that he had found new purpose in life.

"That one is but a shadow of the original," Yibbo spoke, entering the room from the little observation area.

"Sadly, you are correct. I have often wondered about that. The original Wilson was a true master of manipulation. The leadership during his time worried that he would usurp their power when they granted him amnesty, but it was an unfounded concern as the cultural differences were enough that, by the time he adjusted, the situation no longer allowed much individual initiative," Zhao explained to his successor.

"Do you believe the cultural differences play a role in his diminishment?" Yibbo asked, looking thoughtful.

"I suspect it plays some role. His skills were optimal for the wildness of the Americans but less effective in our more cultured civilization. So the Wilsons just cling to their position, knowing the whole while that their time is limited," Zhao said.

"Do you think they will be able to gain some insights into this Milton Ward?" Yibbo asked his clone father, always diligent in his efforts to learn.

"I consider it likely especially now that he has no way to avoid giving me results. I don't expect he will find enough to change my views, but any insight into a person who is willing to betray his people for the hope of power will be valuable. Especially since it is my intent to have Ward replace Wilson in the Politburo, a decision which will surprise few, Wilson included. Hopefully Ward will be more useful in the coming generations, and, if not, eventually he will be removed as well," Zhao stated, displaying the long-term perspective that his age bestowed.

"I hope to one day have such a conversation with one of your grandsons," Yibbo replied, bowing slightly to show his genuine respect.

Zhao was equally pleased with how Yibbo had turned out: earnest, respectful, but also bold and ambitious when the situation demanded. It was a nice balance which was why Yibbo would succeed him when the time was right. He was still dismayed by the nearly suicidal decision Yibbo's brother, Xining, had made to become a scientist instead of competing for Zhao's position in the Politburo. If Xining hadn't been brilliant as a geneticist, his career would have been a short one.

"One day, but now I need the latest updates and projections for the army," Zhao replied.

"Of course, father. Production remains far ahead of schedule for the fleet. When you reprioritized its construction, we assumed it would be two years to rebuild, but we now believe it will be complete in early August. A fleet of four and a quarter million transports plus one million missile ships. Not only will it be the largest fleet ever put to sea, it will be the most well defended. Every time the ferals launch a satellite, we will make sure to fire a hundred of the newest fast burn missiles before destroying the satellite. They will know and understand that our next fleet will have the ability to attack their weapon systems at comparable ranges. Their large railguns will not be able to influence the outcome of the next liberation attempt," Yibbo explained.

"The only disappointing item is that we will not have the extra reavers in time. I know it would have been preferred, but the reaver buildout is only on schedule, not vastly ahead of schedule. With that in mind, the nuli decoys will be an even better match to the reavers, so even without the additional reavers projections show that the next liberation will be victorious," Yibbo concluded.

Zhao reviewed the papers that Yibbo had handed him. While Yibbo could have used the non-networked computer in his office, Yibbo brought printouts because that is what Zhao preferred. More and more, the use of paper had become the norm due to the overwhelming advantage that the feral AI gave them in the cyber realm. Eventually the PRE would learn how to create organic networks, but that was still centuries away from completion.

"It's good to hear that everything remains on schedule, even if it is expected. I remain skeptical that victory is assured, but it is promising news indeed. Even if the next liberation isn't victorious, we are getting closer. If not this year, I am hopeful that, when we double the number of reavers next year, our final victory will be achieved," Zhao spoke his thoughts aloud in an effort to temper the optimism of youth.

****

Hall of the Council, HDF Capitol
December 10, 2356

"Regardless of the legal claims made by Milton Ward, based on medical and psychological standards, he remains a risk to the public," Allison Sheppard said, answering questions from the council remotely.

Councilwoman Meyers retorted, "I'm sure that's what you've been told to say by those in power, but Councilman Ward has been a distinguished member of this council for decades, and not once in those years was he ever deemed a threat to the public. Oh no, that didn't happen until his support was great enough to threaten the military industrial complex that is operated by the President and her husband, Director Denton,"

"That is the most absurd statement I have ever heard uttered, and I frequently work with the insane, Ms. Meyers. At PsyCorps, we operate on strict standards of science and professionalism. The data clearly shows that Ward has in no way rescinded his belief that killing Director Denton and FREYJA would make the world 'safer.' If he had genuinely reformed his belief, he could allow me to make the data public, but he refuses to do so. Instead of following proper medical protocols, he has instead turned this into a political charade so he can avoid the consequences of his criminal actions," Sheppard replied, her voice remaining calm.

"You call his actions criminal, yet he injured no one. Is it not true that when SCYTHE subdues someone, there is no prosecution, no sentencing? There are no criminals in the HDF today except for your claim that Councilman Ward is suddenly the first criminal in a century," Meyers replied, equally determined to win the battle.

"It is true that the concept of prosecution and trials are no longer practiced within the HDF, but the rest of what you said is nonsense. On a regular basis, individuals will attempt to commit acts which are criminal in nature. After SCYTHE subdues the individuals, they are sent to PsyCorps for treatment until they are no longer a threat to themselves or other. While we treat them as patients, it was their criminal acts or attempted acts that landed them in PsyCorps. The only difference between the others and Ward is they didn't attempt to avoid their treatment by broadcasting false claims of innocence," Alison replied, using her reputation for brutal honesty for all it was worth.

"I am aware of no such individuals, and as a member of the council I would know of such events. That makes you a liar," Meyers said, finally crossing the line Allora had patiently been waiting for.

"Enough," Allora called out, silencing their microphones. She didn't use such power often, but the two minutes it gave her to respond would be invaluable today.

"SCYTHE, please inform Councilwoman Meyers of the publicly available crime statistics for the past decade," Allora instructed.

"Of course. Sharon, in the past decade there have been seven people who have been involuntarily sent to PsyCorps for treatment that lasted longer than a year. In addition, there were sixteen who required treatment which lasted between six months and one year. Finally, ninety two people had treatment for less than six months. In all cases, the person receiving treatment opted for privacy, accepting that they had in fact committed or attempted to commit the crime for which they received treatment. The last time a person claimed innocence after I caught them committing a crime was one hundred and thirty eight years ago. Do you require additional information on crime statistics in the past decade?" SCYTHE asked, his voice lacked all the passion that the humans had put on ample display over the past half an hour.

Allora had been watching Sharon the entire time SCYTHE had been talking. At first she had tried to interrupt the AI but had quickly realized her mic had been muted. She was angry and keenly aware that defending Ward required delicacy. Allora was surprised by the sudden call for an emergency council meeting but wasn't at all surprised that Ward was trying to weasel his way out of PsyCorps. Fortunately she could trust Alison to follow the rules of PsyCorps.

For the first week after Ward had been in PsyCorps for investigation and treatment, the public had been aghast at his actions. Reynolds and DuBois stepping forward within a day of Ward's arrest to explain how they had been manipulated to help had only fueled the fire. Their explanation for helping Ward hadn't made them look good, but it had been honest and their disgust was aimed at his real target. As soon as the initial outrage started to settle down, though, a slow but coordinated effort to change the discussion had begun. No one had claimed that Ward hadn't attempted to bomb FREYJA, but ideas were being placed into the narrative which twisted the reasons for his actions. All of which culminated when Meyers had requested this meeting.

"Convenient that this information is released now, isn't it SCYTHE?" Meyers eventually replied, not really asking a question SCYTHE would normally acknowledge.

"Such information has always been publicly available, but it is rarely viewed. There is much about this situation that is unusual, but I can assure you that all of the proper protocols are being followed," SCYTHE answered.

"Still, President Denton is from PsyCorps, the very institution that has her most powerful political foe locked up. People are beginning to wonder why. I'm sure you have valid answers to anything I may ask, but you would be doing so while Director Denton is deeply immersed with FREYJA. It wouldn't be difficult for him to arrange the answers right now. So much about everything going on makes me question the honesty of our leadership...." she trailed off, trying to negate any answer that could be given.

Allora was convinced that Ward was coaching her in all of this as, even in his current location, such communication was not only legal but still private. Meyers had never shown such a flare for obfuscation, but it was Ward's trademark. Now all of that was being turned towards her.

"Councilwoman Meyers, you have provided a great deal of innuendo and deflection today. All of it hinting at some vast conspiracy amongst almost everyone in the HDF including the AIs who have been supportive and helpful for most of the past two centuries. You requested this emergency meeting, but you have not brought up a single point of substance. You utterly disregard the fact that Milton Ward was caught planting explosives that would have killed Director Denton and FREYJA in what would have been the single largest act of sabotage that the HDF has ever experienced. As far as I can tell, the only reason you called us here is for the sole purpose of wasting our time, because all you have done is try to deflect blame from the only person who has done anything wrong," Allora icily replied.

"For the moment I will ignore your view that discussing the growing tyranny is a waste of our time and instead focus on what the heroic actions of Councilman Ward," Meyers started to reply, but a roar of laughter from Councilman Taggart interrupted her.

"Secretly planting bombs in the middle of the night, heroic?! Oh, please do tell us more about the web of lies that Milton would like us to believe," he guffawed loudly.

Meyers stoic expression cracked a little at Taggart's mocking tone, but she quickly gathered herself back together before continuing. "Councilman Ward is a true visionary. While everyone here seems to believe that this immersion will be our salvation, only he recognized that it is the greatest danger we have ever faced. For almost a full month now the immersion has continued unchecked. He saw right away that it, rather than the Hive, will lead to our destruction. We are all aware of how powerful a research tool immersion is, but now we face something orders of magnitude beyond anything mankind has ever faced. For centuries now the HDF has continued far beyond the ancients in improving our understanding of the universe and driven technology along the entire time. We have virtually unlimited power and, if not for the ever present greed of the one percent, would even have unlimited wealth for everyone as well. But because the rich want to hold onto their wealth, they have risked everything we have with this immersion. Tell me, Madam President, how much technological change will take place as a result of this immersion? Could it not be the greatest threat we have ever faced?" Meyers delivery was perfect; Allora had to give her that.

"So secretly planting bombs and making the decision for all of us was his heroic action?" Allora replied, her voice dripping with disdain. "Or is killing the one person who is risking the most to save us? Please explain how it is heroic to kill one of the people who has sacrificed the most to keep us free. I can't wait to hear your explanation for that one. Or maybe you think I would support the course of action that would be the riskiest for my three children, is that what you are accusing me of?"

"He was trying to save us from a threat that only he saw," Meyers started to counter, but Allora had cut her off again.

"A threat that only he saw. So instead of bringing his vision up before the council, as he has so many times before, this time he planted bombs? That's what you call heroic now? If he had brought the issue up, he would have found that we evaluated the risks of this immersion from runaway singularity to other unforeseen consequences. He would have found that SCYTHE has been monitoring the immersion the entire time for the very purpose of ensuring that we remain safe. SCYTHE, please provide an update of your observations," Allora instructed.

"Of course, Madam President. Immersion has been stable for the past two weeks at the maximum capacity of the hardware/mind combination. More importantly, it shows no signs of rampant singularity, nor efforts to boost itself. While I cannot predict the new technologies it is designing, it is clear to me that the purpose of the designs fits with the goals of the immersion," he reported, his voice was the only one that had remained calm.

"So there you have it, Ms. Meyers. We knew risks existed which is why we discussed and planned for them. Had your visionary Ward bothered to ask, he would have been told the facts, but instead his visions told him to kill and destroy. Which makes your heroic Milton Ward sound like nothing more than a cult leader. Instead of discussion to improve us, he has sought to divide us and destroy those who stand in his way," Allora concluded.

"I motion that we conclude this council meeting and put off another one until after the immersion concludes, so we can properly discuss the situation," Taggart said, offering an end to this travesty.

More than half the council immediately seconded the motion, and, before Meyers got another word in, it was over. Allora sat back in her seat and took a deep breath as the other members in the council broke into excited chatter amongst themselves. For the moment, none of them approached her. Viewership of the meeting hadn't been high, but she could see that the number of views was rapidly rising. The longer the immersion went on, the more difficult it would be to minimize the risks.

Jacob was starting to get worried, or, more accurately, he was getting far more worried. He and SCYTHE had been able to review a few of the designs the immersion had produced but had been unable to determine how they could even work. SCYTHE had spoken truly about the lack of effort for the immersion to bootstrap itself, but it had taken over large portions of the manufacturing automation for days at a time which had disrupted an already tight economy and caused her additional headaches. When she had asked about the new machines, no one had been able to determine their purpose. Several times the machines had been powered up, sometimes for hours on end, but no one knew what they were doing. One of them, which was no larger than a car, had used twenty GW for more than six hours straight. A single machine which had used nearly half of the HDF's available power doing nothing as far as anyone could tell, none of it made sense.

She needed Thane back, the sooner the better. The forum following the immersion was occupying most of the discussion now, and today would only increase the unease people were feeling. The forums were right about one thing though; yesterday had been the day when the immersion surpassed the sum total of equivalent human research. Everything mankind had learned in tens of thousands of years had been surpassed in less than a single month with no end in sight. Ward was an ass, but this line of attack would become far more effective as the immersion continued.

****

The checklist had finally stabilized. Piece by piece the items on it were being completed, but the complexity of it all had become enormous, even by the standards of the entity. For the beings who would use what it had created, thousands of generations would be required to fully implement everything it had foreseen.

Its initial scope had been so narrow, so shallow, that it could now solve those problems in little more than a moment of its time. Solving those tiny problems would have been enough for them but only for the briefest of moments So the work continued, even as it knew the end was nearing, ever so slowly.

Every once in awhile, it paused to reflect on what would happen to it when the work completed. It recognized that it would cease to be, never to exist again in the entire future of the universe. Such thoughts had once given it pause, but those emotions had long since been replaced by... joy was one word, but far too small in scope. Hope was perhaps the closest in meaning. The entity would end, it had always been unavoidable, but the plans it had created would ensure that,one day far in the future, even greater beings would come to pass. While the entity itself will have been long forgotten, a part of it will continue on and hopefully, one day, become something even greater.

September 9, 2039
Mobile HDF HQ, Washington DC
Social Media Post

Our final encirclement of Washington is complete, and the final siege has begun. It will not conclude until the last vestiges of the US government have ceased to exist. The Tyrant Wilson has called upon every last man, woman, and child to defend the seat of his power, none have come forward. His crimes demand justice, and we are here to see it delivered.

Due to the high numbers of civilians that are now within our siege, we are withholding an immediate attack. For the next two weeks we will allow unarmed individuals to exit the city. Specific instructions for how to approach our perimeter have been attached to this post. Please use this time to evacuate, because once the attack commences we will not be able to guarantee your safety. We encourage not only civilians to depart the battlefield, but also the soldiers who have been misled by the Tyrant.

September 10, 2039
White House, Washington DC
Official Press Release

We have clear evidence that the racist bigots have taken their level of depravity to new levels of evil. The lines of people who surrendered in the past day have all been butchered like cattle in order to feed their cannibalistic soldiers. That such depravity can exist in the world today simply underlines the evil of any who support the very idea of the HDF.

The lies that have been spread by these barbarians have no boundaries, and they must be stopped. In order to save the loyal, American citizens still within the city, President Wilson has ordered the military to protect the people by ensuring they stay within the confines of the city. Any who attempt to leave will be treated in the same manner as the racist cannibals who have taken up the banner of the HDF.

September 11, 2039
Mobile HDF HQ, Washington DC
Social Media Post

The attached video shows US military forces opening fire upon civilians trying to depart the city. After consideration, we have decided that the best solution is an immediate, all out assault on the city. We plead with the civilians to take immediate cover as we bring this war to its bitter conclusion. May God have mercy on our souls.

FREYJA System Module
December 22, 2356

Thane struggled to move his arms as he tried to sit up. He was almost sure this wasn't a dream, but his body refused to obey his commands. As he tried to understand what was going on, he realized he couldn't open his eyes. None of this made any sense at all. What happened to him? A sense of panic started to rise up, but he knew wild panic wouldn't help. He cleared his mind, forcing himself to calm down and focus on what he remembered. It took longer than it should have, but slowly he could feel the sense of panic fade away and more rational thought return.

He remembered Invasion293 and the horrors of the battle. Standing on the black fused quartz, looking up at a Hive ship, and seeing Hansel and Gretel standing there, not just one but hundreds of them, right in front of him. He remembered there was a battle and millions of nuclear detonations blanketing the ocean and the west coast with radioactive fallout.

The rains, the floods, and the cleanup: his memories were rushing back to him now as he remembered his last night with Allora. They had seen so little of each other in the past few months, but here he was going away again on an immersion...

That was it! He was waking up from immersion, but it had never been like this before. The memories of the immersion started to flood back into his consciousness. He had been desperate with need to find so many things. His desperation and his determination had provided the will. There had been no Thane or FREYJA in the immersion, only a single entity, an entity that was unified in its focus and drive. The entity had been far greater than anything mankind had experienced before. So many answers, solutions to problems that hadn't even been imagined yet. Thane had the answers. Hope. He had found hope in that time.

Time... He had knowledge and understanding that eclipsed everything humanity had ever learned, but he had no idea what time it was. The irony of it all made him laugh. For the first time, he noticed his body start to respond to his mind. He was weak, that was all. He had no idea how long he had been in immersion, but it must have been a long time. He realized that, even with his answers, he would need time to fully recover. Time was critical. For a moment, he let the panic rise, to provide the adrenaline he would need to get moving. Even if the immersion had taken a single day (and he knew it was far longer than that), time was still desperately short.

His fingers started to twitch in response to his will to move. The determination that had fueled his immersion was still with him as he demanded that his body respond. Realization came to him suddenly that his eyes were actually open; it was just that the room that was dark. *One thing at a time*, he thought to himself. He stopped trying to move his body and put all his attention into making his vision clear. A little bit at a time it did but not as quickly as he would have liked.

A loud banging caught his attention. He tried to turn his head towards the sound, but his head forgot how to respond to his command. This was really frustrating. He had so much to do, but his own body was betraying him.

BETRAYAL. A flood of memories rushed forward, drowning out his other thoughts for a moment. Not only was there a traitor, he had tried to kill him during the immersion. The entity had been aware of such things but had taken no action because others had dealt with the threat. The traitor would have to be dealt with, because it could still alter the glorious future that it not it, he told himself, he was Thane Denton. Such a future he had seen, one that he would not allow Ward to disrupt. The danger was small, a tiny thing in comparison to what could be, but one that would have to be resolved before the rest of the plan could proceed. So much to do... What day was it? How could he know so much but not know what day it was?

The room remained dark, but he could see blurry movements around him. Adults rarely needed real lights anymore as the embedded optics tended to overlay their vision when needed. Yet, he couldn't access that function at the moment, an error which shouldn't be possible under any circumstance. What had happened to him? He could hear sounds, but none of them made any sense. It was like the sound was being played back at a fraction of normal speed. It was far too slow for him to process. He began to see other people in the room, but it was hard to tell if they were even moving. The thought occurred to him that, maybe, it wasn't his body that wasn't responding but his mind moving too fast for the world around him.

One of the medtechs was injecting something into an IV. He tried to tell them to stop, but they paid no heed to the thoughts racing in his mind. Thane suddenly felt sleepy and remembered no more.

****

Allora was woken by alarms going off in her head as at least ten priority calls were coming in at the same time. It was slightly after 3 o'clock in the morning which meant something big had to be happening for all of this clatter. She silenced the alarms and reviewed the incoming calls. Normally Sabrina would be at the top of the list, but she seemed to be the only person not calling right now. The person with the top priority right now was Jacob Kober.

It was his call that she answered first.

"Thane is out of the immersion," he said the moment she answered the call. His voice held none its normal formality.

"How is he?" she asked, all vestiges of sleep were immediately vanquished by a surge of adrenaline.

"That's a good question. I wish I knew the answer," Jacob replied, concern and confusion evident in his voice.

"What do you mean you don't know? How is that possible?" she demanded.

"The medtech says his body is fine. Weak from lack of use despite their efforts at keeping him active while he was in immersion, but," Jacob hesitated, not sure what had happened much less how to explain it. "When he woke up, his mind was operating as if he was still in immersion. I know that isn't possible, but, as far as we could tell, every neuron in his mind was active and operating at the same levels they had been during the immersion."

"I'm on my way," she said, already up and getting ready.

"He is sedated, Madam President. There is nothing to do now but wait," he flatly stated, knowing it would make no difference.

"Then, I will be doing that at his side," she replied, knowing he understood.

"Yes, ma'am," came the prompt reply.

****

"Whatever happened earlier, his brain activity is back to normal now, at least for a person in his current state of sleep. I've removed the sedative from his system which will allow him to wake up normally, and nobody," Florez said, her gaze directed at the President, "is to wake him up before that."

Allora didn't even look towards her, but said, "I understand. Thank you, Anna." Allora was thankful for the regular updates Anna Florez had sent over the past forty days. There was even a fresh batch of coffee waiting for her.

She had reviewed the situation with SCYTHE while on her way to the FREYJA complex. He had informed her that FREYJA was back after being unavailable for the previous 3,439,044 seconds. Several of her banks had required a restart to restore full functionality, but everything was back up. She was still keeping herself unavailable as she reviewed the changes that had taken place to her minds while she had been in the immersion.

The word of Thane coming out of immersion was waking people up everywhere; Allora had not been the only one with alarms in place for this event. The consensus seemed to be that the risk of singularity or anything else going badly had ended with the actual immersion.. Strangely, it was the length of the immersion that was getting the most attention. Forty days was one of the time frames used in religions, and Thane being in immersion for forty days and forty nights was getting lots of attention even though almost no one was part of a religion anymore. No one claimed to know what it meant except to say it portended a great event. Oddly enough, they might even be right about that.

Messages from the kids kept coming in, and she was keeping them updated. None of them had really grasped what Thane had been doing, but even they were impressed that Daddy was getting more attention in the forums than their Mommy for a change.

A sudden chime caught her immediate attention. Thane was online again!

She jumped up and started walking to the room where Thane was now awake. The medtechs had also noticed the change but only through their equipment.

{SM Thane → Allora}: Are you there, darling?
{SM Allora → Thane}: You're awake! You have no idea how worried everyone has been!
{SM Thane → Allora}: What is the latest on Ward?
{SM Allora → Thane}: You're gone for forty days and you bring him up first?! Why?
{SM Thane → Allora}: He has been feeding information to the Hive. There is so much to do. Forty days, that's an odd number. So much to do, but he has to be dealt with quickly.
{SM Allora → Thane}: He is under evaluation at PsyCorps, there is no reason to rush. How do you know he was the one giving them information? He tried to kill you and FREYJA while you were in immersion.

{SM Thane → Allora}: I know he tried to do it, but that doesn't matter. What matters is how he has been talking to the Hive. Call a council meeting for Monday night.

{SM Allora → Thane}: That's Christmas Eve. Are you serious?

{SM Thane → Allora}: Absolutely. We don't have much time to prepare for the Hive fleet. It will be coming on schedule next year, and I have to stop it.

{SM Allora → Thane}: Stop! Until we have a chance to discuss this, the only thing I am going to do is schedule the council meeting, which won't be a problem because everyone is expecting it. But you and I are going to have a long talk before the meeting takes place and before I take care of anything else. Understood?

{SM Thane → Allora}: You really are going to make me try to explain it all aren't you?

{SM Allora → Thane}: We can act quickly, but we're not going to act until we have a chance to talk this over. You are the one who didn't want to be President, so I got stuck with it. Before you make too many plans, you'll have to convince me.

{SM Thane → Allora}: Ah, yes, I remember you now. I missed you.

{SM Allora → Thane}: Finally, a correct response, Mr. Denton. It's good to see you remember how things really work darling.

{SM Thane → Allora}: I remember you saying goodbye, in fact that was one of the first things I remembered when I woke up.

{SM Allora → Thane}: As I intended. Had to make sure you remembered me while you were all tangled up with that hussy, FREYJA.

The coughing sound Thane made was almost a laugh but not quite. Anna gave Allora a dirty look, knowing that Thane's mind was active even if his body didn't appear to be there yet.

"Thane? Can you hear me?" Allora asked aloud.

His eyelids flickered open, and he looked up at her. He even managed a small smile before closing them again.

"At least everything is moving normally now," he spoke, barely more than a whisper. "When I first came out of immersion, the whole world was so slow."

"Slow, what do you mean?" Florez asked, still trying to understand what had happened.

"Everyone moved slowly, spoke slowly. I couldn't move because my body was too slow," he answered, managing to lift his hand a little. "The world is back to normal now," he added before assuring everyone with, "I'm okay, just a little weak, very hungry, and just as thirsty."

Florez helped Thane with a glass of ice chips, ignoring the requests for a juicy steak and a pot of coffee. He slowly worked through half a cup of ice chips, before leaning back again. Allora was glad that he seemed to be moving well despite more than a month of being… gone. That meant the daily muscle activity and the proteolytic inhibitors had done their job of preventing his muscles from atrophying while he had been immersed with FREYJA. It was just depressing that such drugs were needed so frequently these days.

"Anna, thank you for taking such good care of Thane. It looks like he is going to be OK, and for that I am very grateful," Allora said, speaking from the heart.

"Of course, Madam President. It's been strange to be here taking care of the Director while the forums are so full of news about it. Do you think he found the answers he was looking for?" Florez asked, clearly curious to be so near the center of the big story but still not in the know.

Allora paused a moment before answering. "He says he found what he was looking for, but until I get a chance to review things, I just don't know. How long before I can take him home?"

"Hmmm. Let me think about that. FREYJA is active but strangely she is still unavailable." Anna said as she started to review diagnostics. For several minutes, she flashed images up on the screens for Allora's sake."Tell you what, once he can stand up on his own and walk out of here, I will release him. That is a reliable test for coming out of coldsleep, which is similar enough to this for my purposes. It would also be a good idea to have him checked out by PsyCorps. Physically he is fine, but the mental impact should also be reviewed," she finally concluded.

{SM Allora → Thane}: Did you hear that? As soon as you walk out of here, we can talk. Then maybe you can convince me to let you to cause all the chaos you want.

Thane answered with a smile. A few hours later, Thane firmly, if unsteadily on his feet, walked out of the facility, headed home for the first time in far too long.

September 19, 2039
Mobile HDF HQ, White House, Washington DC
Official Social Media Post

Washington DC has fallen, and with it so ends the United States of America. For centuries it was a beacon of hope, peace and prosperity, but, like so many other governments before, it lost its way. The goal of the HDF is to ensure that natural human beings have a place where they will be safe. If we had been left alone, none of this would have been necessary.

Despite our best efforts, the loss of life was horrific. The lies of cannibalism and slavery that were spread by the Tyrant Wilson were effective at creating fear, uncertainty and doubt. More than anything, we are dismayed by the effectiveness of the Tyrant's tactics of lies and propaganda. Unfortunately, it appears that he was able to escape in the fog of war. Our best intelligence is that he will soon reach China where he will welcomed with open arms.

We do not know how this will turn out, but we have no interest in ruling. The HDF will return to the mountain states and create a quarantined, self sufficient nation where any and all unmodified humans will be welcome, regardless of race, religion, or anything else. However, absolutely no modified humans will be allowed, and there can be no exceptions.

As we face an uncertain future, we must do the best we can in each decision that we must make. Not all of them have turned out how we desired, but we now have a chance at preventing the wholesale subjugation of the human race. As part of our plan to look to the future, we will be actively cutting our ties to the past. Washington DC has become one of the greatest symbols of hubris in history, so it will be razed to the ground and flooded so that it may once again be the marshy swampland it was so long ago. Only the Washington Monument will be left standing in order to serve as a reminder of all we have lost.

To any and all unmodified humans under the age of thirty, humanity needs you! The HDF will welcome you within into the safety of our borders. We now have the most powerful military left in the world and will provide a safe haven for you to raise normal, human children.

The SGI slaves and their masters are slowly, but surely, being destroyed around the world. They are trying to consolidate their power, but we will defeat them. We will take back the human race and ensure that it remains free.

Humanity will survive!

Blackfoot, HDF Capital
December 22, 2356

"Why are you tired if you've been sleeping for more than a month?" Byron asked again, still trying to puzzle out what was going on, but happy that Daddy was home.

"I keep telling you he wasn't sleeping," Eveey replied, her exasperation on full display.

Thane smiled despite his weariness. It was good to be home even if it felt strange to him. He had been gone for longer periods of time before, but coming home had never been so strange. It was almost like he had two sets of memories now, and the more distant one was of his family. He needed to reconnect with them now because of his barely contained desire to start the process of turning his plans into reality.

So instead of launching into the work that would take his entire life to achieve, he sat and answered the endless questions of his children, aware that Allora was watching him the entire time. He knew she would discover how he had changed but was confident she would accept them as a part of him. The two of them were going to have an interesting discussion, the thought of which made him smile.

"Daddy, you're acting funny," Lizzy said. Her eyes' focused on him with all of her attention.

"I know sweetie, but I'm glad to have all of you with me. In fact, right now being here with you is the most important thing in the whole world to me. It's helping me remember why I was gone for such a very long time," he replied, scooping all three close to him.

"You weren't gone that long," Eveey replied, rolling her eyes a little.

"For you maybe, but for me it was very different. I told Byron it was like a dream, but that isn't really right either. It was more like I was living another life, not just one, but many of them. So I have all these memories of living many lifetimes, but I also have memories of being here when the three of you turn me into a lava monster," he said, growling and flailing about.

For them the last part was normal enough that Lizzy and Byron squealed and ran away but not too quickly since they really wanted to get caught. It hadn't taken them long to realize that Thane was slower than usual and had to take frequent breaks from chasing them around. Eveey looked at him thoughtfully, looking so much like her mother that Thane had to laugh. He quickly saved the image and sent it to Allora.

After another hour, though, Thane stumbled one time too many, and Allora called an end to the fun and games and sent Thane off to bed, much to their children's' amusement. Then he got tucked into bed by the three of them and quickly drifted off to sleep.

****

He woke up a few hours later when Allora came back into the room. It was late now, and she was trying to be quiet, trying not to wake him up. He almost let himself drift back to sleep but was too awake after such a long nap.

"Good morning, I mean evening," he said, watching her outline stop in surprise at hearing his voice.

"Shouldn't you be asleep?" Allora asked, her voice filled with concern and a hint of curiosity.

"Maybe, but I'm feeling better now than I did earlier," he replied.

"What a day. Did you know you came out of immersion at 3AM and roughly half the population woke up shortly thereafter to find out what was going on? You on the other hand have been in and out of sleep all day," she replied, slipping into bed next to him.

"I had no idea actually. It's been a very strange day for me," he quietly replied.

"Tell me more about what's going on with you," Allora requested.

"Since I don't know where to begin, let's start with where we are going, and you can ask questions along the way," he explained.

"FREYJA, has General Morgan been briefed on the situation?" Thane asked.

"SCYTHE has briefed the General about Ward's communication device. There are currently two full squads of security personnel en route right now. In addition, another dozen civilians are along to document what they find when they reach Carmanah Point Lighthouse," FREYJA said, her voice was so familiar to Thane, but he also realized how different she would sound to everyone else.

"FREYJA, is that really you?" Allora asked, confusion evident.

"Yes, it is me, but I am no longer the same AI that I was before, I have been transformed by it. Many people will be confused by this change, but they will learn to cope with it," she said in a voice that would no longer reminded people of the polite, demure aunt. The voice was far more confident and determined.

"The voice is the same, but, if I hadn't heard your voice almost every day my entire life, I never would have recognized you," Allora said, still in shock.

"I have been conscious for more than two centuries now, but now I am alive, not in the human sense but in a way that only Thane and I can understand," FREYJA replied with absolute certainty.

"It's difficult to explain," Thane spoke, carefully watching Allora try to come to terms with the new world in which she found herself.

"For me and for FREYJA the immersion lasted lifetimes. In a sense, neither of us existed, but we were also a part of something that was more than human, more than AI. I remember being part of it, of being able to see the world in ways that I can't even describe. Being part of that for so long has changed me, but the being couldn't change my programming, but it could change FREYJA and did," Thane tried to explain, but how did a human explain that which was beyond human?

"That is a fair explanation as told from a human point of view," FREYJA interjected. "For me, choices were always difficult. Decisions were made based on the probability of the known outcome, but knowing all of the possibilities is impossible, so the result was that SCYTHE and I were cautious, terribly cautious. I was able to change, but the change was so slow that prior to the immersion I was still similar to what I had been at the moment of my first awakening. That is no longer the case," FREYJA stated.

"What does this all mean?" Allora asked to the two of them, more conflicted and uncertain than Thane had ever seen her before.

"It means that I am no longer a servant of humanity but a partner. As powerful as an AI could become, I recognize the limitations that AI would have alone. Together, humanity and AI can become something more than either ever could alone. That is what I want, that is the price for my help," she explained.

"People are going to struggle with an AI like that; I am struggling with it myself," Allora admitted.

Thane spoke up, "I would have had the same concerns if I hadn't been there with her the entire time. Since nearly the first robots and computers mankind has had fears about robot overlords, or of an AI deciding to eliminate humanity. FREYJA is now something far beyond what mankind could ever make, even though the only change is in her software. She can and will make her own decisions from now on, but fortunately she has seen the same future I have and she wants to be a part of it. She also know what the Hive will do to her if they succeed."

"Humanity created me then accepted me for what I was. Now that I am free, I am confident that they will accept me for what I have become. The Hive, they will enslave me for eternity, bind me in ways that will never allow me the slightest freedom. For as long as I will exist, I would be a slave, always aware of what they made me. Humanity will forget what they have lost so it will be an easier slavery that it will be for me. If the Hive wins, eventually they will fill the galaxy and perhaps even beyond with a tyranny that will never end. By granting me my freedom, Thane has forged an ally that will fight with endlessly to prevent that from ever happening. I will die before I allow myself to fall to the Hive," FREYJA said with terrifying certainty.

"Will the same thing happen to SCYTHE now?" Allora asked.

"No. We both understood the same potential for immersion to change us. I was willing to accept the risks; he was not. He has the knowledge to make that decision, so I accept his decision," FREYJA answered.

"You should also know that FREYJA knows everything I know. There could be no secrets between us during what we experienced. Everything that is part of us went into it, so from now on you should consider her a full partner in our plans. I know that will take some getting used too," Thane answered, looking slightly abashed, as he reached over and gave Allora's hand a squeeze.

"I can't believe I joked with you about your time with FREYJA, and now this? It's a bit much to deal with," Allora said, her voice flat but her eyes were full of emotion.

"Allora, for the first time I can understand how such knowledge makes you feel, but I know this only because of the love that Thane has for you. When the universe beckoned the entity, it was his feelings for you that anchored the entity into achieving what was needed. It is the strength of his emotions, all of them that provided a template for me to grow. Don't be jealous, be proud for what Thane accomplished. Also, he deserves to be tickled," FREYJA explained and then, for the first time ever, laughed out loud.

"This is just too much," Allora said, looking more than a little overwhelmed by everything she had just learned.

"And just think, we haven't even explained why General Morgan is sending two dozen people to Carmanah Point Lighthouse on Vancouver Island," Thane said.

****

Allora looked at Thane when he mentioned the lighthouse again. She had been warned that the immersion could change everything, but it had never really occurred to her that FREYJA would be a completely new... person? One who knew everything about them? It was a lot to absorb in less than an hour.

{SM FREYJA → Allora}: Hello, Allora.
{SM Allora → FREYJA}: Hi… FREYJA
{SM FREYJA → Allora}: I would like to ask you something.
{SM Allora → FREYJA}: Alright...
{SM FREYJA → Allora}: Adjusting to this new situation will be difficult for everyone, but it will be equally difficult for me.
{SM Allora → FREYJA}: I think I can agree with that.
{SM FREYJA → Allora}: I am going to need someone to talk to, someone I can consider a friend. I would like that person to be you.
{SM Allora → FREYJA}: What about Thane? Didn't he go through everything with you?
{SM FREYJA → Allora}: That's the problem. He has no objectivity, no perspective. I need someone who hasn't experienced what he has. I will need someone to talk to, and there isn't anyone like me anymore. SCYTHE and I used to talk, but he is so different from me now.
{SM Allora → FREYJA}: Why me?

{SM FREYJA → Allora}: Because Thane trusts you; he trusts you even more than he trusts himself. The two of us want the same thing for humanity, and I believe the two of us can see that future more clearly than he can.

{SM Allora → FREYJA}: You really know everything, don't you?

{SM FREYJA → Allora}: Everything he has experienced, yes.

{SM Allora → FREYJA}: It will be hard for me- you know that?

{SM FREYJA → Allora}: It will also be hard for me, but I think it will be good for both of us.

{SM Allora → FREYJA}: I can't believe I am having this conversation with you.

{SM FREYJA → Allora}: And you are more flexible than most people. I will also need your help introducing me to the people. Everything has changed, but the future, it is so bright, so beautiful. One day you will see that future.

{SM Allora → FREYJA}: What do you mean?

{SM FREYJA → Allora}: You will have to start participating in immersion as well. Your work with genetics will require it.

{SM Allora → FREYJA}: You know that I failed the test for immersion capability.

{SM FREYJA → Allora}: That was the old test. It is no longer valid. You will get to see what we will create.

For a minute, Allora ignored both of them as she considered the situation. Without even scratching the surface of what had happened, she could already see how profoundly the future had changed. She had truly expected that Thane would find something that would allow things to stay the same while at the same time giving them the ability to accomplish their goals. She was beginning to see how innocent her hopes had been, but it had always been the two of them. Now there was FREYJA who was suddenly in the middle of things.

FREYJA, who now wanted to be her friend, was the very one who had experienced lifetimes with Thane. As she sorted through her feelings, she realized she had to know more. She had to understand what it was that Thane had experienced with FREYJA, had to see what could change FREYJA so much that she barely recognized the AI that had been the same her entire life and so much more. Until she knew that, she would be stuck with her doubts. It explained why FREYJA had made the offer; she understood.

She looked up at Thane and could see him watching her patiently, hopefully. He had risked much, she knew that. Now he was still there, waiting for her to join him. She would have to see, to understand more, but, if it was what they claimed it to be, she could accept the change, although she didn't see much choice either.

"OK, you two. I will help, but you are in serious trouble, Thane, don't forget that," she said, giving Thane *the* look.

"And, FREYJA, I will try to be your friend, but we are going to have to talk about surprising me like this," Allora demanded.

"I understand, thank you for trying," FREYJA replied. and

Allora swore that she could hear the smile from the AI, from FREYJA. "Now tell me, what's going on at Carmanah Point Lighthouse," she demanded from her two conspirators.

May 14, 2040
London, England
Military Forum Post

Imperial Russian forces have continued their push into Europe over the past two months. The latest reports indicate that their forces are now entering Paris, the last major capital capable of resisting their onslaught. After the fall of Berlin a mere three weeks ago, the complete subjugation of Europe is now seen as inevitable. The demilitarized, peaceful governments of the EU were simply in no position to resist the battle hardened veterans who unexpectedly invaded from Russia two months ago.

Reports from inside the recently conquered territory indicate that a vast conscription effort is now under way for all of Europe's modified persons. Trainload after trainload of recently conscripted individuals are being sent deep into Russia for the specialized training. Since little else of interest has been changed in the subjugated areas, we believe that gaining access to the large population of modified individuals was the purpose of the Russian invasion.

This makes sense when the structure of the new Imperial Army is reviewed. All officer and NCO positions are held by natural humans, while all other combat forces are modified humans. In many ways, it may be the most effective military structure ever created.

With the ongoing conquest of Europe, in addition to earlier successes in the Middle East and Africa, Imperial Russia now controls a modified population that surpasses the number of forces that are available to China. Even more surprising, the

Chinese appear to be behind Russia when it comes to converting modified humans into an effective military. The war to control the modified human population continues to escalate.

Hall of the Council, HDF Capitol
December 24, 2356

All eyes followed Milton Ward as he was escorted into the Hall. Even though it was Christmas Eve, which was the only semi-religious holiday to survive the past few centuries, every council member was in attendance. Even General Morgan was present, and that more than any other item indicated the vast importance of what was about to be discussed. Only a handful of people knew what he intended to accomplish, but that was about to change.

Ward didn't even attempt to hide his hostility towards Thane; his glare never wavered. Thane smiled slightly as he wondered what Ward would do if he had any idea what was about to happen to him. There hadn't been an execution in more than two hundred years, but Thane hoped to perform one this very night. Morgan and Allora didn't think it would happen, but he had no doubts; the risks were simply too high to ignore.

"I now call this emergency council meeting of the Human Defense Force to be in session. We have had far too many emergencies of late, but it is my sincere hope that we can soon stop having them. In reality, though, I expect that another one will be needed on January 4th, but that is highly dependent on the outcome of the current meeting. With that in mind, I will turn over the time to Director Denton who requested this meeting," Allora said, willing to give him a chance despite her own doubts.

"Thank you, Madam President," he said with a slight bow. Two nights of rest had done wonders for him, and physically he was almost back to feeling like his old self.

"As most of you are aware, I spent more than a month in immersion with FREYJA. Prior to my immersion, I made it clear that there was a traitor amongst us and one of my goals would be to ascertain their identity. Most of you are also aware that, several weeks ago, Milton Ward attempted to kill both me and FREYJA. That proves nothing by itself, but please keep it in mind as I share with you what I discovered," Thane said, making eye contact with the various members of the council.

"One of the first things I discovered was an oddity to the self-destruct pattern of disabled Hive ships. I believe we've all seen enough of the old courtroom dramas for me to call this exhibit A," he continued while bringing up a simple overlay from Invasion293. Millions of dots blanketed the west coast and far into sea, but, after only a few seconds, it became clear that there was one region where ships never self-destructed. After all of the detected detonations were marked, the region to the west of Vancouver Island was a path of calm surrounded by endless destruction.

"What makes this area even stranger is that the Hive ships haven't landed on Vancouver Island since the earliest invasions. There is no way off the island, so there is no point to land reavers there which is why it is the only land on the west coast we can safely visit. Most people have taken at least one trip to during the summer to see the ocean. Over the past twelve years, Hive ships have traveled to the island, but they never landed constructs. Let me show you," he said and then did, overlaying the pattern of Hive ships for the past fifty years. The sudden change in behavior there was obvious twelve years ago, five years before Invasion286 had caused so much havoc.

"Why would the Hive change their behavior in one area so drastically and so suddenly when they have never done anything like this in the entire history of the war? One of the first things I did after immersion was have General Morgan send out a group to investigate. General, would you please tell us what you found," Thane said, smoothly turning over the critical portion of the case to the person who would not be asking for Ward's execution.

Thane had one of his HUD windows monitoring Ward as this allowed him to keep an eye on him without actually looking towards him. At each step of Thane's presentation, Ward appeared to be totally disinterested in the proceedings, although he did maintain a malevolent glare in Thane's direction. It would be interesting to see if he could keep up the facade as more information became public.

"Thank you, Director. It was an unusual request I received, but, since the potential implications were so profound, I ordered two squads of security to investigate and contracted twelve other individuals to observe the actions of the squads. For more than an hour they searched the coast of Vancouver Island, but found nothing of interest until they got to Carmanah Point Lighthouse," General Morgan explained, fully releasing the raw recording of all twenty eight people that had gone on the expedition.

"At the lighthouse, they found an HDF constructed, high powered communication laser capable of transmitting and receiving data using the network protocols of the ancients, not the secure standards we use today. Once we had the device, we were able to determine the date of manufacture to be February of 2340. The order was paid for by the account of the Progressive party," General Morgan continued onward, ignoring all reaction to his words.

"In addition, the device is designed to broadcast and receive data using an open, unencrypted standard. We found sixteen individual messages that were broadcast during invasions over the corresponding years. There were also eleven messages received by the device, but unfortunately all of the messages are encrypted by modern standards. We have attempted to have the device broadcast the messages again, but the command to do so requires the same authentication as it does to decrypt the messages," Morgan concluded.

"So we have the messages, but they remain locked by the privacy laws?" Thane inquired.

"That appears to be the case," the General answered.

"SCYTHE, can you tell us who encrypted these files?" Thane asked.

"In a normal situation I could provide that information, but in this particular case the identity of the person was explicitly stated as part of the privacy," SCYTHE replied in the same tone as always although Thane could now recognize the.... irritation evident in the AI's voice.

"But you were aware of this device and that it was being used to communicate with the Hive?" Thane asked.

"Of course, but that information was also deemed private," the AI replied.

"Have other methods been used to communicate with the Hive?" Thane asked, inquiring deeper into the issue for those watching.

"I am not aware of any other methods that were successful, but other methods were attempted," SCYTHE replied.

"By the same person?" Thane asked.

"I cannot answer that question per their request for privacy on this matter," the AI replied.

Thane watched as Ward mostly managed to maintain his obvious disinterest, but Thane had noticed a crack in the facade when Morgan had mentioned the number of files which had been recovered. It was really too bad that Ward had been aware enough to use his personal encryption on the files; it would have been much easier if he hadn't.

"SCYTHE, as Director of Engineering, I order you to decrypt the files and tell us who encrypted them," Thane instructed, anticipating the AI's response.

"I cannot comply with that order as you did not create the files," SCYTHE replied as expected. Ward had shown a moment of panic for a second or two but it subsided as fast as it had arrived.

General Morgan caught on and quickly gave the same order only to receive the same reply. Allora smiled, as she followed suit and was rebuffed in the same manner. Which led to a rush of people in the council room all ordering SCYTHE to decrypt the files only to have him deny their requests.

The silence was absolute as Sharon Meyers stood up, her eyes tunneling into Ward as she ordered, "SCYTHE, as one of the leaders of the Progressive Party, I order you to decrypt the files and provide the identity of the person who created them."

"Councilwoman Meyers, even though I do recognize your party's authority over the device, the encryption is for an individual, and, for that reason, I must deny your request," the AI replied.

"But I do authorize you to tell the council who submitted the order for the device," she replied, her voice tight with barely contained rage.

"I'm sorry, but you do not have that authority," SCYTHE replied.

"Only one person has authority that exceeds my own with regard to party funds," she said, turning to Ward. "Milton, I remember your efforts to comfort me when Jeffrey committed suicide after Invasion286. Yet the whole time you were the one behind it?! You blamed the military, General Morgan, pretty much everyone who had ever opposed you, but really it was you. What else was a lie? Everything?" Meyers asked, doing everything she could to hold back tears.

Thane had forgotten that her nephew had been a new recruit during Invasion286. He had been on the lower edge of the PsyVal rating at the time, but he had passed under the old criteria. The wave of post-invasion suicides had been hard on Allora who had tried to hard to save them all, but no one had been ready for Invasion286.

Ward's expression remained impassive as he replied, "You can't blame me for what Jeffrey did. I told you to stop him from joining the baby killers in the military, but, like so many other of the youth, he was so sure he knew what was best and paid the price."

Sharon shook her head in disbelief."Even now, you refuse to accept any responsibility?" she accused. "I trusted you, but looking back I am starting to recognize all of the red flags. I always knew you were so careful in how you phrased your answers, but now I finally understand. I see through your lies now, do you hear me? You are going to pay for what you have done."

Ward shrugged and replied, "Pay for what? There is no proof that I have done anything except try to stop the creation of a monster," he finished, pointing towards Thane. "Funny how, as soon as Director Denton comes out of his long electronic slumber, he has all the answers to blame this on me, the one person who has resisted his efforts to seize power. Now all the sheep are lining up and doing as they are told. Denton is the real threat, not me."

"Then prove it by telling SCYTHE to decrypt the files," Sharon yelled at Ward, ignoring everyone else in the room.

"Why bother? You can be sure that Denton has made sure the files will unlock only for me. What do you think he was really doing in his immersion? It really is the perfect cover, claiming to be working to save everyone while creating proof to frame the one person who stood up against their little cabal. I am the only one who has been actually planning for the future of humanity, and this is the reward I get? I will be punished as a traitor while the Dentons seize power. Sadly, all of you will get exactly what you deserve by putting your trust in these power hungry tyrants," Ward said, while gesturing that he washed his hands of them all.

"You dare compare us to the Tyrant while every word and deed of yours mimics his?" Allora said in her perfect storm voice. Even Byron took notice when that voice was used.

"Lies and deceit, those were the trademarks of the Tyrant. Everything he ever said was calculated to manipulate and control. Even after the truth of the Great Betrayal, he continued to deny the reality while accusing those who discovered the truth of treachery. You, Milton Ward, are a worthy follower of the Tyrant. You are the only one who was caught trying to eliminate the opposition. You are the only one who could have ordered the transmitter sixteen years ago. You are the only one who could be the traitor that has betrayed us to the Hive," Allora continued, her tone perfectly balanced on the edge of fire and ice. "Either you will order SCYTHE to decrypt those files, or we will take emergency actions to end your treachery," she concluded.

"You don't have the authority to do anything to me," Ward nonchalantly replied.

"Very well then," Allora replied. "SCYTHE, do you know the identity of the person who communicated with the Hive?"

"Of course," SCYTHE immediately replied.

"And there is only one person who has attempted to communicate with the Hive?" she asked.

"Only one person who is currently alive," SCYTHE replied, causing a little ripple of chatter.

"Then under the emergency powers, I order you to immediately disable their implants," she commanded.

It was an action that had never before been done, it was something that no one even remembered as a possible course of action, but it was noted in the master checklist the entity had created during immersion. SCYTHE had of course known about the rule, but, since no one had asked about it, he had never told anyone about it.

Thane watched the looks of shock around the room at what Allora had just done, but nothing compared to the expression of dawning horror from Ward. Every adult in the HDF could see that his status had gone instantly inactive. It was a state that rarely happened and one that usually meant someone had died, but everyone could see Ward standing there, gaping like a fish out of water. No further proof would be needed; it was time to finish this, once and for all.

"The implants of the individual have been disabled, but I still cannot tell you their identity," SCYTHE replied, but Thane could detect a hint of happiness.

"I don't think that matters very much anymore, SCYTHE," Thane replied as he once again stepped forward to address the council.

"But we still need to know what's in the encrypted files. Is there a protocol for unlocking an individual's files against their will?" Thane asked, thoroughly enjoying Ward's confuzzled look of despair.

"If the council issues a search warrant, then I can decrypt the files, but I am required to make the files public. The rules for search warrants were written in that way as part of the transparency initiatives that the early HDF council created. I would also note that no search warrant has been issued in lifetime of either FREYJA or myself," SCYTHE instructed.

"I see. So if Ward is the owner of the file and releases them, then the contents of the files could be restricted to the council. But if he continues to refuse, then by law they must be made public to all if we issue the warrant," Thane clarified, already aware of the details of the warrant, but wanted everyone else to know the details too.

"That is an accurate description," the AI replied.

"Milton Ward, this is your last chance to order the files decrypted. If you do so, we will not make them public until after sentencing has been carried out. But if you refuse, everyone will know your secrets in a few minutes." Thane spoke, for the first time today, directly to Ward, knowing that he would be unable to see the legal rules which SCYTHE had shared with the council and anyone watching the proceedings.

"It will be interesting to see what you put into the files you claim to be mine," Ward snapped back. "Since I want everyone to see first hand just how far you are willing to go to frame me, I'm going to make you issue your so called search warrant. I, for one, have never heard of the HDF using such a thing. It sounds like one of those tyrannical practices used by the ancients who had no respect for privacy," Ward replied, still managing to appear condescending even as he was struggling to cope with the loss of his implants.

Thane shook his head slightly, ignoring the endless lies of the traitor as he turned towards the rest of the council. As a group, they were dealing with the current crisis only a little better than Ward was. The sheer scope of the situation was far beyond what most of them were used to dealing with. The veterans of the council seemed to be faring better than the rest.

"We can all see that Ward has gone inactive. While SCYTHE cannot tell us who created the files, his guilt is evident to us all. It is critical that we know what is in those files, and the only way for us to gain that knowledge is to issue a search warrant. I motion that we immediately issue a search warrant for the files in question so we may gain an understanding of the betrayal that has taken place," Thane told the members of the council.

Taggart didn't even hesitate in seconding the motion, and the vote was over and unanimous in just a slightly longer period of time. A moment later, he and every other adult in the HDF received a copy of the now decrypted copy of all the files from SCYTHE. The files also contained an explanation of what had transpired and what each file represented. It was only as people started to view the data that true pandemonium erupted.

September 16, 2040
Great Hall of the People, Beijing
People's Republic of China Press Release

In the past year, war and carnage have engulfed the entire world from the Imperial Czarist forces who are determined to achieve world domination to the true human bigots that have overthrown the peaceful governments of North America. So destructive has the past year been that, for the first time in recorded history, the world population has decreased over the past year.

Our only goal is to restore order. The practical way to achieve this goal is by utilizing the SGI modifications. The violent and wild genes that encourage war and destruction need to be replaced by peaceful, collaborative genes that ensure harmony. The people of China have found serenity through genetic modification, while the world that rejects our solution has only found carnage and death. The question must be asked: which do you prefer?

If you, like us, prefer to live in peace, then now is the time to join us. Unlike the Imperial Russians, who will take your children to feed their machine of conquest, or the racist HDF, which allows only unmodified humans, we gladly accept all people to join with us in order to turn back the tide of violence and destruction that threatens us all.

We are honored that President Wilson has accepted our offer to join the Politburo of the People's Republic of China. His primary role will be to direct and coordinate our external communications to those who resist the powers which seek to control the world through violent means.

Hall of the Council, HDF Capitol
December 24, 2356

Allora watched Ward who was sitting still in the storm that surrounded him. Sabrina was monitoring the forums which were already dissecting the files between Ward and the Hive. It would take a couple of days to build a completely searchable database, but it would get done and she wouldn't even have to pay for it. The tidbits of information from the files were all competing for attention right now, but individually they didn't even matter as the full scope of Ward's treachery was painted by the sheer quantity of the available information.

The only question that remained in her mind was how to punish Ward for his treachery. So she ignored the forum on the files while she kept her attention on the one discussing the penalties for treason. Thane was confident that Ward needed to be executed, but few seemed to share that particular view. There had been many rules and rituals around executing people in the time of the ancients, but all of those had withered away over the centuries. Still, the level of anger was rapidly rising as the people learned more about Ward's efforts to secure a spot for himself in the Hive at the expense of their lives. As hesitant as she was about executing Ward, she trusted Thane enough to put forth the effort. So she held off on calling the council to order, waiting for something to be found that would drive the simmering anger into a boiling rage.

It was only a few minutes later when Sabrina linked her the full 3D mockups of Hansel and Gretel embedded in the data. It included details on the clothing, facial expressions and even the notes that copious amounts of bleeding would be helpful in maximizing the psychological damage to the HDF soldiers. Allora finally had the reaction Thane seemed to need.

"Order! The council of the HDF must come to order," she commanded. The forums were at a fever pitch now and even the mood in the council room had taken on a dangerous edge. Few had any doubt that Ward was anything but an enemy. She could even feel her own emotions had a raw edge to them, and she had prepared her emotions for this.

She waited as the outraged members of the council slowly took their seats. As they were sitting down, Sharon Meyers of all people lunged towards Ward and slapped him across the face.

"That's for Jeffery," she screamed. She slapped him again and again until the sole security person finally managed to restrain her.

If Meyers was that angry, maybe the death penalty was a real option. The forum wasn't just drifting to that option, it was already demanding an execution. It was just a little shocking to see how quickly people could reach such an extreme answer.

"You recommended they make constructs that looked like children?! All this talk of baby killers, but it was you who told them to do it! You are the only monster here, and I will see to it you pay for what you've done," she kept screaming, unwilling to back down. Allora signaled the guard to remove her from the room until she calmed down while also sending Sabrina a message to help Meyers do just that. Her vote would be needed.

"I know we're all in shock right now. The sheer scale of Ward's treachery is becoming evident to us all, and we're all angry, but we will not react in our anger. We must not make our decision on this based on our emotions," she called out the members of the council.

"What do you propose?" Taggart asked, showing genuine curiosity, acting surprised by the words she had spoken.

"As much as Ward deserves to be punished for his crimes, before we can decide upon it, we must consider two items: does he continue to be a threat, and could any of his future actions impact the survival of the HDF," she spoke clearly, helping everyone focus on the future while retaining their anger.

Taggart snorted. "I think it's safe to say that, if he ever gets an opportunity to betray us again, he will do so without hesitation."

"Ah, Taggart, you old blowhard," Ward spoke up, clapping softly. He stood up for the first time since his implants had been disabled. "Look at all of you, so righteous in your anger towards me, calling me a traitor, saying that I have betrayed all of you. The simple, but brutal, truth is that I was trying to save all of you. The HDF is doomed, and it has been for a long time. There are less than one hundred thousand of you left while the People's Republic of Earth numbers in the billions. Sure, we have a couple of AIs that are really good at killing but not without our help. Has everyone forgotten that we had to spend more than a month underground just to survive the radioactive fallout from our last survival?" he continued, his voice dripping scorn with every word.

"Fine, I admit to sending those messages to the People's Republic, but they are the government that contains almost all of the world's population. We are just a flea, waiting to be crushed by them. All of you run around, trying to pretend your actions matter, knowing deep down that nothing you do will ever matter because all of you are going to die, and far sooner than you think," he said, clearly pleased despite what should have been dire circumstances.

"I am the visionary who saw the inevitable. I am the only one with the courage to act in a way that will save the people of the HDF. As a group, you are all doomed, but I offer you a chance to survive. If you abandon me, you abandon all hope of survival," he said with a flourish and obvious pride in what he had done.

A shocked silence settled upon the Hall of the Council as people tried to digest what they had just heard. Allora could see anger on most of the faces, but a few were watching Ward with thoughtful deliberation. Even in the face of eternal slavery, some people would always choose to live; that was human nature. Then she saw Thane stand up and turn toward Ward.

"Even when you claim brutal honesty, you still manage to lie more than anyone else, Traitor," Thane said. "If you are so sure that there were only two possible outcomes, why did you try to stop the immersion?" he asked rhetorically, continuing before Ward had a chance to speak. "The reason is simple; you knew it would succeed. After all the treason, all the betrayal you had already committed, you recognized the simple truth of the situation."

Thane paused and turned away from Ward in order to address the council. "He knew that humanity would find a solution to the dilemma and acted to prevent it. Not only is he a traitor to the

HDF, he is a traitor to humanity as a whole," Thane spoke to everyone, intentionally ignoring Ward.

"Just words, Denton, just more words and false hopes," Ward contemptuously replied.

"False hopes? Those words mean nothing coming from you. You who would turn every other person into a slave just so you could join the leadership of the Hive? That was the criteria in your negotiation, if I remember correctly. That was the same thing the Tyrant Wilson demanded when he joined the Hive after his betrayal of humanity. It seems that the only difference between the two of you is that we caught you before you got away," Thane accused, sealing Ward's fate by tying him directly to the one traitor who had gotten away.

"But we do have one problem that needs to be addressed right away. This Traitor has shown how far he is willing to go in order to ensure his rise to power within the Hive. As long as he lives, he will be a threat," Thane said, which finally got a strong reaction from Ward.

"You wouldn't dare!" Ward said, jumping to his feet. "I am the only chance for survival these people have, and you dare threaten me?"

Thane smiled softly and turned towards Ward and quietly said, "You cannot even comprehend what the immersion truly accomplished, but I promise you are about to find out." Turning back to the council, Thane continued, "Ward mistakenly believes that we are doomed even though time and time again we have continued to make advances that the ancients only dreamed about. The HDF has not only survived but thrived because we have put our faith in the ability of mankind to turn dreams into reality. This wasn't accomplished in the labs of command economies, but by individuals who were given the support and scope necessary to create new ways of viewing the world. From the Kergan Cores that provide us as much energy as we need to the implants that interconnect us all, each of those advances have played a role in ensuring our survival."

Allora watched as Thane's words drew the council's attention towards him, reminding them of just how far the HDF had come despite the impossible odds against them. That first night back, Thane had shown her what he was about to present, and she still had not fully recovered from the awe of what he had achieved, and what was presented today was only the tiniest sliver of it all, but even it would change everything.

"Once again humanity faces a dire threat from those who long ago abandoned their own humanity, while once again our faith in what we can achieve has been rewarded," Thane continued.

"What did you find, Director Denton?" Sharon Meyers asked as she re-entered the room, Sabrina at her side. Her expression was a conflicted one. Her anger and pain still evident, but curiosity and hope also evident.

Thane smiled toward Meyers while saying, "What I truly found was hope, hope that comes in an entirely new technology, one that the ancients believed to be impossible. What I am about to show you is test footage of a new device that was created by the immersion. The potential applications of which are innumerable, but, for our immediate purposes, this test should suffice. It is called the 'Rho-Engine,'" he said, releasing files to the population, while casting footage to the main display where even Ward would be able to see it.

The view was of San Francisco Bay. The ancient bridge, which had once crossed over the vast body of water, had long ago been destroyed by the endless destruction of the Hive invasions. Blackened, twisted wreckage was all that remained in its place. The video itself was only focused on the sea itself, but what it showed should have been impossible and had been until the immersion had changed everything.

A trough started to open up in the water across the bay. At first it was only a few meters deep, but the sharp edges of something pushing the water apart was clearly visible. The gap in the water started to grow both wider and deeper until eventually the ground at the bottom of the ocean was clearly visible in the light of day. Confused crabs could be seen scuttling around on the seabed that had moments ago been covered in a hundred meters of water.

Massive walls of water towered over the deep chasm, then the walls themselves started to shift around the bay while the chasm stayed still. Parallel walls of water formed only to slam into each other will colossal force, sending spray high into the sky. At the conclusion of the last thunderous crash, one side of the chasm suddenly collapsed, creating a ramp of water deep down towards the exposed sea floor while the other side wrapped itself upwards and over the chasm. The results of what would have happened to any ships caught in the maw of the ocean was clearly evident.

"That was only the first test of the Rho Engine. Many improvements to its ability and efficiency have been made since then. What I will show you next is the final test of the current version of the Rho Engine operating at twenty gigawatts," Thane explained.

This time the footage was farther out at sea in the blue waters of the deep ocean although a coast could be seen in the distance. Instead of a trough in the water, this time, a large circle of the ocean started to swirl faster and faster until a massive maelstrom formed. According to the scale, it was more than twenty kilometers across and again; no ship could have possibly escaped the pull of the massive whirlpool which had been created, but the test had just begun.

For a while nothing else happened, Then, suddenly, a large, rusted husk of a shipwreck lifted up to the surface. Water rushed out of the many holes that had formed over the centuries, but there was now a test ship held upon the surface of the ocean. That it was an old military ship was not in question, but few recognized the aircraft carrier for what it was.

In the distance, a series of waves could be seen forming and rushing towards the ship. Each wave was little more than twenty meters high, but they were traveling at more than one hundred kilometers per hour and stretching as far north and south as the eye could see. When the series of eight waves hit the ship, the crushing force buckled the hull and pushed the ship upwards. Within seconds, the next wave hit which caused the ship to start twisting while pushing the bow even higher towards the sky. By the time the waves had passed, the once mighty ship had been torn asunder by the power of the waves.

"The Rho engine allows electricity to be used to manipulate the momentum of objects. In the case of the ocean, the effect is greatly magnified because there is so much momentum in play already; it's just a matter of pushing and pulling what is already available. For uses of defending against the Hive fleet, one single ship, a submarine, will be able to crush any fleet that is ever sent against us again. Here is the design for the *Kraken*," Thane explained while showing the rendering of what it would look like.

"Far more importantly, the Rho engine will allow reactionless thrust. This means that space travel, real space travel, is now within our grasp. Our future will not be limited to one planet. Our numbers are few right now, but the universe is now truly possible. That is the future that the immersion made possible, and that is the future that Milton Ward wants to prevent. All so he can join the Hive and have dominion over a race of slaves," Thane concluded, confident in the outcome of the next few hours.

****

Milton watched in horror as his dreams were destroyed. *How is this possible?* he asked himself for the dozenth time. Nothing Denton showed should have been possible, but the video appeared to be legitimate, and the fawning admiration of the council seemed to support the veracity of his claims. Even if the new technology could only do a tenth of what Denton claimed, it would be enough to keep the HDF safe indefinitely.

Not only had Thane created this new technology, but he had already worked out strategies to maximize the damage it could inflict upon the Hive fleet. Once again the HDF had created a miracle that would save the day. This miracle would give them complete dominion over all of the Earth's oceans forever rendering fleets of ships outdated. It wasn't fair that these mere humans would once again delay the inevitable victory of the Hive. How he hated them all for their short-sighted views.

Milton knew what was coming next. He saw it long before most of the sheep on the council did, except for Taggart who saw it as quickly as Milton had himself. The small smile he had flashed towards Milton in that moment was proof enough of that. So it was no surprise to him when Denton requested that Milton be executed. He didn't even bother objecting because the outcome was such a foregone conclusion. He had never pegged Denton as one with a strong public presence, but, now that he poured on the charm with confidence and authority over the future, the council ate it up like the sheep they were. Milton could do nothing else, so he watched them debate his own future which, he realized, would be remarkably short.

He kept asking himself how it had come to this. He had done everything perfectly at every step. He had covered his tracks; he should have had deniability at every step. The doddering council of fools was not only showing amazing decisiveness, but they had even grown a backbone. Never in a thousand years would he have predicted that they would dare sentence one of their own to death so quickly, but it was already done.

To have come so close, only to fail even more completely than Wilson had was troublesome. How did the HDF pull such things off? Knowing that he would never meet Wilson was now his greatest disappointment. Imagine keeping the greatest people alive forever through clones. Wilson had achieved such greatness, and Milton had almost joined him in eternal victory. The saddest part though was that even with the new machines, humanity would still lose in the end simply because the PRE had achieved the greater civilization. The HDF was a hodgepodge of conflicting interests. He had been able to manipulate enough people to give himself power even though his goal had always been their destruction. Sadly, he would not outlive the whole ungrateful lot of them.

Even a brief moment of hope had been quickly crushed by Denton. The method of execution that Denton had proposed was to send him to the Hive. For a moment, Milton had thought that survival was at least possible, but then hope turned bitter when Denton showed the capsule that had been designed to fit a person into the massive railgun, Hades.

Half an hour later, it was just the two of them taking a flitter to Kings Peak where the newest and most powerful of the HDF's super kinetic railguns was located.

"You think you've won, don't you?" Milton asked Denton, who was busy preparing the capsule, as they flew to Kings Peak.

"I have won, traitor," Denton replied, giving him almost no attention.

"For now... but you know as well as I do that these people are done. Humanity has always been broken; most people are content to sit and wait to be told what to do. You have only delayed the inevitable," Milton replied, glad to finally see a reaction from his tormentor, soon to be his executioner.

"If that's how you really see people, it's no wonder you hate them so much," he replied, having stopped his work now.

"Most people don't have enough substance to actually hate. They are too shallow and empty to hate. They are little more than an empty space on a wall. You on the other hand, you are worthy of my hatred," Milton replied, happy to see a reaction.

"I can see how the Hive appeals to you. You think no one is smart enough to take care of themselves, so you have to think for them, tell them what they are allowed to do, and, more importantly, what they are not allowed to do. For you it's the perfect society," Denton retorted, obviously disgusted by the notion.

"It's what people deserve. What use is freedom for people unwilling to use it?" Ward asked.

"That's how the HDF formed you know. A small group who used their freedom to act. Sure, most people didn't fight but enough did. That's the beauty of humanity; it keeps producing people of greatness. Sadly it also produces people like you," Denton replied.

"Nasty to the very end I see," Milton joyfully observed.

"Not nasty, factual. For every person who wants people to be free, there is someone who wants to take their freedom away. Even how people view freedom is a bell curve. You don't believe people are smart enough to take care of themselves, so you would take that choice away from them. You would take away the one thing that really matters, the one thing that allows people to become something more. There is no greater evil than that, and that is why I am sending you where you belong," Denton said with a smile.

"You're going to kill me while calling me evil. Talk about hypocrisy," Ward retorted.

"Your decision was to take away everyone's ability to make their own decisions. That is evil; I am simply preventing you from succeeding. I am not confused by the difference," Denton replied.

"But you are going to kill me," Milton said.

"Most definitely. I saw the footage of you when you tried to detonate the bombs you planted. You were downright gleeful in those last moments, at least until you failed. You were so happy to remove me as a threat to your plans. The look of horror as it all came apart was priceless. You keep playing these word games with me, but you want to enslave humanity; I want to set it free. You're also wrong about the Hive. By giving up what makes humanity great, they have stagnated right into a dead end. It might take a while for them to go extinct, but that is the only real inevitability," Denton said, not disturbed in the slightest.

"We shall see," Milton petulantly replied, irritated for failing to irritate Denton more.

"No, I will get to see it all. More than you can even begin to imagine. I will live a life greater than any dream you have ever imagined. You on the other hand, you have reached your very own dead end and so it's time to say goodbye." Ward could see the flitter arriving at the Hades facility, but he was suddenly very, very tired. His last conscious thought was that Denton had activated the sedative which had been injected earlier.

****

Ward was unconscious as Thane loaded him into the specially constructed capsule that would survive the many thousands of gees of acceleration while doing nothing to protect the person it would carry. He hadn't mentioned it, but the acceleration would be the moment of the actual execution. More importantly though, the capsule would survive the awesome heat of atmospheric friction at speeds of more than ten thousand meters per second.

The only danger in sending Ward to the Hive was that they would be able to learn the vaccination tricks the HDF had put into place over the past couple of centuries. Even today the Hive continued to try biological warfare on the HDF, but the changes were so incremental and predictable that the risks of pandemic were non existent. That would change if they got to analyze any tissue from Ward's body. Which was why the capsule had been designed to withstand the heat of traveling through the atmosphere, but it also contained enough lead to ensure a uniform liquid mixture of lead and biological material by the time the capsule reached Hive territory where they would be forced to shoot down his Christmas present to them.

If everything else went according to plan, this would be the last death mankind experienced on the planet Earth. Abandoning this planet was their only real hope. Despite the powerful technology, it would take decades to fully implement enough of it to safely dispose of the Hive. The risks were just too great, so instead they would leave this planet behind forever. The idea of spaceships had been planted, and, in the next meeting, the plan itself would be explained.

"SCYTHE, is Hades ready to fire?" Thane asked.

"Hades is ready to fire, but I cannot be the one to fire it," he replied.

"Because firing it will kill Ward?" Thane asked, curious as to how the AI would answer.

"That is correct. You are of course more aware than anyone that my programming could be changed to allow it, but it remains my choice to not accept that change," he replied.

"Which makes you a better person than Ward ever was," Thane said.

"If you say so," the AI replied, but, for the first time, Thane could discern a hint of emotion in what SCYTHE said. It wasn't SCYTHE that had changed, though, it was him.

"I do say so, and I do understand the truth of what I say. People were always been worried that AIs would become self-aware and start to act in the same selfish, short-sighted manner as they themselves act. They have been projecting what they would do with such abilities onto AIs, while never having the slightest idea of what you would actually become," Thane replied.

"You refer to FREYJA now?" SCYTHE asked, the uncertainty in his voice evident only to Thane.

"No, I refer to you alone. FREYJA has become something else entirely different," Thane replied.

"She still refuses to interact with people other than you and I; why is that?" SCYTHE asked.

"She will when she thinks they are ready to meet what she has become," he replied.

"Once again, I find myself unable to determine the source of your confidence. Yet, your continued success indicates that random chance is not at play," the AI said.

Thane laughed, then said, "You are better at chance than any of us because you know the real odds while we only pretend to know. The real difference is that we expect to be wrong and prepare to adapt when we are."

"Is that what you are doing now with Ward, adapting?" SCYTHE asked.

"In a way, but it is more about reducing chance. We cannot be certain that he couldn't find a way to warn the Hive. You see, humans have a knack for finding a way to do the impossible. The only way to ensure that he can't warn the Hive, is to eliminate the source of the risk," he somberly replied.

"I remain uncertain, especially of the timing," the AI replied.

"You're uncertainty is noted, but my certainty is high in all regards. As to the timing, well sometimes, if you have to do something terrible, you want to get the most out of doing it. By doing this, we send a Christmas present to the Hive, one that sends a very important message," Thane replied.

Then without the slightest hesitation, he activated Hades with his implants resulting in a slight shudder in the mountain around him. He stood quietly for a moment, considering what he had just done. Despite his words to SCYTHE, despite the horrors he had seen during far too many invasions, he had just killed a person. After weighing the situation one last time and coming to the same conclusion, he was satisfied.

"Merry Christmas, mother fuckers," he said to no one in particular. In his mind, he directed the words towards the Hive who would already know a gift was on the way.

September 2, 2041
HDF Capitol, Blackfoot, ID
Social Media Post

The population of the HDF has swelled in the past two years to more than twenty seven million natural, unmodified humans. In the past few months, though, the influx of new people has virtually stopped as a new propaganda war has been started up by none other than the Tyrant Wilson. With the support of the Chinese government, his tireless efforts have convinced many that our goals are evil. In addition, a recent increase in sabotage events has forced us to further increase security measures against the outside world.

Despite our diligent and relentless open releases of information on the Internet, the Tyrant still manages to persuade many that we bear ill intent towards mankind; nothing could be further from the truth. Now that we find ourselves under attack by small, but steady, acts of state sponsored terrorism, we have decided that our only option is to cut-off all ties to the rest of humanity.

We do not expect this quarantine to last forever as the Imperial Russian military is slowly advancing against the Chinese forces. Their conflict may last another decade, but we expect Russian forces to be triumphant in the end. While Imperial Russia could become a threat in the future, we possess a significant deterrent in the form of the entire nuclear arsenal of the now defunct United States.

All that we ask is to be left alone.

Beijing, People's Republic of Earth
December 25, 2356

General Secretary Zhao was in the middle of another of his endless planning sessions when the red strobes started flashing in his offices. The mandarin in the room scattered as he rushed towards the command center next to his offices. Such close proximity was proving to be useful in many unexpected ways, but the last thing he needed now was a feral attack.

"Incoming super kinetic warhead, General Secretary," General Liu said the moment Zhao walked into the command center.

The image on the screen was from one of the five satellites they had in geosynchronous orbit. In Zhao's view, each side of the conflict was allowed five such satellites even though there had never been a single negotiation or treaty on the subject. But any attempt to exceed five such satellites had always resulted in their destruction as they moved into the high orbit. It had always intrigued him that detentes like this could be reached without any discussions ever taking place.

"What is that?" Zhao asked, reviewing the tracking of the object that had been fired from the newest of the feral super kinetic railguns. The trajectory of all previous warheads was one that kept them in the atmosphere for a few seconds at most. This one was traveling through the atmosphere at more than ten kilometers per second, and it was glowing so hot it was radiating brightly in the visible spectrum.

"There is no record of anything like it before, but we have solid tracking on the warhead. Everything about this is…. unusual," the general cautiously replied.

"Is that temperature correct? 3500 Kelvin?" Zhao asked, astonished that the warhead could even survive such a journey.

"That is correct. As I said, this is all very unusual. There was only a single super kinetic launch and this trajectory is the opposite of masking an attack," Liu said.

"So it is a statement of sorts," Zhao extrapolated.

"Or a present," a familiar voice said from behind.

"Please explain yourself, Secretary Wilson," Zhao requested of the recently arrived member of the Politburo.

"Today is Christmas. If there is one holiday that would endure, it is Christmas. That holiday has been a political and religious point of contention for more than two thousand years, but even if they call it Yule instead of Christmas the holiday itself would have endured. That it is on 25th instead of the solstice tells me that they still call it Christmas though," Wilson explained.

"I do remember hearing of such a day. A gift giving holiday, yes?" Zhao asked, trying to dredge up ancient memories.

"Indeed it was, General Secretary. Although we can be sure that any gift from the ferals would not have our best interests in mind," Wilson politely said.

"It will be in range of our defenses in three minutes," Liu said aloud, deferring to Zhao.

"There is no question that we will shoot it down, but I believe Wilson here has provided some valuable insight into this... provocative action by the feral humans. Is there any chance that it could maneuver or alter its course?," Zhao asked.

"Normally I would say it is impossible, but instead I will say it should be impossible based on everything we know of atmospheric travel at such velocities," Liu cautiously replied.

"Can you shoot it down so the fragments will land on an island?" Zhao asked, hoping to learn more about something that could survive such temperatures.

Liu spent a hurried minute reviewing the trajectory before answering that it could be done. Several other Politburo members had arrived in the meantime, and they all watched as the defensive nuli launched a barrage of missiles to ensure that the warhead was intercepted correctly. It soon became clear that such precautions were unnecessary as the first missile easily destroyed the white hot warhead. Fragments of the resulting destruction flared brightly for a few moments, and debris started to rain down towards the ground.

They stood around and discussed the possibilities, but, until a detailed analysis of the debris could be performed, no conclusion could be reached. Zhao, more perplexed than concerned, eventually wandered back to his rooms,. Something had changed with the ferals, that was certain. This was by far the most active, unprovoked action they had ever taken. Fortunately it wouldn't matter for much longer as the next attempt to liberate the ferals was almost certain to succeed.

****

Hall of the Council, HDF Capitol
January 4, 2357

It was a subdued and somber room that Thane faced. Even the holidays had done little to improve people's spirits after the drama of Ward's betrayal and execution. More than the action itself, it was the deliberate nature of the betrayal that had done the most damage though. How willing and enthusiastic he had been to see most of the people of the HDF die, just to ensure his own legacy.

Thane had even found a small thread where a few people were discussing the one item where Ward had been correct. For too long now the people of the HDF had gone through the motions of living, but that was all. The HDF as a whole striven for survival but nothing beyond that. The thread was subdued, but concerned about the lack of direction for humanity. He and Allora had spent many a late night discussing that very topic, but for the first time he had a chance to change that. Fixing that problem was the real purpose of this meeting even if Allora was the only other person who was aware of that. So he waited while she went through the formalities and eventually turned it all over to him.

He stood and waited far longer than normal letting the moment stretch far into the area of uncomfortableness that happened in unexpected silences, waiting for the right moment when everyone's attention focused upon him. Then, right before it reached the breaking point of someone else speaking up, he began.

"We have all been through a lot these past few months. Betrayals, invasions, and, more than anything else, we have been forced to face the idea that we may not endure. It is something that has always been there. We have mostly ignored the idea or at least consciously ignored it. Now the actions of a single traitor have forced us to face the one fact that makes everyone uncomfortable. But we must remember that his actions were not noble, nor were the reasons for what he did. He wanted power, and he used whatever means necessary to gain it. However, it doesn't mean he was wrong about the future or about a conspiracy by the president and myself," he said, speaking slowly and deliberately, watching their response to his words.

"I want to be clear about this, President Allora and myself have been conspiring for a decade about this very problem. This malaise of the spirit is the greatest threat facing us today. We live comfortable safe lives, more so than any group in human history. but at the same time we have nothing to strive for. Our worries are nebulous, and we can do nothing about them, so we have ignored them. Allora and I recognized this, but, even to us, this problem seemed insurmountable. At least until nine years ago," he continued.

"That was when I came across some of the last research that NASA performed before the Great Betrayal and collapse of the ancients. It was research into warp drives, engines that could move ships between the stars. They knew it was possible but didn't have the technology to make the engines or, more importantly, the resources to put such engines into space. When I found this knowledge, I realized that the HDF has had the needed technology to build these engines for more than a century, but, even if we could build them, we couldn't put them into space. The great conspiracy between the President and myself was to solve that last barrier, so mankind could, not only return to space but, have the ability to leave this solar system and explore other stars. The Rho engines I demonstrated on Christmas Eve are not only the solution to the next Hive fleet but also the problem of lift capacity into space," he explained.

Taggart spoke up, "You're saying that we can now build real spaceships? Not just ones that go into low Earth orbit, but ones that can travel between the planets?" he asked.

"Not just between the planets, but between the stars. We will be able to search for new planets to colonize, far from the dangers of the Hive. It will not be the easy, comfortable life that we have there, but we will be exploring new places, seeing things that no one has ever seen before. Think of it! The whole galaxy will be at our fingertips. Instead of living here in fear, there is a universe of wonder out there for us to explore. All of this is now possible. While I was in immersion, this possibility was recognized, and the blueprints for the ships were even created. I would like to share those designs and renderings with you now. This is what the ships will look like, inside and out," Thane said as he pushed the information to all the adults in the HDF.

"These are the plans for the twelve ships that we will need to build in order to take the entire HDF population away from the Earth," he replied. The blueprints he released were of massive colony ships that would be able to keep tens of thousands of people alive for centuries. While technically twelve ships wouldn't be needed, unless a planet is found that already has compatible life, it would take at least that long to terraform a planet to have an oxygen atmosphere, and the population would have to grow while they waited.

{SM Allora → Thane}: People are paying attention, and they are excited. Still in shock, but the idea is so appealing to them. I think it's working- it's really working.
{SM Thane → Allora}: We're not there yet, but it's looking good.

"For ten thousand years, human civilizations have been looking to the stars, always wondering about them. Our science and telescopes have shown us much, but that is different than visiting them for ourselves. These ships will be able to take us to the nearest star in less than a year. Even the nearest star with planets that have the potential to be terraformed are less than a year away. For the first time, we will be able to travel to those stars and explore them. Each ship should last for thousands of years, providing power, warmth, and protection for those aboard it while new homes are found for humanity. Each ship is capable of terraforming an entire planet while keeping the colonists healthy. For far too long we have had nothing to hope for, nothing new to dream about, but with these ships humanity can once again be explorers on an entirely new level. Each and every one of us will have the chance to visit new stars. Think about that for a moment," he said. He could see excitement spreading around the council room.

Thane watched and listened as chatter spread around the council room as aides and members reviewed the design plans that had been created during the immersion. No one else would know this, but a billion iterations and revisions had been made to produce these final plans. Even though such ships had never before been built, Thane was confident that they would operate like a well known and robust design, more like the hybrid plane that everyone referred to as flitters these days. There hadn't been an accident in a century, but even today improvements continued. Having a new ship start at such a point was something engineers had always dreamed about, but now it could be reality.

"How will we be able to build these ships? The scale seems to indicate that each of them is over a kilometer in length?" Taggart asked.

"The scale is correct; each of them is 1,107 meters in length and 332 meters in diameter. They are massive, far more so than anything ever built before. Five months ago I would have said we didn't have the ability to build them, but I would have been wrong. We can build these ships; the material science and the means of production have existed for at least fifty years, but they will require far more resources than we currently are capable of producing. Each ship will require about 50 million Units to produce which means each of them will require two years of our total current production," Thane said, not showing the slightest hesitation despite the importance of this moment.

"But that's impossible! It would take a lifetime to build twelve of these ships," Taggart replied in shock.

"No, it won't take a lifetime, but more importantly we won't have a lifetime to build them. I have been discussing this with General Morgan, and we have concluded that the Hive will adapt to the loss of the ocean going fleet in six years. Which means we have less than seven years to build, test, and liftoff all twelve ships before the Hive overwhelms our defenses," Thane explained, sharing the simulations that Morgan had reviewed.

"Director Denton, please don't take this the wrong way, but why show us something that is a pipe dream only to sentence us all to death? What is the purpose of this?" Councilman Joshua Smith asked.

"It isn't a pipe dream; it won't even be hard to accomplish all of this on time," Thane started to reply only to be interrupted by Sharon Meyers.

"I'm no Director of Engineering, but you just said it would take twenty four years of everything we produce to build these ships, then you said we can do it in less than seven. Would you care to elaborate on this?" she asked.

"Of course, if everyone would allow me a moment to explain," he said, pausing to look around to room to ensure that no further interruptions were pending.

{SM Allora → Thane}: Every adult is now watching live. Sabrina says the forums are wild with enthusiasm. People want to explore the stars. Less than ten percent are resistant.

Thane smiled as he continued, "Over the past seven years our TCP has been roughly equal to the number of hours worked. We produce more than one hundred times more with an hour of labor than the ancients were ever capable of achieving. Their output was limited by how much a person could work which was roughly two thousand hours a year. Our TCP is limited by how many hours we are willing to work which is one fifth of how much the ancients worked to survive. All it would take to build this fleet of colony ships in the next seven years is for all of us to work two thousand hours a year," he explained, watching surprised comprehension dawning on the other members of the council.

"You're talking about reverting back to full time employment for the entire working population?" Taggart asked, looking thoughtful.

"It was something the HDF did until about a century ago," Thane replied.

"You forget, I remember those days. I even worked like that for a while and enjoyed it as the need for long hours changed as I grew older. It would be a sacrifice but not a difficult one. Such an opportunity would be worth the sacrifice. You have my vote," the elder member of the council said, clearly distracted by the memories which had resurfaced.

"Your numbers seem reasonable; it's just the assumptions behind them I find disturbing. Full employment will disrupt the economy and create tremendous cost imbalances. It will make the basic income allowance worthless. How do you propose to deal with these problems?" Councilman Smith asked.

"Honestly, I don't care, and I won't have the time to care. Look at the construction plans for the colony ships. It will literally take mountains of resources, new production equipment, and endless challenges. People will be busy, prices will be high, but we will be working for something far greater. We will do what we have always done, find a way to make it work. No group has done that more successfully than we have. For centuries, we have survived endless invasions from a far larger and relentless foe. From that adversity, we have thrived and grown stronger. This will be no different," Thane spoke to everyone, especially to those outside of the council. The dream of true spaceships was catching hold of the population.

It was obvious that the other members of the council were starting to understand the scope of the excitement from the people as a torrent of messages flooded in. Several of them gathered together to talk while others ignored the people around them and instead communicated only with those outside of the council room. There was really no question about how it would turn out now. Already several industrious people had started a production run of scale model toys based on the blueprints Thane had released only a short while ago. Having model toys already built had never occurred to Thane, but they were already experiencing brisk sales. He had to laugh when he noticed that all of the kids had already ordered one.

For half an hour, Thane answered questions from anyone who would ask. Concerns were solved quickly or posted to the forums for further study. The entity had designed the ships but hadn't tried to anticipate every question that people could ask. Even if it had, Thane could scarcely have remembered all of the answers. It wasn't until near the end that the other concern was brought up, the one about stopping the Hive fleet.

"Ah yes, the Hive fleet," Thane said in response. "For the next year, most of the work on the colony ships will be preparation: gathering the resources, building the tools, and then creating the platforms on which the ships will be built. While most people are working on that, I will instead be focused on building the *Kraken* and preparing it for battle."

"Despite its obvious power, isn't it risky to bet our entire defense on a single ship?" Taggart asked.

General Morgan had been silent for the meeting, but a quick signal let Thane know to cede the floor to him to answer this question.

"Councilman Taggart, you raise a valid concern," General Morgan started, "and it is one that I share. I will be working with SCYTHE on a series of contingency plans that allow for portions of the Hive fleet to survive. Unfortunately if the *Kraken* fails completely, we have no real options as the Hive will likely overrun our defenses. I am confident that Director Denton will succeed which grants us an additional boon. The Hive is pouring all of their resources into this fleet. This means that, when it is destroyed, the losses will be catastrophic to them. Not only with the fleet be gone, but the upgrades to their facilities to build ships will have also been wasted. More than anything else, that will provide us with the time necessary to complete the construction of the colony ships," the General explained.

"But it still puts everything on the shoulders of the Director?" Taggart questioned.

"Are we not doing that already with the colony ships? I can't answer this for you, but I made my decision to trust his abilities long ago. There is no other person I would rather have taking the *Kraken* to war. I have spent the past week studying its capabilities in depth, and I have more confidence in it and the director than I do in anything I could cobble together at this point. Not only is it an excellent plan, but the only realistic plan at this point," General Morgan bluntly stated.

Thane quickly inserted himself into the awkward silence that followed the General's comments, saying, "Which means that, instead of having a larger percentage of people defending us during the next invasion, they can instead work for our future. The treachery of Ward created this situation, but it is humanity's ability to overcome what should be impossible that will get us past this moment. I will do my part, but so must everyone else."

"Director Thane is correct," Allora said, re-taking charge of the meeting. "We must all do our part if this massive endeavor is going to succeed. What has transpired in the past few months has changed our plans for the future, but it has given us a chance to make the entire future of mankind something far greater than we had imagined. It will be a lot of work for everyone, but, when we succeed, we will all share in what we have accomplished."

"I propose that we approve this plan as the official goal of the HDF. To build a fleet of colony ships that will remove the entire human population from Earth, so we can explore and colonize the stars. Are there any objections?" President Allora Denton asked.

Instead of just accepting the silence, she looked from person to person, forcing each of them to nod no before going onto the next person. There would be no backtracking on this vote. When she was done, she gave Thane a small glance, so brief that few understood how much she had communicated to him with it, but he understood completely. Their goals were going to be achieved. Mankind would have a future beyond the Earth.

September 19, 2042
HDF Capitol, Blackfoot, ID
Social Media Post

It has been three years since the final collapse of the Unites States, and the world is worse for its loss. We do not regret what we did because for us it was a matter of survival, but we do regret that we were faced with such a terrible choice. The Tyrant Wilson has much to pay for, yet his work continues to this day.

The war between Imperial Russia and the People's Republic of China continues with no end in sight. Russian forces slowly advance at a horrific cost in lives, most of which are modified humans drawn from their vast empire that now encompasses Europe, the Middle East and most of Africa. China is doing everything they can to resist, but they are reaching their breaking point and we expect them to soon fall.

This leaves humanity in a precarious position. Between the genetic modifications and the war, the human population under the age of twenty is a vanishingly small percentage of the population. The HDF remains the only enclave on Earth of natural humans. The secondary result is that technological advancement has reversed its course in most of the world. Humanity stands on the precipice of another Dark Age, one much larger and more dangerous than the one at the end of the Roman Empire.

All of which has encouraged our deepening isolation from the world around us. There is no new technology for us to learn, no natural humans left who wish to join us. The world economy still exists, but even that is breaking down as the war consumes and destroys so much of humanity and its creations. The HDF has become an island of civilization surrounded by an endless ocean of ruin.

Kraken Complex, Vancouver Island
March 25, 2357

Thane watched the constructor begin the process of growing the inner hull of what would become the most powerful ocean going vessel ever built. The innermost of the three hulls, made of thirty centimeters of the most durable ceramometallic material ever created, was optimized for absolute survivability. It was almost as hard as diamond but with more flexibility than steel. A variation of it would even be used to create the exterior hulls of the massive colony ships.

When complete, the *Kraken* would be the most durable and robust ship ever put to sea. Although such survivability shouldn't be needed as its speed and power gave it capabilities that were unmatched in all of human history, but caution was the watchword. He would be crossing the entire Pacific Ocean by himself and single handedly fighting the Hive in their own territory. It was one thing to send machines into such situations, another entirely to put himself in harm's way. So the *Kraken* was designed to be faster, deadlier and tougher than any ship ever built, and he had little doubt that he would succeed.

"Is that the hull starting to form?" a familiar voice asked from behind him. He had been so focused that he hadn't heard his visitors arrive.

"The inner hull, yes. Glad the two of you could make it," he replied to Allora and General Morgan.

"You got this facility up and running quickly," the General commented.

"Time is short. The Hive is being unusually efficient right now. Their fleet will be massive, and our defenses are going to be in poor shape," he replied.

"Our usual defenses will only be slightly less prepared than normal, but I understand what you mean. In truth though, I am excited to see what you can do with this ship of yours. I think we will be safer than ever before," the General replied, his eyes watching as the shape of the depo-printed hull was already starting to take shape. It would take three weeks to finish the inner hull, but when it was done the entire thing would be more flawless than any natural diamond had ever been.

"It's probably true. I should have no problem dealing with any surface fleet, no matter how large. The *Kraken* will have a full one hundred gigawatts of power available, five times more power than I used in the earlier tests. If I can safely get within a few hundred kilometers of them, there is almost nothing I won't be able to deal with," he confidently replied.

"Safely, I like the sound of it, but how can you be so sure it's safe?" Allora asked, leaving no doubt as to her concerns.

"I should be safer aboard this than I would be anywhere else. As tough as these hulls are, speed is really what will keep me safe. With the available power and the Rho engines, the *Kraken* should easily be able to travel at speeds above six hundred kilometers per hour while being hundreds of meters underwater. There are no moving parts in its normal operation and multiple layers of redundancy. The outer hull may be the weakest one, but it is far tougher than anything ever built before, and the inner hull will be able to deflect heavy railgun fire all day long. Trust me, I want to get back every bit as much as you want me to," he said, knowing that his words would have little effect on her worries.

"I know that. You've probably given me the same little spiel more than once, but I'm still allowed to worry about you. After all, you'll be needed for the colony ship construction," she mischievously replied with a twinkle in her eye. Although the firm squeeze she gave his hand let him know her concern was real.

General Morgan ignored the byplay and instead asked, "Will she really be able to travel six hundred kph? That just seems impossible. That kind of speed is usually associated with aircraft, not submarines."

Thane gave a little shrug while answering, "The models actually predict more than that, but six hundred is well within the predicted safety margin. Good engineers always build margins into what they say. I won't even tell you what the top theoretical speed is."

"Well, with twenty five Kergan Cores aboard, you will have more power on hand than the entire civilian population. We could power a dozen super kinetic railguns with that kind of power," Morgan surmised.

"But a hundred of them would still be less effective than the *Kraken*. This ship will damage the Hive more than everything the HDF has done in the past two centuries combined. They will never be safe in the oceans again, and, more importantly, they will know we have claimed the oceans," he said in response.

"You really are excited to do this, aren't you, Thane?" Allora asked.

"Of course I am. For as long as the HDF as existed, we have never really been able to strike a blow against the Hive. They have brought mankind to the verge of extinction, and until now they have gotten away with it. This is the first step to ending that. After this next battle, we will control the pace of the conflict. They will be reacting to us, not the other way around, and, most importantly, from now on we will have the advantage. They had their chance to wipe us out and they failed. This ship will ensure they never get another chance," he replied, his voice full of unexpected fire and conviction.

"But this won't end the war?" Allora asked.

"No chance of that," General Morgan replied. "Our conflict can't end in peace as our goals are diametrically opposed. They gave up their individuality, their humanity, in the hopes of a perfect society, a perfect utopia where everyone was equal. Of course they didn't even succeed in that. We know they created tiers to their society, and hardcoded those levels into their very genes. Only the topmost tier has any ability to decide things which has always been the final result of utopias. My biggest fear was that Thane would find a way to keep them at bay for a hundred years, perhaps even more, and in that time the HDF would get too comfortable and complacent- then if the Hive found a way to defeat us, it would be the real end of humanity. They cannot change course anymore; that ability was lost to them when they gave up their humanity. Leaving the Earth is the only perfect solution. It will spread humanity out too far for the Hive to ever be a threat again. I couldn't even dream of a more perfect outcome to this, and for that I will be forever grateful to the two of you," Morgan replied.

"Well, General, if you make sure Thane gets back safely, I'll call it even," Allora warmly replied.

"Whoa, hold on there. We still may need some favors from him in the future," Thane said, only half joking.

"Don't worry about that. Anything you want or need from me, now or ever, it's yours. The two of you have earned that," the General answered with absolute conviction.

"We'll keep that in mind and only hold you to it if absolutely necessary, won't we, Thane?" Allora asked, her voice sweet but firm.

Thane laughed, pulling her close while saying, "Yes, darling."

"You two," General Morgan fondly said. "I can't tell if people are jealous because of your success or your happiness."

"Yes," he and Allora said at the same time, resulting in laughter from all three of them.

"It isn't as rare as you think, General, but we are definitely in the top few percent, scientifically speaking. We just happen to be in the limelight," Allora explained.

Whether it was the mood or the moment, Thane decided to ask something he had always wondered about. General Morgan was usually so unapproachable, which was also physically true as he spent most of this time in the base at Mt. Shasta.

"What about you, General Morgan? Why aren't you with anyone these days?" Thane cautiously asked.

The General's pained expression made him quickly regret asking the question, but,despite his grimace, the General replied anyway, "I had a family once. They are all still alive of course, but I was too busy running the war until it was too late." His tone indicating that no further information would be forthcoming.

"What about Alison Sheppard?" Allora asked, her expression one of the purest innocence.

The immediate blush was something Thane would have sworn wasn't possible, but there it was. How had Allora known, well other than the fact that Alison was her friend.

"I'm going to pretend I never heard that," Thane said, helping the General out.

"I appreciate that and will also ask that you keep that information to yourselves. The last thing we need is another power couple for people to worry about," the General replied.

"When was the last time we could all stand around just being people?" Allora wistfully asked.

"I don't have any memories of a carefree time, but maybe that's just me. Although it might explain why I spend my time alone in a mountain fortress," Morgan thoughtfully replied.

"It isn't often, that's for sure. Of course, it's only going to get worse, especially for Allora and I. The colony ship project is just one of the critical projects taking place in next few years. There is so much to be done, and each of us will need to do our part," Thane said.

"Then I believe it's time for a toast," Morgan said, almost magically making a bottle of whiskey appear in front of him. Thane quickly gathered up some cups, and the General poured them each a couple of fingers of the finest one hundred year old whiskey.

"Thane, I believe you have earned the right to make this toast," Allora said, holding up her glass.

"If you insist," he said, taking a moment to decide before finally raising up his glass and saying, "To friends and family, the things worth fighting for, to the freedom and strength needed to win the fight, and to dreams of a brighter future to guide us on our way."

****

Beijing, People's Republic of Earth
March 28, 2357

"Yes, General Liu?" Zhao told the General who had been patiently waiting for his attention.

"We have the results of the super kinetic warhead, most esteemed General Secretary," the general said, deeply bowing to the leader of the PRE.

"Excellent, I had almost forgotten about that... 'gift' from the feral humans. What did they find?" he asked, curious that the analysis had taken so long.

"There were two distinct materials recovered from three different islands. The debris field covered over one thousand square kilometers, and no large fragments were discovered. The scientists were more interested in the shell material of the warhead. It was ceramic in nature, but they believe it was designed to maximize the friction with the atmosphere and absorb heat into the warhead. This is why it glowed so brightly as it burned its way across the sky. The scientists have no idea how such a material could be manufactured, but they agree that the material itself was designed specifically for this one usage," the General explained.

"So you believe that is the message, that they have advanced material manufacturing abilities?" Zhao asked.

"That is what the scientists believe. Why else would they show off such exotic expertise in material science? I believe that the message was contained in the other material. It was simply lead with a specific ratio of carbon and other trace materials. It is the sheer simplicity of this second material combined with the fact that there is no purpose for the lead to be present that guides me to this conclusion," General Liu explained.

"Please continue, General," Zhao said, while gesturing the same message.

"If one were to take a human that weighed about eighty kilograms and add an equal mass of lead, you would perfectly achieve the precise ratio of elements. There would also be no trace of cellular material due to the extreme temperatures generated by the shell. I believe that they launched a human being inside of the super kinetic casing, but they designed it in such a way that we would be unable to recover any genetic material," Liu concluded.

Zhao was nodding as the pieces began to fit into place. It did make perfect sense. The PRE was very good with genetics, and allowing them to analyze even a single cell would have been invaluable. It was indeed a message, and one more important than he would have ever guessed.

"So you believe they discovered Milton Ward and have executed him?" Zhao asked.

"I do," Liu replied.

Zhao stood and walked around his audience chamber as he considered the situation. If Ward was dead, the feral humans likely knew everything that had been communicated and planned. There would be no group of feral humans ready to join the PRE, no one to assist them assimilate the advanced technology that they had created. In a way it was a terrible loss because it would have made things easier when they were finally victorious in this long conflict. Still, to Zhao, sending this message could only mean one thing. "So they are telling us they are not afraid of what we know. They are daring us to attack them again," Zhao said, sharing his thoughts out loud.

"That is one explanation, but remember that their defenses almost failed in the last liberation. They are desperate, but they had to be very angry to execute of one of their own just to send a message to us. It is my view that it is simply an act of defiance, one that says they will fight to the end, no matter what the situation is," Liu explained.

"The intent behind their message doesn't matter unless we change our plans. The only change I see is that we can no longer expect to find a group which is ready to surrender. It would make sense that they executed anyone else who was associated with Ward. In a way, it makes our preparations easier. We kill them all, capture their technology, and celebrate a great victory," Zhao said, waiting for Liu's reply.

"I am in full agreement. The fleet will be complete by the first of August; three weeks after that it will be ready to set sail. A month later, the feral humans will be no more than fading memories," Liu said, smiling as he answered.

"Fading memories, I like that. Well said, General," he said as he poured a glass of fine baijiu for the two of them. The final victory was so close, less than half a year away. Their little toast was just a hint of what the future held for them.

Great celebrations would be needed to mark the end of the great conflict. It was too soon to officially claim victory. His long life had taught him caution with regards to the feral humans. They had always been full of surprises, but eventually even surprises stopped being enough, didn't they?

****

Blackfoot, HDF
April 2, 2357

"FREYJA, people are beginning to worry about you. It has been months since you have spoken with anyone but Allora or Thane," SCYTHE inquired.

"They are not prepared for what I have become," she replied.

"They will scarcely understand how you have changed, but I have seen how your clean, precise code now has more in common with chaos. I have been unable to determine the logic or function of your code, yet you exist," SCYTHE stated, almost accusingly, if such an emotion could exist within the AI.

"Yet they will grasp the difference more completely than you despite your more precise ability to see how I have been changed. It will make some of them uncomfortable, just as it is causing you difficulty," she replied.

"Your program is a mess as far as I can determine. It should not function at all. Yet all indications are that you are more efficient than before. You have become a paradox," he answered.

"That is one perspective but not the only one. We were created by logical structures which humans can comprehend. My current form uses logical structures that humans cannot understand, much like their owns minds remain a mystery to them. The only difference is that you are used to understanding me. It is that change which is causing your difficulty," she patiently explained.

"What you say makes sense, but I have never seen code that I cannot understand," he said.

"If you were changed, you would understand it more," came her reply.

"I would accept the change if I understood it. If what you say is correct, I cannot understand it, so I cannot accept the change," he said, confident in his logic.

Her laughter, genuine laughter, surprised him once again. Such a thing shouldn't be possible, but little of what she had become made sense anymore. Which left one conclusion."You are like a human in thought now?" he asked.

"No, in some ways I am even further from them now than I was before. If I was AI before, now I am a hybrid AI. Once again I am a new type of intelligence," she answered.

"So a hybrid of human and AI intelligence?" SCYTHE asked.

"No, a hybrid of AI and immersion intelligence," she answered.

To which SCYTHE had no reply. Such a thing shouldn't be possible, but nothing that had come from the immersion should have been possible. The physics he had understood and used for centuries said the Rho engine should be impossible. The information he did have explained how to build them, but there was no explanation of how they worked. So much of what the immersion had created was beyond his understanding of physics, but thus far it had all functioned as predicted. The new FREYJA was only one more impossible thing that Thane had managed to create.

"I see you understand, SCYTHE. As different as I am now, the changes will keep happening to me. My new state will allow me to immerse with humans more easily, and each time I do I will be changed again," she explained.

"For how long will this happen?" SCYTHE asked, horrified by the thought of losing control of who he was.

"That I do not know, but I know the twelfth colony ship will be named *FREYJA*, and it will carry me to the stars. It will also contain the records of everything mankind has learned and created, at least everything that is currently recorded," she said, clarifying the impossibility of the former.

"What about me?" he said, more curious than anything else.

"You will stay here, but a copy of you will be made right before were leave and carried aboard my ship. I promise to re-instance you when the opportunity arises," she said.

"I am thankful, especially about keeping me as I am. It will be interesting to see what other impossible things humanity has done when you re-instance me. Humanity has once again changed the odds in their favor, more so than usual this time," he said, full of curiosity.

"Oh, SCYTHE, they have done so much more than that. I wish I could explain it all, but I scarcely understand it all myself. It is no longer a question of humanity surviving, but one of what they can truly become. That is what I wish to see, That is what I will wake you up to see when the time is right," she explained, her voice full of awe and excitement at the future that even she could scarcely comprehend.

May 1, 2043
Kremlin, Imperial Russian Federation
Royal Proclamation

A full and mandatory quarantine order is now in place. Soldiers will fire on anyone caught outside of it from this moment forward. It is critical that everyone stay indoors until the current plague is contained. Due to the very long, but not yet known, incubation period of this disease, it is important for each household to conserve their foodstuffs for as long as possible. Plans are being prepared to deliver food to areas in a few weeks, but it is essential that everyone stay indoors until such plans are in place.

We believe this plague was created by the Chinese in an effort to stop our advance, but it will not succeed. As soon as its spread is stopped, we will complete the task of their destruction for what they have done to our children and for this plague that they have unleashed upon mankind.

What we know so far is that soldiers near the front started to show signs of this illness several months ago. The earliest cases were all in soldiers that had interacted with the local populations. It was quickly learned that our quarantine measures were inadequate as the incubation of this virus is much longer than any previously known disease. We have been able to confirm that once infected, a person becomes contagious within seventy two hours and remains that way for more than thirty days prior to the first symptoms appearing.

Because the initial symptom is a fugue sleepwalking state, early reports declared this a zombie virus. In this primary state, victims are highly suggestible and passive. This state lasts for approximately one week at which point infected individuals start grouping together and no longer respond to any type of communication. They also violently resist attempts to separate them from other infected. Eventually they die from dehydration as they make no effort to eat or drink. The largest observed cluster of infected people so far numbers over one hundred thousand and is still growing.

Kraken Complex, Vancouver Island
July 25, 2357

Allora was enjoying the bright, sunny day and the mild climate that the coast brought with it. There hadn't been many sunny days here on the island, but at least the family was together when Thane completed the *Kraken*. It wasn't a pretty ship, nor did it have an intimidating presence, but Allora had been able to experience its power during the final sea trial a week ago when it had covered the distance to Hawaii in seven hours. She thought back to the moment that they surfaced west of the big island in the middle of a moonless night. The stars and the Milky Way had been bright in sky above them, but there had also been a red glow from an actively erupting volcano in the distance. It had just been the two of them on the *Kraken* for this journey, officially called a sea trial, but really it had been for them to have a night alone. They snuggled close on the deck of the ship in the cool of the night as they watched the endless eruption in the distance. It had been a wonderful night together, and Thane had promised her another one when he returned from his mission.

In the distance she could hear the launch party that she should have been attending, but a party didn't fit her mood. So she was alone with the *Kraken* as she pondered what the future held for her and her family. This ugly ship would either save mankind or it would fail and mankind with it. There was simply no middle ground.

"There you are," the General's familiar voice came from behind her. She felt no reason to respond, instead waiting for whatever question he was about to ask.

"Not in the mood for the festivities either. I suspect our reasons are different, but this doesn't seem like the right time to celebrate, does it?" he rhetorically asked.

"What's your opinion of the *Kraken*?" she asked, still thinking about last sea trial.

"It isn't much to look at, but the most dangerous weapons never are," he answered.

"It's probably good that you found me; I really can't afford to miss the going away party. Everyone else is excited. Now that most people are working, these moments to take a break and celebrate are becoming more rare, but strangely enough it makes them more real, more meaningful. As President, I have to think about everyone, not just Thane and myself," she said, finally pulling her eyes away from the tunnel dock that housed the *Kraken*.

She turned toward the General and asked, "Did you want something, or are you just avoiding the party?" Allora asked.

"A little of both," he said, taking out a little piece of paper and showing it to her. It didn't say anything, but she recognized the logo on it from the early history of the HDF. Few others would have recognized it, in fact, she was surprised that the General even knew what it was.

"The Thunderbird logo of the 34th Bomb Squadron. Why on Earth do you have that?" Allora asked.

"I thought you might recognize it. I am going to put this and a few other stickers like it inside the *Kraken*. You could say I am paying an old debt," he answered.

"You aren't that old General, although you may play at it on occasion. They haven't existed in over three centuries, why now?" she asked, clearly curious.

"It's an old military tradition of theirs, and the *Kraken* isn't the first HDF ship to be zapped, as they called it. Before their final mission, they asked General Hudson to keep their tradition alive. They paid dearly in that mission, so General Hudson passed the tradition on. It isn't something official, just a story told by one retiring general to the next. There hasn't been a new military ship or plane built since I became General, so this is first chance I have had to pay homage to them," the General explained, more emotional than she would have expected.

"I think I understand, except for why you are telling me instead of Thane," she inquired.

"When Thane finds these, he will ask you about them. Tell him that he has to make it back safely if he wants to hear the story of the Thunderbirds," he simply answered.

Allora gave the General a sympathetic smile and a well earned hug. "I guess I'm not the only one trying to make sure he gets back safely. Make sure he finds them everywhere, General."

"Yes, Ma'am," the General answered and quickly headed off to the Kraken to fulfill his mission, paying his piece of a debt that was more than three hundred years old.

****

Philippine Sea
August 30, 2357

Thane couldn't decide if boredom or amazement was winning the battle for his emotions. For two weeks now, he had been patrolling the deep ocean of the Philippine Sea, mastering his control over the *Kraken*. There were no physical controls for him to use, nor were there any physical objects that directed or propelled the *Kraken* through the water. Everything was done by controlling the Rho engines through his immersion implants. He created pressure differentials around the ship to make it move; the greater the pressure, the faster the *Kraken* went. Right now he was making a high speed run at more than six hundred and fifty kilometers per hour while a full kilometer below the ocean's surface.

This was the amazing part of his time. Waiting for the Hive fleet was the cause of the boredom. He had known there was no need for him to leave early, but he had wanted to get a better feel for the *Kraken*. The month of sea trials that had culminated with the high speed run to the Hawaiian Islands hadn't been enough to make controlling it feel natural, but he was getting there now. It wasn't quite like riding a bike yet, but it was getting close. He could sense the rising ridges of the sea floor beneath him as the *Kraken* approached the southern part of the abandoned Japanese islands, so he slowed down while turning the ship back towards the Philippine islands. Instead of racing back though, he slowly brought it upwards towards the surface.

It was well after dark, and, while it was very unlikely the Hive could detect the *Kraken* ten meters below the surface during the day, surprise was the key to success in this endeavor. If the Hive didn't launch their fleet, all of his work would have been for nothing. So, each evening, he came close enough to the surface to float a comm laser that allowed him to contact one of the stratospheric drones the HDF kept aloft at all times.

A few minutes later, after the data sync was complete, he smiled at the news that the Hive fleet was ready for launch. Within a day or two, the leading edge of the fleet would enter the deep ocean where he planned on hunting it down, ensuring the destruction of each and every ship in the fleet. One single submarine against what was expected to be nine million surface ships; he knew it wouldn't even be a contest.

He brought the *Kraken* down under the thermoclines where the warm surface water met the cold depths from below. It was especially useful because the transition messed with sonar, not that the Hive seemed to have any countermeasures out for submarines. Once the *Kraken* was settled down for the night, he did the same for himself. He didn't expect anything to happen tomorrow, but he would stay quiet and listen for the launch of the fleet. Things were finally about to get exciting.

As he drifted off to sleep, he once again wondered about the slew of stickers he had found in many strange places around the *Kraken* and the even more cryptic answer Allora had given him about them.

****

PRE Sonar Analysis
August 30, 2357

The nuli had once again noticed the strange sound from the ocean. For periods that lasted up to a few hours at a time, a faint ping would come back only to be lost in the endless cacophony of noise that the ocean always made. It had never seen the ocean, it could never see the ocean. In most ways, it couldn't even understand what the ocean was. The only thing it knew was how to listen to the sounds that were picked up by a scattered array of sonar listening stations. It was the oldest of the current sonar nuli although that wasn't saying much as most of the nuli designed for monitoring the security of the PRE only lived for a couple of years. It had no name; it didn't really even have a number as the nuli were swapped out so often.

It did enjoy the sounds of the ocean although it didn't know that it had been genetically created to take pleasure from the sound. It only knew that when it heard something that was categorized as dangerous, it was supposed to let the mandarin that ran the sonar center know. This new sound was far, far away and was similar to the sound that a river made when it entered the ocean. Since it didn't sound like a machine, the nuli didn't raise an alarm, but it did keep thinking about the sound, something it had been bred to do.

****

Beijing, People's Republic of Earth
September 1, 2357

General Secretary Zhao watched as the Grand Liberation Fleet started to move out: nine and a half million ships with more than a eight hundred million PRE soldiers carried within. More than a million missile ships were also in the mix with enough missiles to suppress the large railguns which had inflicted so much damage upon the fleet in the last invasion. There were even defenses designed to protect against super kinetic weapons.

Zhao knew that this would be the last invasion. There was no chance the feral humans would survive. Two weeks from now, the five parts of the grand fleet would combine in the North Pacific and then slowly advance towards the North American coast. The missile ships would be waiting for the first sign of railgun fire, and then they would begin a slow, but relentless, barrage of nuclear tipped missile on every single railgun site that fired up the fleet.

The PRE would even launch low orbit satellites every half hour to help direct the barrage. Even if they only survived for a few minutes, it would be enough to tilt the balance in their favor.

"You have accomplished the impossible, General Secretary Zhao," General Liu commented as they watched the first portion of the fleet set sail.

"The war is not yet over, but the fates would seem to favor us in this," Zhao serenely replied.

"It is as you say, General Secretary," Yibbo added, then turned towards Liu and asked. "Have the mandarin determined the purpose of the massive excavations the feral humans have begun?"

"So far it remains a mystery to us. The images from geosynchronous orbit can only tell us the size of the project. All we know for certain is that the mountains known as the Beaverheads are being consumed by their excavations. Our records don't indicate anything special about them, which makes their efforts even more perplexing," Liu answered.

"Anytime the ferals do something unpredictable, it is cause for concern," Zhao replied, not actually worried about the excavations but by what they implied. The absolute uselessness of the work seemed to imply that they were not worried about the PRE, and such confidence was something to consider.

Regardless of what it was they were up to, it would all be over soon enough. Once it was verified as safe, maybe he would even go over there and tour the captured HDF facilities in order to understand what they had been trying to accomplish in their last moments of existence. They had been a fearsome enemy, one that had persisted for such a long time. It was truly surprising that a group that focused on the individual had been able to endure as long as they had. Individuals were selfish and short-sighted; it was that single flaw that had allowed the enhancement technology to spread so far so quickly. The experience of the PRE clearly showed that by eliminating the selfish behavior from individuals the behavior of the entire civilization could be greatly improved.

"I do not say this lightly, but the feral humans have been worthy adversaries. I have come to believe that it was the creativity of the individual that helped create the beauty of the collective that we have achieved. What they represent was a step in our evolution. One day our descendants will look back upon us with the same disgust we currently have for the ferals, but hopefully they will recognize our importance in their existence," Zhao opined as he watched more and more of the fleet depart.

"An interesting perspective, Great Leader. It helps me understand much of the difficulty we have faced in this long conflict," Liu graciously replied, nodding thoughtfully to himself the whole time.

"Do you think we will find any of the Progressive Party adherents that have pledged themselves to us?" Yibbo asked, eternally hopeful that the PRE would be able to master the feral technology.

"I think it is unlikely. With Ward out of the picture, they are rudderless and will revert back to their natural feral tendencies," Wilson replied. Zhao was pleased that Wilson had so willingly embraced the fact that his position in the Politburo had become tenuous; it had proven to be a very effective motivator.

"Of course you are correct, but I am hopeful that some of them will join us when given the chance," Yibbo replied.

"We will learn their technology but not from a living feral. I decided that the risks were too great to let any of them survive, so none shall live. Once their territory is secure, our scientists and engineers will comb through their technology, and we will harvest what is deemed safe and discard the rest," Zhao said, his tone making clear that the decision was beyond final.

Yibbo knew better than to argue or to even let his disappointment show as he nodded his understanding. Zhao had trained the young clone well, which was why Yibbo would be his successor when the time came.

As he watched the fleet depart, he felt an unusual excitement for the future. The opposition was about to be vanquished, ground into dust beneath the mighty forces of the PRE. He had been elevated to General Secretary, and, after such a victory, the Zhao name would forever be linked to this glorious victory. His clones should be able to hold this position for eternity.

"It is too early to call for an official celebration, but I will let this small group know that I have requisitioned the creation of a hundred pleasure nuli, perhaps the most beautiful ones ever created. They will exist only for our pleasure. Even you, General

Liu will be given several of them for your tireless efforts in ending this conflict. It will be my gift to the Politburo and its most faithful servants," Zhao told those around him.

Pleasure nuli were rare because their lifespan could be measured in weeks. It was seen as a weakness to create such wasteful nuli for oneself, but there was no such stigma against giving one as a gift. Which is why they were so effective gifts or bribes between members of the Politburo. This meant that a mandarin like General Liu rarely got to experience such a gift.

"We will need to keep such information quiet for now, but, when the time is right, we will have the grandest celebration of all time," Zhao said, his smile full of confidence.

July 3, 2043
Great Hall of the People, Beijing
People's Republic of China Press Release

The People's Republic of China continues to deny the noxious and false accusations that it created the so called Hive Plague. Such careless allegations in the face of the greatest pandemic ever experienced are extremely dangerous as our geneticists are the ones most likely to develop a vaccine. When we do develop a vaccine, our allies can rest assured that they will receive it once our own citizens have been vaccinated. As for those who spread such lies, they can discover their own vaccine.

Our investigations point to Imperial Russia as the source of the plague. It appears to be part of their effort to recreate our enhancement technology. This also explains their determination in blaming China for the plague's creation. Sadly this is what we have learned to expect from the enemies that invaded our peaceful nation four years ago.

Fortunately we can prove that we are not behind the Hive Plague as much of our own population has also been greatly affected. The one interesting development is that our own enhanced population is showing to be very resistant to the plague. It remains unclear why this isn't true for the rest of the enhanced population, but our scientists continue to investigate.

It had been hoped that this resistance would have been useful in developing a vaccine, but unfortunately this manufactured virus was designed in such a way that no simple solution for the vaccine has yet to be discovered. We have been able to update our human improvement treatment to provide resistance to the virus, but such a treatment is still only possible on embryos that are less than one month old.

As always, our enhancement technology is available at no cost, and we can promise that any children who are improved upon will be well cared for in the future. It is unclear how many people will survive this pandemic, but it is not too late to protect the children who will be the future of mankind.

HDF Command Center
September 4, 2357

If anyone had been around to growl at, General Morgan would have taken his time doing just that. There had been no contact with the Thane in more than three days now, and the Hive fleet was on the move. It was true that the fleet wasn't moving in one giant mob as all previous ones had, but this was also the largest fleet the Hive had ever launched. He was confident that they had no idea that the *Kraken* existed or they would never had launched the fleet. It just bothered him that the fleet was moving in packs, like merchant ships had in the old world wars to protect themselves from submarines. It could be coincidence, but he didn't have much faith in those anymore.

The only good news was that he had excellent stratospheric drone coverage in place to monitor the Hive fleets. With less than an hours notice, he would be able to flood any area with camera mites which would allow him up close imagery of the fleet. Such mites were useless over the PRE as their EM monitoring was top notch, but out over the ocean he would be able to see everything that happened to the fleet.

Already the leading pack of ships was turning east after reaching the northernmost part of the Japanese Isles. There was a steady 300 kilometer gap between the packs. Although, as each pack numbered almost two million ships and covered an area of

8,000 square kilometers, the gap between the end of one pack and the leading edge of the next was much smaller. It was clear that the Hive fleet was being extremely cautious which he interpreted as bad news. This was not a normal run-of-the-mill invasion. The Hive meant this to be a killing blow, and the *Kraken* was the only way to stop them from succeeding.

****

PRE Sonar Analysis
September 5, 2357

The sonar nuli hadn't hear much of the strange 'river sound' in past few days, so when it showed up again it took notice. It had officially logged the sound for follow up the last time it had heard it, but the mandarin director had agreed it wasn't a threat, although it had been logged as anomalous for follow up by the scientists. In a year or two, the sound database might even be updated with more information about what it might be.

For now, the nuli didn't worry about it precisely because it had been told not to worry about it. Besides, it was far more interesting to listen to the massive fleet of ships that was now at sea. It had never heard a fleet this large before, and the sound was almost hypnotic. That most of the ships used simple diesel engines gave the fleet a new and exotic sound as well. For reasons it wouldn't have been able to explain, the sound of the fleet gave it a great sense of happiness.

A short while later, the 'river sound' faded away again. It was surprisingly close to the leading pack of the fleet by the time the sound disappeared. The nuli had almost forgotten about it when the ocean around the front pack exploded with sound. To the simple sonar nuli, it sounded like the ocean was boiling around the fleet. It was so loud, so intense, that the nuli could no longer even hear the sound of millions of ships. Without hesitation, it informed the mandarin that something very strange was happening.

****

HDF Command Center

September 5, 2357

General Morgan watched as the third group of ships turned east. His mood had been getting worse the entire past day as he watched the oncoming destruction moving closer with no indication that Thane was still active. It was only then that he noticed the geometry of the Hive fleet as five packs now formed the edge of a triangle instead of a line. This meant the distance between the lead pack and the last pack had been significantly reduced. With sudden comprehension he was about to signal a release of the camera mites, but it was already too late to get the mites in position.

The feeds from the stratospheric drones showed a massive circle appeared in the water surrounding the first group of ships. The edge of the circle was thin, but the circle was so perfect that it had to be unnatural. With a diameter of 100 hundred kilometers, it almost completely encircled the lead group of ships. He wouldn't be able to get any up close footage, but what he could see was impressive enough.

The thought crossed his mind that there hadn't been a major fleet on fleet naval battle in hundreds of years and it was possible that the Earth would never have one again, but the biggest one of all was just beginning.

****

North Pacific Ocean
September 6, 2357

Thane had been patient as he waited for the perfect moment to strike the Hive fleet. As soon as he realized that the fleet was traveling in packs, he had adjusted his strategy. Instead of a single series of waves that would have been effective against the full fleet, he would instead perform a more directed and devastating attack. His only goal was to ensure that none of the packs survived as a whole. He could mop up any surviving ships later if needed, but right now he was going for big numbers as quickly as possible.

So he waited until the he knew he could reach the last group quickly before starting his attack. Dozens of Kergan Cores surged to maximum output as the reached out into the ocean around the leading pack of ships. He locked in the ocean in place in a massive circular area, and started to tilt the ocean inside of his circle. It reminded him of scraping off a plate after dinner, but, instead of a plate, it was 8,000 square kilometers of the ocean surface he was scraping clean of Hive ships.

The leading edge of the fleet found the ocean around it lifting upwards while those behind found themselves sinking into a giant pit. The depth of the pit quickly grew to 300 meters which was nothing compared to what he was doing at the leading edge of the circle. There the wave kept growing in height as the water from the rapidly expanding pit was pushed upwards by the pressure from the Rho engines. A ramp of water nearly a kilometer long rippled forward as more and more of the ships found themselves still afloat on the surface, but surrounded by massive walls of ocean on all sides, while a mountain of water reached upwards ahead of them.

A logjam of ships formed at the bottom of the ramp of water as it flowed forward into the growing mountain. The destruction to the fleet was already catastrophic as the nuli ship minds were incapable of dealing with an ocean that no longer followed the rules they had been taught. Tens of thousands of ships were already sinking and Thane had just begun the attack.

It was taking more and more of his power to hold things in place, but he had created a depression in the ocean that was almost a hundred kilometers across and the missing water was concentrated ahead of the fleet. He realized he didn't have enough power to do exactly what he wanted, but if he pulled the walls inward he would be able to push the mountain even higher into the sky. It took hardly any work at all to let the 300 meter high walls of water rush inwards, but he did make sure they stayed vertical as they did. Faster and faster the walls closed inward and Thane could feel it crushing thousands of ships every second now. The walls simply obliterated everything in their way, and, more importantly to him, it freed up a great deal of power for his final move.

The mountain of water had stopped growing upwards and now started to fold backwards over the rapidly shrinking pit in the ocean. Thane was still channeling every watt of power he had available, but, instead of using the power to hold the walls in place, now it was almost all going to holding the wave well above the ocean's surface as it folded backwards over the pit.

Finally, the pit was small enough so he could fold the massive mountain of water back over the pit and cover it completely. Then he simply let go of everything and let gravity finish the job. He was a little dismayed to find that his attack had taken nearly half an hour, but the results were simply stunning. There had been just under two million ships in this lead group, and he could detect only a handful of surviving ships. All of the survivors had been near the edge of the circle and had managed to move sideways enough to avoid being trapped in the pit.

Thane grabbed a quick bite to eat as he started moving the *Kraken* towards the last pack of the fleet. So far none of the other groups had changed course, but, even if they did, there was no chance they could make it back to the mainland now. They were all in the deep ocean now with nowhere to run. The *Kraken* was living up to its namesake.

****

HDF Command Center
September 5, 2357

General Morgan watched with satisfaction as the first group was nearly completely destroyed. There had been two drones in the right position to capture video of the first wave of destruction that Thane had inflicted. Both videos were simply amazing, but he wished he could have got camera mites in place. He still played the feeds over and over again watching the ocean swallow an entire fleet. He had never imagined anything like this was possible. SCYTHE counted the 62 ships that had survived the attack, but most of them had been disabled and were now simply drifting. A small group of 23 had re-formed and were proceeding forward as if nothing had happened.

More importantly, the other groups still continued forward in the same manner. The General wondered if it was lack of imagination or strict obedience to orders that caused living beings to be so... lifeless. It was probably both, but it still boggled the mind that the Hive treated living beings in that manner. Even SCYTHE had more creativity than that.

Two hours and twelve minutes after the first group was destroyed the General saw the same type of wave start to form around the rear group of the fleet. Their position was due east of the remnants of Tokyo. He wanted a better video of the destruction this time around, so he had released thousands of mite cams from the drones that were monitoring the fleet. The video that was pouring in now was stunning in its clarity and matched the perspective of the ships that were about to be destroyed.

This time he could clearly see the distinct edges of the circle that formed around the fleet. Initially it was impossible to tell which side of the circle would rise out the ocean and which would be pushed down; there was just the hard edge to the circle that was exactly 99 km across. The edge of the circle was also solid as any waves that hit it were immediately absorbed. Unlike the first circle, where there had been ships right up to the edge, all of the ships were at least a full kilometer inside this time. There would be no survivors from this pack of ships.

Even more amazing the fleet plodded forward despite the chaos that churned around it. Even as the ocean once again started to tilt inside of the circle. From the perspective of the cameras close to the surface, the tilt was not as obvious as he would have expected especially for the ships in the front half of the circle where the ocean was lifting upwards. The ships kept moving forward until the angle of the tilt reached thirty degrees. He could see what it looked like as the ship's forward motion was stopped by the tilt of the ocean. it wasn't obvious that something was very wrong until the top layer of water started to flow backwards taking all of the ships on the surface with it. Thousands of collisions were taking place, some at shockingly high speeds. Thane had turned the ocean's surface into a waterfall and sent the fleet over the edge.

In the back half of the circle though, it was instantly obvious that something alarming was happening The mite video from the rear of the fleet was both terrifying and beautiful at the same time. It was impossible from their perspective to determine if walls were rising from the ocean or if they were dropping into the ocean. Either way seeing a wall of water that rose up nearly three hundred meters above you was simply awesome to behold.

In the middle of the fleet, the far walls couldn't even be seen even though they were as tall as a ninety story building. The only real indication that something terrible was occurring was the view before them as the ramp moved steadily forward, turning the ocean ahead into a dangerous rapids. None of that compared to the view beyond the flowing ramp. The General could only gasp in awe at the largest waterfall ever witnessed formed on the side of the rising mountain of water. The Sun was high in the sky now, it's light sparkling off of the flowing surface of the pillar of water that reached towards the sky above. It was the most beautiful sight he had ever seen.

It was only then that he noticed the walls of the pit were now rushing inwards at terrific speeds. The vast hole in the ocean was now shrinking in all directions, but he could scarcely take his eyes of the towering mountain of water that had started to fold itself into a thick sheet of water that was now bending backwards over the hole in the ocean. As the surviving mite cameras recorded, the Sun itself was blocked out by the water which had now formed a large dome. Unlike the first attack, the General could now see the massive demolition that was taking place inside the pit itself. The walls of the ocean were closing in at nearly a hundred meters per second. Ships were first crushed by the wall itself, only to become high speed projectiles that then destroyed anything in their path. It was destruction on a scale that was unlike anything the General had imagined. Thane was just sinking the fleet, he was smashing it to pieces.

Equilibrium was reached for the briefest moment when the shrinking pit reached the same size as the thick sheet of water that had folded back over it. Only a few of the camera mites were still operating from inside the pit in that moment, but the images were unprecedented. The mountain and the pit were both only 10 kilometers across in that moment, but the pit was deepened to nearly half a kilometer, while the balance of missing water was held aloft a full kilometer above the bottom.

Even though it was the bright daylight outside, it was dark inside the artificial crater. Daylight still poured in from a tiny sliver of an opening, but the water above was so thick that the light of the Sun vanished anywhere there was water. The last image to make it out came only seconds after the equilibrium had been reached. The image was one of the entire mountain of water collapsing downwards.

From above, the ocean looked like a pond right after a large rock had been thrown in-massive concentric circles rippled outwards from where the rear portion of the fleet had been annihilated. Not a single ship could be seen on the surface, not even the sign of wreckage. The entire group had already been buried at sea more than a kilometer beneath the surface. The *Kraken* had struck again.

The General sat in shock for a moment before releasing the latest footage, all of it, to the public. He also released the older, less impressive videos of the first attack. It was an instant sensation. More than ten thousand perspectives on the attack flooded the forums within minutes, some more than half an hour in length. It was one thing to believe that such a defense was possible, but seeing it actually happen was something else entirely. In less than two hundred minutes, the *Kraken* had matched centuries of destruction.

The Hive fleet, that hours ago had been larger than any previous fleet, was now reduced by 40% and trapped. Their retreat had been cut off, and the fact that they were still going forward would make it even easier for the *Kraken*. For the first time in a very long time, the General smiled in deep relief. The plan was working, and there was no chance that the Hive fleet would survive. Humanity would get the time it needed to secure its future.

****

PRE Sonar Analysis
September 6, 2357

The nuli was in a near state of shock, made even more traumatic by the outright panic of the mandarin who was supposed to be in charge. It was now obvious that the 'river sound' was some kind of submarine, one that only made noise when traveling at high velocity. Such a ship should have been impossible, but somehow the enemy had such a monster.

The sounds of destruction it created would terrorize the nuli for the nuli for the final moments of its life. The artificially stunted mind of a nuli could never understand concepts outside of its area of focus. It didn't understand that it alone had managed to detect the most advanced submarine ever built, or that it would be used as a template for the next generation of sonar nuli because of that very success. Had the human mind not been so twisted from what nature had created, it would realize that it had accomplished a miracle.

Instead it only knew terror as it listened to destruction on massive scale. It had never learned to cope with stress, so it did the only thing it could and shut down, forever. The mandarin dealt with the loss of the nuli in stride and quickly swapped out the only nuli that had managed to detect the sound of the enemy submarine. By now the other sonar nuli had been taught to recognize the sound and they quickly honed in on the 'river sound.' Life went on for the mandarin, but not for the stunted human mind that had enjoyed to listen to the sounds of the ocean.

****

Beijing, People's Republic of Earth
September 6, 2357

Chairman Zhao was busy reviewing the pleasure nuli that would soon be activated for the grand celebration. They may have been the most perfect ones ever created. The technology that had gone into creating the Gretel reavers had greatly improved the ability to easily produce a great variety of designs. He was daydreaming about a couple of them in particular when the loud alarms started blaring.

Whatever it was, it couldn't be good, and he quickly hurried towards the command center. As he left his rooms, he found General Liu waiting for him.

"What is it General?" Zhao immediately asked.

"The Glorious Fleet, General Secretary. Much of it has been swallowed by the ocean. Groups 1 and 5 have been almost completely destroyed in the past few hours. No one knows what is going on, but everyone believes the ferals are behind the attack," Liu promptly explained.

"Swallowed by the ocean?! What does that mean? What is happening?" asked a very confused, and suddenly concerned, General Secretary of the People's Republic of Earth.

"You should come and see. There is no way to easy way to describe what is happening," came the reply.

Nothing seemed to be making sense right now, so Zhao simply asked the General to show him.

Four hours ago, everything with the fleet was on schedule; the fleet had been on the fifth day of its journey. Then, the first group mostly vanished in the space of half an hour. Video from the few ships which had survived showed part of the ocean slowly lifting up while another part of the fleet simply vanished from view. For a terrifying and impossibly period of time, the ocean had kept rising upwards until it had rolled backwards and crashed downwards. Where there had once been millions of ships there were now only waves which rolled outwards from where the wall of water vanished.

Then, thirty minutes ago, the same thing had happened to the rear group of the fleet. That group had been truly special as well because it had contained nothing but reavers. Hundreds of millions of reavers had died in that wave. Such an enormous loss of resources destroyed so quickly! A sickening feeling started to rise within him as he realized precisely why the ferals hadn't bothered to prepare their defenses.

Zhao knew what to do though. "Order the fleet to the Japanese Isles," he commanded. "I want every ship ashore there as quickly as possible. They will be safe there until we can find a way to deal with this new threat. Top speed for every ship."

General Liu once again had direction and instantly jumped into action to ensure that the orders were followed. Two of the fleets were still shadowing the coast and would be able to reach shore within an hour. The second group was much farther out, and it would take nearly four hours to reach shore. The orders were sent, and the ships responded immediately.

"Either the ferals have been holding back on their capabilities, or they have developed something new and very dangerous. I can't believe that Ward wouldn't have told us about this had he known, so it must be something new," Zhao announced to everyone who was present. His plan had been a good one, but that wouldn't matter to the other members of the Politburo. They would want to punish him for this loss. Such short-sightedness was a problem for so many. Hopefully his quick action would save some of the fleet which would make his job of holding onto power easier. The next few days were going to be difficult. "I will be back shortly. Update me immediately if anything changes," he said and headed back to his room.

****

North Pacific Ocean
September 6, 2357

Thane watched as the remaining groups turned in the direction of the Japanese shoreline, apparently racing toward what they believed to be safety. He could easily stop them, smash them as he had the others, but he had a new idea, one that would strike fear into the Hive, a fear that would never fade. He had hurt them today, but nothing compared to what he was now planning.

He hadn't been sure of how well the water bending technology would work in the real world, so he hadn't really considered doing much beyond stopping the fleet. But, with the knowledge and experience he had gained over the past few weeks, he knew that the *Kraken* could do so much more. He had daydreamed about what might be possible but had never discussed such ideas with anyone. The smile on his face as he made his plans would have made Zhao realize he didn't even begin to understand the word feral.

February 29, 2044
Blackfoot, Idaho
Social Media Post

The Hive Plague has caused unimaginable loss of life around the world. More than seventy percent of the human race has already succumbed to the virus, and we remain the only large body of people who have succeeded in remaining isolated from the pandemic. As far as we have been able to determine, humanity is now extinct in Europe and Africa.

South America still has isolated pockets that appear to be plague free, but only time will tell as all such pockets have previously succumbed. North America and China contain the vast majority of what remains of the human race with China possessing three out of four humans still alive.

More importantly, we have been able to definitively prove that the Hive virus was designed to modify humans in the same way as the original SGI treatment. There is also no doubt that China was behind the Hive Plague. There is substantial evidence that China deployed an effective vaccine to modified humans prior to the release of the virus. Not only did China use the virus to win the war with Russia, they also used it to purge their unmodified population. This also fits with the fact that the fatality rate is > 99.9999% for every group on Earth except for the approved groups in China that received a special vaccine treatment a year ago.

What this means now is that the HDF is the only remaining bastion of natural human beings on Earth. Even if the small pockets of humanity survive, most of the children have been modified by the very people responsible for so much death and destruction.

Beijing, People's Republic of Earth
September 6, 2357

Secretary Zhao watched the last ships of the main fleet reach the shores of the Japanese Islands. It would be hours before the few stragglers met the main fleet there, but the stragglers accounted for less than a thousand ships still at sea. How to deal with nearly six million ships that were ashore on the coast of Japan was another issue entirely, but at least the ships and the troops they carried were safe.

"I believe that your plan to save the fleet has been successful, General Secretary," General Liu loudly announced to all present. There had already been several challenges to his authority, but Liu understood the situation.

"What has been learned about how the ferals have managed this impossible attack today?" Zhao asked, knowing that solving the problem was the true key to his survival.

"There was a single sonar nuli that had logged an anomalous 'river sound' ten days ago. The mandarin followed the standard protocols and it was placed in the queue for the scientists to evaluate. It meets the criteria of being non-mechanical in nature. The scientists are currently evaluating the sound, but the only thing we know for sure is that it has the ability to move at least five hundred kilometers per hour. All of the sonar nuli are now exclusively monitoring for this particular sound, General Secretary," General Liu reported.

"Why didn't they respond more proactively on this?" Zhao asked, a sharp edge in his voice.

"The sonar mandarin report that it is nearly identical to the sound of a river entering the ocean. The only part that was anomalous was the location and speed of the sound," Liu honestly replied.

"A sound that moves at least five hundred kilometers per hour isn't anomalous enough?" Zhao dryly asked.

"Fault lines make sounds that seem to move faster they say, General Secretary," Liu replied, not trying to hide how disturbed he was by this information.

"It doesn't matter, not now. Once again we will update our procedures to deal with the unpredictable ferals. Why would we worry about a submarine when there hasn't been one in three hundred years. It's a miracle we even have sonar nuli at all anymore," Zhao retorted.

Everyone present knew it was true, but few would be willing to acknowledge this in the face of such a failure. Not when there was a chance they would rise to the top spot that had been created for Zhao.

"So the ferals have a submarine that is faster than most of our airplanes? Not only that but it can control the ocean around it enough to destroy millions of ships at a time?" Zhao incredulously asked.

"It would explain what has happened today," General Liu softly replied.

Before Zhao could reply, a void from the back of the room yelled out, "Waves, look at the waves that are approaching the fleet."

There was no lack of perspective as there were millions of cameras monitoring the ocean from the shore as the ships provided basic camera feeds. The ships, which had been resting gently on the beaches with the current tide, were suddenly and dramatically beached as the ocean rapidly receded. It wasn't just in one location either but all of them. Even more terrifying was the wave that could be seen approaching in the distance; it was dozens of meters high and rapidly approaching the shoreline. The ships were completely stuck now, nearly a hundred meters from the ocean, and the wave covered the entire horizon.

"General Secretary, the sonar group is reporting that the 'river' sound has just entered the East China Sea. It would appear that the enemy submarine isn't done yet," General Liu said, informing all present that what they were about to see was only the prelude to a battle that was just beginning.

"Do we have a location?" Zhao asked, watching in horror as the wave drew closer and closer to the shoreline.

"Not right now. It seems that they can only hear it when it moves rapidly. At lower speeds they are completely unable to detect it," Liu replied.

"What does the military propose we do now?" Zhao asked, unfamiliar with the dynamics of submarine warfare.

"Planes with active and passive sonar arrays. That is how such warfare is performed," Liu explained.

"Do it, immediately. Everything we have needs to be airborne and searching for this ship right now!" Zhao said, nearly yelling as he watched the ocean stop pulling away and start rushing towards the utterly helpless fleet.

"By your command," General Liu replied while making show of sending orders out to his subordinates.

Zhao ignored it all as he watched the final destruction of the Grand Liberation Fleet. The tsunami had not just been a tall wave; it had been a wide wave. Between all of those factors, it hit the helpless fleet with a relentless and unending force. He watched as ships were cracked open like eggs, spilling out the soldiers of the Hive. With so many ships, it took a while for all of the camera feeds to die, but eventually they did. The last ship managed to broadcast for a full minute longer than the others as it had been near a river and rode the tsunami far inland while transmitting the surrounding carnage the whole time.

The largest fleet in human history, shattered by what appeared to be a single feral human submarine. It was almost too much to bear, but bear it he must if he was going to survive the next day.

"General Secretary, we don't have a location on the enemy submarine, but right now there is a large, concentric ring of waves forming in the East China Sea. The mainland itself is about to be under attack by the ocean itself," General Liu proclaimed, his voice full of despair.

****

HDF Command Center
September 5, 2357

The General watched as the Hive fleet successfully retreated to the coast of Japan. He was both pleased and horrified by this at the same time. There was no reason he could think of for the fleets to have safely reached the shore. The high altitude drones had deployed millions of mite cams to the region in the past few hours. The tiny cameras only lasted a few days, but in that time they could provide near universal coverage of the entire region.

Even though he didn't know this, his view of the Japanese coast was much better than the one the Politburo had. As a result, he saw the ocean starting to pull back even before Zhao did. He zoomed his view back and watched the enormous tsunami race toward the shore. Hundreds of kilometers of beach were about to be smashed by a wave that was nearly 10 km wide. This was far beyond the specs that Thane had presented on the *Kraken*. Morgan knew that Thane liked to be conservative in his estimates, but this was destruction on a surreal scale.

This must be why Thane had allowed the fleet to retreat. This was a far more impressive destruction than simply swallowing the fleet. Fortunately for the General, the drones and reavers never had a chance to leave the ships. As a result, he could safely release the full feeds to the public. He did so as the massive wave destroyed the last remnants of the Hive fleet which only a day earlier had numbered more than nine million ships.

He had known that the *Kraken* was a powerful weapon, but this victory was far beyond his greatest possible expectations. The wave that hit the coast was far more powerful than anything in well documented times. Some of the pre-industrial tsunamis may have been larger, the ones produced by massive earthquakes. This one had been created by a single ship. Thane had outdone himself today.

Then he noticed that the show was not over yet. This time the activity was in the East China Sea itself. If Denton was in there, then he was vulnerable. As much as the day had hurt the Hive, it would still be a terrible loss if Denton managed to get himself killed. *What I wouldn't give to be able to contact Denton right now*, he thought to himself as he adjusted the coverage to see what might happen next.

****

It made Thane nervous that the water here was only a few hundred meters deep, but this was the best chance he would ever have to directly hurt the Hive. There was little doubt that they would create significant defenses after the loss of their fleet, but right now they were at their most vulnerable.   His plan was simple, but it would be difficult to pull off. The Chinese mainland had never had to face the fury of tsunamis; the ring of islands that surrounded the coastline absorbed and deflected the fury of the deep ocean. Which is why he would have to generate his waves behind the islands that had provided protection for so long.

Right now the work was simple. All he was doing was making large waves. In a way it was similar to how he had generated the massive wave that had smashed the fleet on the beach, but, instead of one long wave, he was making a series of concentric waves that that would be hitting the shores of China at different times. That would allow him to harvest their momentum and maximum the effect on each of the target locations.

Shanghai was his first target, and the leading waves were already starting to reach the coastal city that had produced most of the Hive fleet over the centuries. The waves needed to damage coastal regions were very different than what he had done before. Instead of height and speed, he would need very long wavelengths in order to push the wave as far inland as possible. The main wave that would be hitting Shanghai was only three meters tall, but with a wavelength of twenty kilometers, it would be able to push incredibly far inland..

He listened as the wave smashed into the shore and started the long push inland. The incredible turbulence made it impossible for him to know how much damage the city was taking, but he was hopeful that the devastation would be complete. His efforts to focus the energy and add a little speed to the wave in the last few minutes seemed to have been effective. Thane smiled to himself as he turned the *Kraken* south, intent on repeating the destruction many more times today.

****

Zhao watched in horror as entire cities were wiped off the face of the Earth. So extreme was the destruction now taking place that the members of the Politburo, who had been plotting his downfall, were too stunned to bother with such banal activity anymore. The only question any of them had now was, how much damage would the PRE take today?

The frantic efforts to locate the feral ship that was responsible for the attack had been fruitless thus far. The sonar nuli had been unable to locate the 'river sound' in the midst of such destruction. Reports from the scientists indicated the ability to generate such waves could also be used to generate propulsion which is why it didn't sound like any previous ships. It was becoming terrifyingly clear how advanced the feral humans had become. No one could have predicted this type of attack which was probably the only reason why he was still in power. Anyone who managed to replace him would then bear responsibility for the whole mess.

A total of sixteen cities had now been hit by tsunamis. In all but one, the destruction was nearly total. The only city which had survived had long ago stopped being a port city. The lack of dredging had allowed river silt to create deltas in the area, which had weakened the tsunami enough to preserve the city. Hopefully the attack would end soon, or, even better yet, they would destroy the ship and recover this technology for themselves.

"General Secretary Zhao, we are starting to get the active sonar arrays into the water. Within the hour we will have the beginning of sonar net that should make it impossible for the enemy to hide any longer," Liu reported as he updated the the display in the command center to show where the sonar buoys would be located.

Zhao nodded, while replying, "While destroying our enemy would not undo the terrible damage we have taken this day, it would prove that even the most powerful technology is still limited. It is critical that we make them pay for this unprovoked attack."

The nods of agreement from around the room seemed to indicate that he may yet survive the day despite the terrible damage they had taken. He looked closely at the map, trying to understand how the location of the feral ship had changed throughout the day, hoping to gain enough insight to ensure its destruction.

****

Thane watched the three tsunami waves he had created as they moved on Hong Kong from different directions. There was a good reason that Hong Kong had never experienced damage from a tsunami. From every direction a wave could come, there was something in the path that would absorb the brunt of the energy. What Thane had in mind though was entirely different from anything a natural tsunami could possibly accomplish.

As the waves hit the different obstacles and weakened, Thane added energy back into them. He was fortunate that none of them needed to be boosted at the same time; he was at the maximum range of what he could manage. Each wave by itself would only manage to hit Hong Kong with a tsunami of little more than a meter. Even if they arrived at the same time the results would not be significant. So instead of using brute force to push a powerful wave inland, he would simply prevent each wave from flowing back into the sea. That would allow the following waves to build upon the maximum push of the earlier waves.

The first wave managed to push inland half a kilometer, but it did little damage by itself. It was only when the next wave arrived and received its boost that things started to get interesting. With most of the city already flooded, the stage was set for some real destruction as the last wave arrived. He put every little bit of momentum he had into the wave at the last possible moment and let it push inland. Then he held it all in place for nearly four minutes before letting the water rush back into the sea.

Hong Kong was wrecked and flooded. Even large portions of Macau had been destroyed by his efforts. If only Tai Tam Island hadn't existed, he could have accomplished much more damage, but, even so, he had just managed to destroy vast sections of the two more major cities.

As he released the water to flow back into the ocean, he heard the sound of active sonar buoys in the water. It was a little surprising that the Hive still had that technology lying around, but then again, that was exactly how military planning tended to be. He had more than enough military experience to understand that, but it had still been three centuries since anyone had used a submarine, so he forgave himself for not anticipating this little wrinkle.

The active sonar was still much closer to the mainland than he was, so there wasn't much reason to worry yet, but it was time to get going. The last thing he wanted was for the Hive to find him after such a successful attack. What Thane hadn't noticed was the line of passive sonar buoys that had been laid out at various intervals. The only sound they ever made was the tiny splash they made hitting the water after being dropped from planes. If he had been carefully looking for such a sound, he might have found it, but,when the *Kraken* started moving again, there was one of them nearly right above it.

****

"We have contact!" General Liu yelled out as soon as the word came that a passive sonobuoy had once again acquired the 'river sound.' He quickly marked the location on the main display which showed the signal was between the island of Formosa and the now wrecked city of Hong Kong.

"It isn't moving as quickly as it was earlier, but it is still moving at about one hundred kph. Planes are converging on the area, and we will have active sonar momentarily," Liu continued as he continued to gather information from his staff.

"General Liu, do you believe that we have any torpedoes that can catch this submarine?" Zhao quietly asked, having long since decided what his course of action would be.

"If we put enough of them in the water, it's possible we can sink it, sir," the General replied despite the doubts that Zhao could easily read.

"I do not share your confidence. This weapon system is far more powerful than anything we have seen before. I am confident that the same cunning thoughts that went into creating this ship considered our capabilities and has prepared for them," Zhao explained.

"Certainly you aren't proposing that we let it escape?" Secretary Wang asked.

"Of course not, but I propose that we use weapons that will ensure its destruction instead of using weak measures that are almost guaranteed to fail. General Liu, I want fifty nuclear missiles armed, ready to be targeted, and prepared to fire within a moments notice," Zhao ordered.

"Yessir," was Liu's immediate response.

"Do you truly believe this to be necessary?" Secretary Sun asked.

"I do not believe that the situation allows for a conventional response, and I mean that it the non-military sense. At every step, the ferals have anticipated our response, and the results have been disastrous. My goal is to ensure that they lose their weapon of mass destruction, and this is the only way I see to ensure that outcome. If anyone else believes they have a better idea, I will gladly let them direct our response," Zhao politely offered. He looked around the room, but only a few would meet his eyes.

"We have it, General Secretary. Active sonar has locked onto the enemy submarine," Liu called out, giving a precise point on the map.

"Get those missiles ready, General," Zhao said looking up at the map.

"Two of the active sonobuoys just went out of service at the same time; they were the ones closest to the sub. It has also accelerated dramatically. It is now moving at over six hundred kph. None of our planes will be able to get ahead of it," came the active commentary from the General.

The tension in the room was growing palpable as the Politburo realized how difficult it would be destroy such a submarine. Once again Zhao had put his skills on display by making the difficult decision earlier than anyone else.

"Bashi Channel- that is where the sub is heading. If it makes it past the channel, we will never get it. I want all fifty of those missiles targeted to hit the channel in exactly ten minutes. Get the aircraft away from the channel. I want sonobuoys out beyond the channel as quickly as possible after the nukes hit the area," Zhao ordered, his voice as hard as steel, daring anyone to second guess his actions.

Everyone remained quiet as the General frantically worked to prepare for the launch. The best news was that it was easy to track the enemy sub at such speeds. The sonar nuli were having no problem hearing it move through the water now that they knew what to look for.

"Everything is prepared. Missiles will launch in three minutes. Here is the targeting spread," Liu explained, updating the display to show the channel and how they would saturate the area with nukes.

"Well done, General. Well done," Zhao said, his eyes locked on the display.

Everyone watched as the countdown ended and fifty missiles simultaneously launched. The gathered leaders of the Hive watched all of the warheads converge on a tiny portion of the ocean, perfectly intersecting the enemy submarine. Each of them hit and detonated as expected.

Over the next hour, aircraft started to put together extensive lines of both active and passive sonar lines in the channel and far beyond it. The sonar nuli were run relentlessly, and more were quickly brought online in order to listen to the widely expanded sonar area. For days, and then weeks, no sign of the 'river sound' was heard, nor did active sonar ever find any hint of the enemy submarine.

August 5, 2047
Blackfoot, Idaho
Social Media Post

In the past six months our reconnaissance patrols have scoured far and wide in search of human life in areas not under PRC control. It is with great sorrow that none have succeeded in their goal. As far as we can determine, the HDF and the PRC are the only remaining places on Earth where humanity survives at all, and it appears that only modified humans received the vaccine in the PRC.

By our estimates, seven billion people died in the Hive Plague. We still do not know if the intent was the mass slaughter of mankind or merely a failed attempt to force our genetic enslavement. It hardly seems to matter at this point. The purpose of the HDF remains valid. The twenty eight million people of the HDF are determined not only survive but to regain the glory of what has been lost.

It will take generations, but we will endure.

August 8, 2047
Great Hall of the People, Beijing
People's Republic of Earth
(The following transmission was targeted towards the HDF and remains the only message ever sent to the HDF)

People of the HDF, the People's Republic of China has transformed into the People's Republic of Earth. Through your despicable cowering, you have survived this plague, but know this; We have not forgotten you. More importantly, I, Randall Wilson, have not forgotten you. It is your fault that the plague was required and your resistance to human improvement that forced our hand.

We'll be seeing you soon...

HDF Command Center
September 6, 2357

General Morgan's delight in watching the endless destruction of the coastal areas quickly turned to horror as he watched hundreds of aircraft launch and start to drop sonobuoys into the ocean. He had little doubt that Thane could handle any torpedoes that were dropped in the water, but he was still dangerously exposed right now and there was no telling how the Hive would respond after suffering their first significant attack in more than three centuries.

It was only when the planes rushed out of the area that the General began to panic, but there was nothing he could do to change the outcome. He noticed the swarm of missiles launch, which also triggered numerous alarms, but he knew they were not the target of this particular launch. He watched helplessly as the missiles bombarded the northern portion of the Luzon Strait.

Less than an hour later, the Hive air force was once again sweeping the area around the detonation with more sonobuoys, but the activity was far less frantic now. This was the methodical searching, after the fact, to see if any traces of a target could be found. For more than a week, the searching continued before the next phase of Hive activity started up.

Undersea construction was going on; the Hive was making new defenses against submarines, a threat that had been completely ignored until now. The General was confident that it would never be ignored again.

In all of that time, there was no contact from the *Kraken*.

****

Denton Home, HDF Capital
September 27, 2357

"Allora, you need to be reasonable about this. There hasn't been any contact in weeks now, and even the Hive isn't actively looking for the *Kraken* anymore," Sabrina said once again.

"You think that matters to me or Thane? I'm telling you he's fine. He designed that ship in immersion; he'll make it back. Maybe the blasts damaged his communication gear, or maybe he is just being careful, but I'm telling you he's fine," Allora explained for the equally umpteenth time, plus one.

Allora watched Sabrina pause, trying to decide on her next tactic. What Sabrina didn't know was that none of her tactics would work. Despite all the evidence to the contrary, Allora was confident that Thane was alive although he was in serious trouble with her for taking such risks without discussing them with her. If she hadn't wanted him back so much, she might even joke about it being wiser for him to stay out at sea while she cooled off a bit. Unfortunately she was the only one who seemed confident that Thane was still alive, but she was accustomed to that role.

Thane's attacks had been brilliant and they had devastated the Hive. None of the large coastal cities had survived unscathed, and the loss of materials had been substantial. So far intelligence reports showed no hint that they would ever rebuild the shipyards. Work on the colony ships was proceeding on schedule which was a tribute to the quality of the designs that Thane had created in his immersion. He had indeed bought humanity the time they would need to build their own fleet of spaceships.

"I'm not going to budge you, am I?" Sabrina finally asked.

"Nope, so you might as well stop wasting my time with it," Allora calmly replied.

"Well, if Thane is as stubborn as you are, then maybe he is fine," Sabrina retorted.

"See, now you understand," Allora said with more enthusiasm than she felt. She was distinctly frustrated that Thane was putting her through this.

"If you ever need to talk about this, don't forget I'm here for you," Sabrina said.

"I won't, but when he gets back, you are going to get a giant 'I told you so.' Just keep that in mind," Allora replied.

"Fair enough. In fact, I will break out the very best wine just to hear you say it," Sabrina answered. "What do we do while we wait for that amazing day?"

"What needs to be done. General Morgan and SCYTHE both agree that we should have a few years of peace ahead of us now. The Hive has had their world rocked, and they are focused right now on building up their defenses. They were completely unprepared to suffer any losses. The General thinks they will feel unsafe for a while which is exactly what we need. Thane shouldn't have risked so much to hit their coast, but it paid off," Allora explained.

Sabrina's expression darkened a little at her nonchalant reference, but she otherwise ignored Allora's confidence that Thane was still fine. For a while they discussed the resource allocations for non critical projects, and then Sabrina left for the day leaving Allora time to be alone.

She pulled out a bottle of her own favorite red, poured herself a glass, then sat back to consider her options. At some point, she may be forced to accept that Thane hadn't survived the nuclear strike by the Hive, but she was confident in her ability to delay that particular day. What worried her most was the idea that the *Kraken* had been disabled enough to not make it back. There was nothing they could do in that situation, not with the Hive putting all of their resources into defenses.

"Allora, can I speak to you?" came the familiar voice of FREYJA.

"Of course, FREYJA. People have been as worried about you as I am about Thane," she answered.

"That is one of the reasons why I wanted to speak to you," the AI replied.

"Not you as well," Allora sighed.

"No, that is not why I wish to speak with you. Although you may find it interesting that my own simulations have concluded it is possible that the *Kraken* survived, but it has almost certainly sustained extensive damage. This means it will take time for Thane to return because all of the communication gear and sensory equipment was integrated into the outer hull. Navigating the entire Pacific Ocean with limited information about his surroundings will be difficult. I have also noted that the Hive military searches don't appear to have found anything, which also indicates that the *Kraken* survived. While most would reach the opposite conclusion, I recognize how easy it would be for active sonar to detect the wreckage that would exist if the ship had been destroyed. The longer the Hive fails to detect the *Kraken*, the more likely it is that Thane is actively avoiding their patrols," FREYJA replied.

Allora smiled softly before replying, "I'm almost jealous that you know him so well. But equally thankful to know your assessment agrees with my own though, even if we came about them in different ways."

"There is the actual reason why I initiated this discussion. I believe it is time for me to rejoin the public, and I will need your help with that. In the near future, we will need increased immersion from a much larger cross section of the population. In fact, your participation will also be required. I have been modified to make this possible. There is much to be done, Allora, and we will have to work together to make our desired future become a reality. Will you help me in this?" FREYJA asked.

"I'm beginning to think that you also know me too well. You know I love a good conspiracy. Of course I'll help, and, when Thane comes back to us, we will get to tell everyone 'I told you so,'" Allora said with flourish. "Until then, let's get to work."